RED MIDNIGHT

RED
MIDNIGHT

Thomas Hal Phillips

UNIVERSITY PRESS OF MISSISSIPPI JACKSON

This book is dedicated to Wayne Mills and Roger Jacobs.

Red Midnight is a work of fiction. Names, characters, incidents, and places are fictitious or are used fictitiously. The characters are products of the author's imagination and do not represent any actual persons.

www.upress.state.ms.us
Copyright © 2002 by University Press of Mississippi

Manufactured in the United States of America

10 09 08 07 06 05 04 03 02   4 3 2 1

♾

Library of Congress Cataloging-in-Publication Data

Phillips, Thomas Hal, 1922–
   Red midnight / Thomas Hal Phillips.
      p. cm.
   ISBN 1-57806-474-0 (cloth : alk. paper)
   1. Fathers and sons—Fiction. 2. Male friendship—Fiction. 3.
Ex-convicts—Fiction. 4. Mississippi—Fiction. I. Title.
   PS3566.H524 R43 2002
   813'.54—dc21   2002006164

British Library Cataloging-in-Publication Data available

PROLOGUE

The taxi driver was young and nervous, and the farther he got from the airport the more nervous he became. He was a student who drove at odd hours and he had never had a trip of fifty miles. He kept thinking: almost a full shift. He had never been to Hammerhead though he knew it was a sawmill town to the east, on or near the state line, in the hills, somewhere near Koslo, which he had passed through on the train when he was in the CCC camp.

He adjusted the rearview mirror to get a better look at his passenger in the backseat. His thumb left a smeared print on the glass, an omen, almost a presentiment. His hand was very sweaty. He wiped it dry on the front of his camp fatigue jacket which he also wore on the university campus.

He was now on the highway and the traffic had cleared, and he could memorize the young face behind him. It was a finely chiseled face, a long delicate nose, deep blue eyes that blazed and dreamed at the same time, though now the eyes were closed, the face quieter. But the wildness, the fugitive quality was still there, and the blood. The driver could see distinctly the thin smear of blood across the cheek and chin, and he could vaguely make out that the passenger still held his hand in the pocket of his topcoat, as if he concealed a gun. The topcoat lay across the only piece of luggage, a large duffel bag.

But it was neither the blood nor the hand in the topcoat that had started the uneasiness. It was the look on the passenger's face when he had refused to part with his coat or his bag as he entered the taxi, and the confused instructions. With a strange expression, a curious mixture of happiness and horror, the passenger had said, "The Peabody." And before the driver could close his own door, the passenger had commenced to talk about Hammerhead, not incoherently, but strangely enough for concern.

"You want the Peabody or Hammerhead?" the driver had said, his hands tight on the steering wheel, his head turned toward the side, waiting.

The passenger had leaned forward, sweat rolling down his forehead, his hands still in his topcoat. He struggled to make up his mind. "Yes," he had said.

"Yes? Which one?" The driver could hear the nervousness in his own voice.

"Hammerhead," the passenger had said. "It's only fifty miles. About that."

Then the passenger had leaned back, wiping his forehead with his free hand, and the driver thought he heard, "Precious are the dead."

The driver had moved into the traffic circle, turned east, thinking for a moment he would reenter the airport circle and tell the passenger to get another cab, he was a student, he had a class that night. But before he could decide he was past the circle entrance, thinking of the amount of the fare, his uneasiness somewhat gone.

By the time he reached the highway, his uneasiness had commenced again, stronger than ever. He looked back at the passenger, as if he could not trust the image in the rearview mirror, but the traffic was heavy and he had only a fleeting glance.

Now the taxi was entering a rolling stretch of clay hills where the right-of-way and trees were smothered with November green kudzu. The rank and consuming foliage of the kudzu formed weird and grotesque shapes in the late soft sunlight. There was little traffic. The driver looked again at the passenger whose face was turned slightly, holding onto a silo and dairy and a pasture of Holstein cows. Those were the first things the passenger had seemed to notice. His head continued to turn back, looking.

The young face suddenly settled back and the blue eyes closed. The driver began to study and remember the clothes. It might be important later. He had already memorized the blue eyes and blond hair and the tiny cleft in the chin.

The passenger wore an Oxford-gray alpaca sweater, a blue shirt, tan trousers. The duffel bag was brown with black leather strips and handles. The topcoat was dark gray. The driver thought he remembered the shoes were black. Or perhaps they were short black zippered boots. And he thought the topcoat had a lining. He was not quite certain. He couldn't swear to it, if called on.

The hills grew steeper. The kudzu disappeared and great waves of pine loomed in every direction. The driver increased his speed. At least it was daylight and he would be there well before dark.

After a while the driver saw the green sign and the white arrow: HAMMERHEAD. He turned off the highway onto a winding, black-topped, farm-to-market road. He looked back again. The passenger might have been asleep, but the driver knew he was not. There was nothing peaceful in that face.

The road now was rough and sharply winding. A great gash of red clay earth appeared directly ahead. The car took the turn severely and the tires squealed. The passenger sat up slowly, not alarmed, but quietly watching the roadside.

The houses were sparse. Those that did appear were small and unpainted, often tin roofed, nestling too near the edge of the road like shacks along the banks of a river. Piles of firewood lay scattered in the bare yards where here and there a few chickens scratched.

Occasionally, discarded pieces of furniture rested on the front porches and sometimes a bright new washing machine stood like a sentinel by the porch swing.

The driver and the passenger had said nothing to each other for an hour. They reached the crest of a hill and a great splash of color stretched out before them. The flaming golds of hickory and maple and poplar, the burning red of tupelo gum, the various shades of oak, all were deeply etched into the vast green of new and virgin pine. The driver could see that the passenger's face had suddenly brightened though the touch of a strange shadow still remained. The passenger was holding in his hand a yellow rose.

"Did you know you had some blood on your face?" the driver asked.

The passenger felt his face. He took out a large, peculiar-looking handkerchief, wet the corner in his mouth and began to rub his face. Then he saw the blood on his hand. He opened his bag and put the rose inside and continued to clean his face and his hand.

"I think you got it," the driver said, watching the rearview mirror. He was beginning to feel easier.

The car wound its way into the valley where on either side of the road the stalks of harvested cotton and corn lay hidden in the frost-struck remains of cocklebur. They crossed the bridge over Dixon Creek and the sound of the car flew down the hollow like a flock of blackbirds.

"You been off at work?" the driver asked.

"No. I've been in prison," the passenger said. He looked at the soiled and curiously shaped handkerchief which he still held in his hand. He knew the driver was looking at him in the rearview mirror. "Prison sounds better than penitentiary," he said.

The sharp grade of the hill was slowing the car. "I don't know the difference," the driver said.

"I don't either," the passenger said.

They began to reach the crest of the hill where new-looking houses, with well-kept yards, stood comfortably away from the road. They reached the level stretch and the houses became old again, sometimes mere shacks with fallen porches and cluttered yards. They passed a deserted blacksmith shop and an old abandoned lumber shed whose once-bright tin roof now seemed to be covered in old cracking leather.

The road curved and suddenly before them was a totally disordered arrangement of buildings, most of them very old. The driver slowed the car to a creeping pace. Directly ahead of them the blacktop ended in front of a long, high-porched, shoe-box building, one of the three stores remaining in Hammerhead. The storefront was covered with fading and peeling signs and the black lettering: TANNERS GEN MDSE. At the back of the store was a small brick building with its flag and the designation: U.S. POST OFFICE. Beyond the store and the post office was the gin and beyond the gin was the Presbyterian church and its weather-beaten steeple. Atop the steeple was a bronze hand with one long finger pointing skyward. To the left of the store was a large building, also high porched, padlocked and abandoned, with the faded lettering: SCHOFIELD LUMBER CO. Beside the Schofield building was a small bank. Other buildings lay scattered in a haphazard fashion with one new neat grocery store in their midst. High on a knoll in the distance was the faint outline of school buildings and playgrounds, and the looming mass of a water tank.

The driver had brought the taxi to a standstill in the middle of the blacktop, directly in front of the high-porched store. He was waiting for directions, left or right, but he gave the appearance of pausing for his passenger to get a look at the town.

A man opened the door of the barbershop, and stood looking toward the taxi. A woman, holding an old black sweater about her shoulders with one hand and a newspaper in the other, emerged from the post office. She paused to observe the strange appearance of the taxi. Suddenly, in the distance, though it could not be far away, the long plaintive sound of a whistle echoed and re-echoed through the hills and hollows.

"Is that a train up here?" the driver said.

"The sawmill," the passenger said.

As if reminded by the whistle, the woman called toward the taxi, squinting her eyes into the sun, "If you're lookin' fer the sawmill, it's thataway." She pointed to the driver's right, pulled the sweater tighter about her shoulders, and started down the gravelled sidewalk.

The driver saw that the passenger was also indicating a turn to the right. He turned the car into the road leading south. "You want the sawmill?" he said.

"No. The cemetery."

The driver did not answer. He looked into his rearview mirror. He was beginning to feel uneasy again.

They passed stack after stack of raw and drying lumber. The road turned sharply and the driver saw below them long low lumber sheds, a mill yard, and mountains of logs. The road turned sharply again around a steep red clay knoll, and before them was a church-yard and a church and a cemetery.

"Here," the passenger said. "Here," he repeated, louder, as if he thought the driver would pass the narrow dirt entrance leading to the churchyard and the cemetery gate.

The driver stopped between the church and the cemetery gate. The passenger got out quickly leaving his bag and his topcoat. He did not look at the church at all. Perhaps he knew it had changed little during his lifetime, and not at all in his absence, except for the new composition roof that had replaced the old cypress shin-gles. Everything else, inside and out, the pimpled weatherboards, the pews of heart pine, the cane-bottomed choir chairs, the walnut lectern draped in its blood-red mantle, had all been waiting in a blue-gray haze of standstill. But he did not look. He hurried toward the gate which was new to him, and half stumbled as he read the lettering cut into the keystone of the brick archway: CUMBERLAND CEMETERY, ESTAB. 1837.

He made no effort to open the cast-iron gate. He grasped the bars, frantically shaking them two or three times. Then he held on, gazing at the gravestones. Great drops of sweat rolled across his forehead and into his eyes and down his cheeks. He heard a voice behind him but he did not turn, did not listen. He held onto the bars, not shaking them now, but gripping with all the strength of both hands until his knuckles showed white. The road through the cemetery was almost gone, but he could follow it distinctly, everything mentally clear, even the wagon ruts which had long since worn and washed away. The old cemetery road had led from the gate, what was now the new gate, curving left off the slope, then straight for a few yards, then curving right to the northwest corner of the cemetery. Gravestones, newer than the others, stood along the old roadway now. But the road was there, forever.

"Is this it? This where you wanta stop?" the driver said.

"Yes," the passenger said, without turning to look.

The driver took the bag and coat and carried them to the gate. "The meter shows twenty-four forty," he said.

The passenger held two bills, a twenty and ten, which he seemed to have ready. The driver took them and remained standing. "Thanks very much," he said, and kept standing where he was.

The passenger picked up his bag and coat, opened the gate and went inside. He put the bag down and folded the coat on top of it. He saw the driver had not moved, and was now looking toward the end of the old cemetery road where wilted flowers lay scattered about a new mound of red clay.

"I can wait, and take you on home," the driver said.

The passenger turned and looked toward the south. "If it wasn't for the leaves, you could see my house. Through there." He pointed.

Still the driver did not move to go. Some final, nagging urge, the power of a secret, the force of mystery, anchored him. "What did you go to prison for?"

The passenger raised his eyes slowly. The driver saw in the young face now a different person, a calmness and composure he had not seen before. The eyes which had been a mixture of blaze and dream were now childlike and compassionate.

"For murder," the passenger said.

"Oh," the driver said.

"That's it," the passenger added quietly.

The driver half-turned toward his car, thinking: He's younger than me. He turned back to say, "Thanks again." He got into the taxi and started away. He looked back toward the gate, thinking about tonight and tomorrow and all the questions that would come to his mind.

The passenger remained standing at the gate, not looking into the cemetery, but gazing southward.

With one final look the driver moved on, wishing he could have taken his passenger all the way home. He had a strange and definite urge to see his house.

I

A Road through a Cemetery

I

I WAS FOURTEEN years old and I couldn't look at it any other way. My father once said, "No, son, you won't be eight for two more days. You're seven until you're eight." So I was fourteen. I wouldn't be fifteen for two more weeks and one day. I had come all the way from France by car and ship and train and foot. By car from Bordeaux to Le Havre, by the *Île de France* from Le Havre to New York, by the Southerner and the Chickasaw from New York to Koslo, and by foot from Koslo to Hammerhead, which was three miles. I had my duffel bag and my binoculars with me and my trunk was still in the station at Koslo.

From the Indian mound, high above the village, I saw a redbird among the apples in my father's favorite tree. I could not hear its singing, though I knew the autumn wind which was strong enough to move ripe apples pushed the sweet sound toward me. It was in the corner of my ear, just as I heard and did not hear the sawmill which had been closed all day no doubt, for it was Saturday.

The sun was almost down, was well hidden behind Hammerhead Mountain. But the railroad I saw clearly through my binoculars which I had purchased at the little shop two blocks away from Vingt-neuf Cour du Maréchal Foch. They were not French binoculars. They were German and like a magnet they drew the bird in so close to my eyes that I could see the brightness of its head against

3

the dull glow of a single apple. I was not looking for birds. I was looking for my father. I was almost fifteen and I had not seen my father or the orchard or the house or the barn since I was almost eleven.

My favorite tree was not in the orchard. It was the pear tree by the lot gate, tall and wide as an oak. My father never had to do anything to the pear tree, spray, fertilize, or prune. And every spring it was the first to bloom as if envious of all the attention my father gave to the apple trees and everything else in the orchard. It bore great golden pears almost as large as a Karo bucket. They got ripe in October. Before my father started working at the sawmill we would come in at night from the sunbaked cotton fields and I would lie on my back in the bitterweeds beside the lot gate, my flour sack half full of cotton for a pillow, and spoil my supper with a luscious golden pear. My mother would scold me in English. When she was really angry I got it in French.

"It was only an hors d'oeuvre," my father would say. That was one of the few French terms he knew.

"Sugar," my mother would say, meaning the pear and not my father. "Pure sugar."

The sun suddenly dropped behind Hammerhead Mountain and all the world was bathed in a pale golden light. It was early October, dry, warm, and ripe. The hiding of the sun, the softening of the light set the hills awash more vividly than ever in a sea of colors. More vividly too because I had come, unannounced, straight from the dark, dull, sultry streets of Bordeaux and the funeral. The red of the tupelo gum and the gold of giant hickory exploded against the ever-present green waves of pine. Oak and elm and maple and poplar dappled the earth as if a million of Aunt Bella's patchwork quilts had been spread precisely over the peaks and ridges.

I moved the binoculars away from all the color and back to the orchard and to my father's favorite tree, tall and old. The redbird was gone, but the apples, streaked with white, seemed to hang with unusual weight, heavy as the melons my father sometimes grew in the orchard. I wished, because it was my father's favorite tree, planted by his father, the apples could hang light as strawberries. He always had a strawberry patch too, even after he went to work at the sawmill. The summer my mother and I went to France he had to give the strawberries away.

From the mound I could see almost everything in Hammerhead except the Negro school and Milltown where most of the sawmill workers lived. To my right was the cypress grove, the cemetery, the Baptist church and the sawmill. At the top of the rise beyond the sawmill was Mr. Galloway's house, and still farther on was Tanner's Store and the bank and the giant hand and finger on the steeple of the Presbyterian church.

To my left was our house, a tin-roofed Gothic cottage which Aunt Bella always called Deer Forks. And a little farther left was Aunt Bella's house, the Elms, and the cabin for Sarah and Brooks. Below the Elms, at the foot of the hill, there gushed from the rocky cliffs a stream of stone-free water so strong and powerful that I could remember many times hearing it in the valley a mile away.

I trained my binoculars on Aunt Bella's house but I saw no sign of my father nor of Aunt Bella. The only living thing I saw was Cleo, Aunt Bella's mare, standing by the barn like the great bronze horse in Shiloh National Park.

Aunt Bella was my father's aunt. My great-aunt. I knew from his letters that my father ate with Aunt Bella often though he lived at Deer Forks. He never wrote much and didn't write often, but his lines were so wonderful that I sometimes burned them without a word to my mother. It was an awful thing to do, because when his brief, factual letters on plain tablet paper came to her she always showed them to me. He always wrote as if he expected she would come home as soon as my grandfather was well enough. That was why we had gone to Bordeaux in the first place, she said, because her father was expected to die.

I suppose he did nearly die for a long time. Nevertheless, he went to his office twice every day, early in the morning before I left for the lycée, and late in the afternoons. He was a coffee merchant. His building with big letters, MAURICE TISSOT & FILS, stood on the docks. Sometimes he took me to the river and let me watch Gilles unloading the coffee. But he was very strict with me and seemed to think I was under his authority more than my mother's. I did not want him to die. I have never wanted anybody to die. Yet, I did blame him instead of my mother for keeping me away from home, from the Elms and Aunt Bella, from Sarah and Brooks, and from Obie. I thought he was the one who had robbed my father of something, and with that feeling I often obeyed my grandfather too slowly. And it rained so much. That didn't help. From my room on the première étage, which is the second floor, I could walk out onto the narrow balcony and see the gray sheets of rain pass across the park and cry all over the Bordeaux Opera House. *Il pleut. Il pleut. Il pleut tout le temps.* Soon after our arrival, anyway, it rained for eighty-three consecutive days. The river was only a few blocks away from our spacious apartment on Cour du Maréchal Foch but I could not see it. I did not have my binoculars then.

I have always had this strange obsession with binoculars. When I was four or five my father and I rode Cleo up Hammerhead Mountain one Sunday looking for chestnuts. He stopped the horse on a ridge near the peak and took from his jumper pocket that piece of magic and searched the hills and valleys. Then he passed the binoculars into my hands and the world changed. It was like the power of prophecy. I had no curiosity about the origin of those binoculars. Knowing my father I could have believed he invented them. But later, when he gave them to me for my very own, I learned he had brought them back from France after the war, just as he had brought my mother who was very very beautiful.

One day, I must have been seven or eight then, I sat in my father's favorite tree when the apples were no larger than my favorite taw and through my binoculars watched my mother in the garden. She was awkward and lost among the beans and potatoes and corn, not like my father at all, but I thought she was the most beautiful person I had ever seen. Yet, she looked very sad.

I imagined she had received another letter from her father. He wrote to her often. There was no one else for him to write to, she said. One of her brothers was killed in the Argonne Forest and the other in the battle of the Marne.

I don't know why I did not take my binoculars to France. I could have. They were all mine. My father had made that very clear. And when he gave you something it was all yours. I could have taken the binoculars. I must have thought we would be gone a very short time. Certainly I did not think it would be four years. And not my grandfather but my mother was dead. Suddenly. It was so sudden that my father could not have come to Bordeaux if he had wanted to.

Why I wanted to see him through my binoculars first is more than I can explain. It was something I had planned carefully. I had some sort of insane notion that such a maneuver would prepare me, cleanse me for my homecoming. Deep inside me was a gnawing, guilty feeling of having deserted my father. My appearance would certainly be a surprise, for my grandfather had insisted that I would remain with him. Immediately following my mother's accident I went to school every day and made no complaint. Then one day, while my grandfather was at his office, I brought the trunk from my mother's room and began to pack. The next day I bought the binoculars and a duffel bag. That night, after I had gone to bed, the door to my room was opened very quietly. I thought it might be Maria Sousa, the maid.

"Are you sleeping?" The lights went on. It was my grandfather. I could never remember his coming to my room except once when I was very sick with a cold.

"No, monsieur."

He stood above me, tall and thin and dark, but his eyes, his whole face had a strange glow in the soft light. He wore a beautiful wine-colored gown that fell neatly but loosely about him almost to his velvet sandals. Around his boyish waist was a black-and-red rope belt with golden tassels. He glanced toward the trunk at the foot of my bed where the binoculars and my duffel bag lay. "What are these?" He inspected the binoculars. "German? *Très cher.*" He spoke English better than my mother.

"Yes, monsieur."

"Is this your mother's trunk?"

"Yes, monsieur."

He removed the bag and binoculars to a dresser and opened the trunk. He lifted a shirt. A book. A golden key. Then he replaced everything and closed the trunk carefully. "The binoculars are quite dear, are they not?"

"Yes, monsieur."

"Did you pay for them?"

"Yes."

"Monsieur."

"Yes, monsieur."

"Where did you get the money?"

"From my father."

"Recently?"

"No, monsieur. I saved it. He sent me the money many times. I saved it. He sent my mother money too."

"Did he?"

"Yes, he did."

"Very much?"

"I don't know."

"She had no need of money. Don't you understand that?"

"I don't know."

"You intend to go away?"

"Yes, monsieur."

"There is no need for haste when one is uncertain of his destination."

"I'm not uncertain."

"You understand you are under my authority?"

"I don't know."

"You don't?"

"No, monsieur."

"You are. Quite." He examined a sleeve of his gown that seemed to have some foreign matter on its cuff. "You will undertake to go without my permission?"

"Yes, monsieur."

"Why?"

"I want to go home."

"Is this not your home?"

"Yes, monsieur. In a way."

"Marcus," he said. I could not remember when he had called me by my given name. It sounded quite strange. "Your mother may have had some premonition, I do not know. But more than once she exacted the promise that if anything happened to her I would keep you here."

"Make me stay?"

"Command you to remain is the way she expressed it. Until you are eighteen. All is in writing. Would you like to see the document?"

"No, monsieur."

"May I sit on your bed?"

"Yes, monsieur."

He sat on the corner of my bed and closed his eyes for a long time. He looked up at me and smiled, which was not like him at all. "My dear child, my dear child," he whispered. "You are so beautiful. Young. Young. Forgive me. Pray for my forgiveness. I have done a terrible wrong. No. I have permitted a terrible wrong. It was not I who did. It was I who gave permission. What would I not give to have her alive in a place she hated rather than dead in a place she loved. And now they are all gone. Oh, you are so beautiful, my child, and you must forgive me. I have been strict with you. Severe indeed. Do you know why?"

"No, monsieur."

"I hardly know myself. I wanted to love you. I do love you. But each time my heart moved toward you I became afraid. I felt a guilt. I felt I might repeat some grievous error. It turned my eyes, not my heart, away from you. I was already the instrument of too much sorrow. The road is so narrow, so crowded, so unreadable, and the slightest detour can harbor disaster. But the young cannot know those things. The young are always innocent. To be innocent is everything. Do you understand what happened to your mother?"

"I know she was never going back, monsieur. She told me so."

"You see, we cannot help what we love. We can help what we hate, but we cannot help what we love. She did love me dearly, and her brothers, and her friends. The symphony, opera, dance, wine, flowers. She loved your father too, I am certain, but without... without the things of her childhood... *C'est-à-dire, c'est dommage. C'est dommage.* I think she could not bear it forever... and that is why..." He stood up. "*Eh bien, alors*, one must not talk all night. You must have your rest. The journey will be a long one. But I have tried to make all the arrangements as comfortable as possible. Gilles will drive you to Le Havre. All the reservations are first class. Some day, if you choose to return of your own volition, I shall be overjoyed... if I am alive. And I may be. My illness was never quite so severe as your mother pretended. Maybe she didn't pretend. Maybe she believed it. Anyway, her pretense was for the benefit of your father. She did love him. You must remember that and give her the benefit of every doubt. There is no accounting for the ways of the heart."

He stepped away from the bed and then turned back. "May I be permitted to kiss you, my child?"

He kissed me and closed the door quietly, and even though he wore velvet sandals I could hear his footsteps all the way to his room.

2

NOW I WAS home, with my new German binoculars, standing on the mound searching the world for my father. Again, why I wished to see him through the binoculars first is beyond my comprehension. I only know that it was so and I certainly did not think of my carefully planned action as being insane or even strange. My trunk was at the depot. And I had walked all the way from Koslo with my duffel bag. It was not a long way. Only three miles. Obie and I had often walked there and back twice in one day. Obie was a great walker. Had been when we were last together. During all the four years he had written me only two letters. I never counted but I had written him a good many more. Sometimes, in a letter, my father would write that he had seen Obie who sent such and such a message. I was anxious to see Obie too but I had no particular desire to see him first through my binoculars.

The whole world was on the verge of twilight. If I expected to find my father with the binoculars I knew it must be done quickly. I turned toward my aunt Bella's house again. The old house had been like home to me until I was five and started to school. My mother had taught French in the high school and each morning my father brought me up the hill, past the big springs, and left me with Aunt Bella. Actually I was left in the kitchen with Sarah, the cook, or with Brooks, her son, who tended the yard and garden, drove Aunt Bella's Buick, and ran errands and kept everybody happy. He looked as old as Sarah though he was always smiling and she was always solemn. If Brooks ever frowned or complained I never saw or heard it.

Aunt Bella had three subjects she discussed with me endlessly during those days: Sanford Galloway; her house, which had not always been called the Elms; and the war. She did not mean World War I, when my father had fought in France and had come home with a wife. She meant the Civil War. She was a Dixon and she told me that the Dixon name appeared on the Honor Roll of the Confederate Dead more often than any other name in the county, thirty-one in all and five of them were her uncles. Her own father, who would be my father's grandfather, was wounded in the war five times and died before he was forty leaving Aunt Bella and my father's mother to the Elms and to the care of their grandparents, William Marcus and Augusta Anne Dixon. The Elms and a trust fund came to Aunt Bella, who was never married. Deer Forks, the cypress grove, and what was left of the Dixon land came to my father's mother.

As I searched the house and the yard and the gardens there was no sign at all of Aunt Bella. She was probably upstairs in the south room working on a patchwork quilt. That room, which extended all the way across the house, still had the beds and patchwork quilts and dressers and wardrobes which the Dixon boys had used before the war. Nothing was changed except the corner of the room where Aunt Bella had her sewing table and quilting frames.

The house, Aunt Bella told me, was built by William Marcus Dixon in the heyday of Hammerhead, when virgin timber covered the hills, sawmills groaned from sunup to twilight, dry kilns blazed night and day, and lumber was moved to the railroads in Koslo by ox-drawn wagons. It was a two-storied house of heart pine weather boarding, painted a light gray and trimmed in dark blue.

Tall, oversized windows broke the gray walls above and below, and chimneys sat on the cypress-shingled roof like isolated trees on a hillside. In front of the house was a grove of giant oaks and elms and cedars, so old that no one living at the time the house was built could remember their growing, only their dying away one by one. There were no more elms than cedars or oaks but eventually the house was known as the Elms, though at first it was called the Springs because of the giant spring below the barn at the foot of the hill.

In the summertime my father and I sometimes bathed at the springs every day. Often in my room at Vingt-neuf Cour du Maréchal Foch I thought about the springs and the Elms and imagined things might have been considerably different if Aunt Bella had lived in our Gothic cottage and my mother and father had lived in the Elms. But I knew in my heart that the Elms had been rightfully handed down to Aunt Bella. She was rather tall, stout and quick, and her gleaming silvery hair and black eyes and beautiful complexion made her surprisingly attractive in spite of her slightly horse-faced image. She looked like a schoolteacher, which she had been until she was fired as teacher of Latin in Hammerhead Consolidated by Sanford Galloway soon after my father came back from the war in France. She was not actually fired. Mr. Galloway, chairman of the board of trustees, simply removed Latin from the curriculum. He had been offended by Aunt Bella's remarks as a substitute teacher in history. "I didn't malign anybody," Aunt Bella told me time and again. "I spoke the truth. I said the first fatal mistake of the war was General Lee's idiotic notion to invade the North. And when he got there, to Gettysburg, Lee was fool enough to ignore Longstreet's sage advice. The second fatal mistake of the war was old temperamental Joe Johnston who sat on his rear in Canton and let Pemberton shrivel up in Vicksburg. I ought to know. I had uncles at both places and they're still there. Their blessed bones are. Ask Sanford Galloway about his uncles."

I understood clearly from an early age that she hated Mr. Galloway, who owned practically everything in Hammerhead, including the sawmill, the planer, the dry kiln, the cotton gin, the bank, Tanner's Store, and most of Milltown where the Negroes and the poor lived.

I didn't hate Mr. Galloway, but I did consider him to be very strange. He was not like my father. Even in the hottest dog days of August he wore a suede jacket, khaki pants, a gray Stetson hat, and black brogans which he made Obie rub with tallow almost every night. Before I went away to Bordeaux, Obie, almost a year older than me, was my closest friend. When he spoke of his father he always called him Sanford. But the strangest thing to me was how Mr. Galloway ran everything with a tight hand but rarely was seen. Lots of times I had spent the night with Obie and never caught a glimpse of Mr. Galloway. If I did see him with Obie, or on the streets alone, or in Tanner's Store, he always started a peculiar laugh and asked me how much I wanted for the melons. It was a joke at first and I didn't mind too much. Sometimes he would reach out with his fore- and middle fingers and pull my nose. I always disliked that even if it was a joke. It was not a joke really. It started one year when my father had some watermelons for sale. They were beautiful melons, not sunburned at all, having been raised in the shadow of the orchard. Because he was likely to be at the sawmill if a buyer appeared, my father instructed me on the price. I think I was eight or nine at the time. A buyer did appear. He wanted a hundred melons and asked the price each. I told him, "My father said ask you twenty cents and if you wouldn't give it to ask you fifteen but not to take less than a dime."

The buyer paid me a dime and I suppose he related the whole tale to Mr. Galloway. Anyway, I kept hearing about it almost every time I met Mr. Galloway. One day, when Aunt Bella was angrily disparaging him, I told her the story of the melons. "The next time he asks you about those melons," she said, "you tell him to kiss your behind."

I did tell him. My father and I were in Tanner's Store to buy a well rope and an axe handle and some fishhooks. The clerk, Nelson Gray, was showing the axe handles to my father. Mr. Galloway came into the store wearing his suede jacket though the weather was terribly hot. He laughed his peculiar laugh which I must admit I would not have minded so much except for Aunt Bella. "Marcus, you got any watermelons for sale?"

My father ignored the question with a grand silence and handed the well rope to me so that he could inspect the axe handles. He made it clear the question was for me.

"What about it?" Mr. Galloway continued. "You ain't got no melons for sale?" He advanced toward me, laughing, ready to go through the whole business of pulling my nose. I wanted my father to turn in anger and tell the man to leave me alone, but I knew he was no more apt to do that than to kick over the barrel of hickory axe handles.

Mr. Galloway reached out and pinched my nose in the usual way. His fingers smelled of coal oil. "Hee...hee...hee...I'll give you a dime fer 'em," he said.

"You kiss my ass," I said in French. I ran out of the store, knowing there would be no fishing trip that Saturday night. I looked around for Obie and couldn't find him. I was angry with Obie too. It was his father, not mine, who was upsetting our lives. I started very slowly toward home. Just before I reached Miss Malinda Marlowe's big house I heard my father behind me, then felt his presence beside me.

"You had no business to do that," he said. He did not understand French, except a few words, but he knew what I had said.

"He had no business to pinch my nose. Like catching a mule," I said.

"Oh," my father said, and I knew he had not seen the pinch. "But he is a grown man. And you told a grown man to kiss your ass. Ain't that what you said?"

"Yessir."

"Was that becoming?"

"Nossir."

"He's your elder. He's my boss. He's Obie's father. Your best friend's father. And you told him to kiss your ass. What do you think I ought to do?"

"I don't know."

"Give me the key," he said.

I took the golden key from my pocket and placed it into the big outstretched hand and felt the world grow darker and darker. He had given me the key on my seventh birthday. As long as I was in his good graces I kept the key, but if I lost favor on any account I had to give it back. The sun was almost hidden behind Hammerhead Mountain but the clock in my mind was tolling midnight. We walked along side by side and I was glad he did not have the well rope. I felt he might use it on me though he had never whipped me in my life.

I ventured to ask, "You won't tell Mother, will you?"

"Why shouldn't I tell her?" he said.

"Because . . . because it will sound awful to her."

"Likely. Likely it will. And likely she won't cater to no fishing tonight."

"You don't have to tell her. And besides, he didn't understand a word I said. I could tell. He didn't understand a word."

He stopped. "You reckon not? You reckon he didn't understand?"

"I'm sure he didn't."

"Likely not. That does make a difference."

"And you won't tell her?"

"No," he said. "I won't tell her. But we'll have to think of something. Maybe have to put you under the bed for an hour. Half an hour anyway."

"Anything. Anything. I'll work with you," I said. He was such a wonderful man, my father, though we both knew that having to crawl under the bed and lie for even a few minutes was a terrible embarrassment.

I don't think my mother ever knew I had to crawl under the bed that day. When we got home and put the new well rope through the pulley, my father went to the barn and sent me inside to my room because he had decided my sentence would be for an hour instead of thirty minutes. I wanted to get it over with as soon as possible. Otherwise I would have gone to the barn with him.

I looked up at the slate and the coiled springs and was surprised how cool it was, the day being so hot, and wondered how many times I would lose the golden key. I didn't want to aggravate my father because every time I did it was as if he had on his Sunday white shirt and I had run up to him with muddy hands. When I did something wrong he was usually very quiet, rarely ever scolded me, and certainly never once whipped me. But I knew well enough when he was displeased. One look could absolutely make me shiver. My mother was exactly the other way, carrying on for ten minutes, half in French, half in English, when I broke a single egg or soiled my clothes carelessly. Sometimes she used the razor strap when she considered the offense serious enough. I really didn't mind the carrying on or the strap but my father's displeasure made my heart truly ache.

I fastened my eyes on a single coil of spring that spiralled endlessly, and I thought of how clean everything was. I could not see that well but I could smell the absence of dirt and dust. That made me think of how clean my father always appeared, except when he came back from cleaning the Baptist church. Other times, in work clothes, Sunday clothes, winter or summer, he always seemed as pure and unsoiled as if he had stepped from the bright waters of the springs. Oh, to be clean, forever clean, and free of my father's censure, worthy of his slow country smile. That was all I ever wanted. No goal seemed higher than to deserve that smile unfolding slowly like a cotton bloom, not soft nor always approving, but straight from the earth. His eyes were very dark and steady, his shoulders broad, his figure tall and work lean, his hands powerful, beautifully shaped with dark hair noticeable on his wrists. His movements, like his speech, were never rushed yet he did everything with such certainty and confidence that he appeared to move, to speak, more quickly than he ever did in fact.

I had been lying under the bed hardly thirty minutes when I heard the sharp, tinkling sound of the golden key on the floor. It bounced and dribbled and slid under the bed and lay there like a ray of sunlight. I had not heard my father enter the room but I knew he was there. "It's not been an hour," I said.

"No," my father said. "Your buddy's coming. You don't want Obie to find you like this."

I snatched up the key, crawled out quickly and ran to the window. Sure enough there he was, coming down the lane between our house and the Pollards', his straw hat set back on his head and half a dozen fishing canes hanging over his shoulder. I thought I could see the late sunlight dancing in his eyes, could hear the music of each certain step on the good earth, and God behind me was saying, "I'll have your mother fix us something to eat to take along while yawl git some catawba worms."

It was our last fishing trip before I was bundled off to France.

3

TIME SUDDENLY SLIPPED away from me. Darkness flooded the mound. I looked up as if searching for weather signs and saw the stars hanging in the sky like cotton bolls that have ripened too late to be picked. When I looked down again a light had appeared in Aunt Bella's house. There were lights in almost every direction although I could not find one in our house. There could be one in the kitchen, I thought, and I wouldn't see it. I quickly stuffed the binoculars into my duffel bag and ran toward home.

The nearest way led through the cemetery. For once in my life I felt no superstitions about the land of the dead. There was no thought of spirits and ghosts, and no more concern about seeing my father first through the binoculars. I just wanted to see him, hear him, touch him, assure myself that the blood flowed unhindered through his powerful body. I was almost crying when I reached the cemetery gate. I ran down the old road that curved from east gate to west gate, vaguely seeing the gravestones in starlight, thicker than the trees in cypress grove, so thick that there seemed to be no vacant plot anywhere.

At the west gate, to find the going easier, I turned away from the direction of cypress grove where whippoorwills had commenced to cry, leaped down the high road bank, and crossed the edge of the sawmill yard. The great stacks of lumber loomed like old haunted buildings, and the only thing on the mill yard that seemed vaguely alive was a new bright-red log truck with boomers and chains hanging on its stanchions like some kind of Christmas decoration. Within a minute I was in the woods behind the Pollard house.

I stopped. The crying of the whippoorwills was behind me. And so was the cemetery, crammed too full of its sad reminders. I was suddenly superstitious again and surprised at my bravery in passing along the old cemetery road. For a few seconds I thought the old black dog was trailing me. My eye caught sight of a single golden leaf falling from a hickory nut tree. Everything came peacefully into focus and I walked on slowly, feeling the unusual warmth for early October. As I neared the edge of the woods and got my first glimpse of the Pollard house the smell of honeysuckle and the sound of voices reached me at once.

"They's things to be done here too, sister, if you was to ask me. Yes, ma'am. Plenty to be done with me in the shape I'm in. And you staying over there till slap dab dark. That in itself don't look none too becoming. Looks like if you got to traipse over there every day you could manage to git back at a decent time. You know how your daddy hates to eat his victuals after dark."

"Couldn't you fix supper? For once?"

"He wanted them tomatoes. You know how he likes late tomatoes. Won't be many more. Frost coming. I woulda got 'em but my feet's been killing me agin. What kept you so late anyways? I know he's home."

I had stopped to listen. I knew the voices belonged to Mrs. Pollard and Shelley Raye. I moved to get a better view and saw Shelley Raye coming out of the garden toward Mrs. Pollard who stood apron in hand on the back porch.

"What kept you so late?" Mrs. Pollard asked again. She limped away from the naked porch light and the soft flabby features of her face became hard and dark. She looked like a fat little mannequin.

"Aw, Mama," Shelly Raye said. "I've got the tomatoes."

"But no answer. You don't have no answer, do you?"

Shelley Raye had reached the edge of the porch. I could not see her that well but I remembered clearly. She was larger than my mother, taller, and several years younger. Her face was too round, too full, like a doll's face, with dimples and magnolia white. Her hands were too large and her nose too long. And yet there was a strength about her, a goodness in her eyes, a warmth in her voice that made her beautiful and appealing. Once when I was five or six I spent the night with the Pollards and slept in the room with Shelley Raye. I remember her rolling up the sleeves of her nightgown and the dimples in the golden flesh of her elbows were so lovely. I thought I had never seen anything so beautiful unless it was her golden hair.

"No decent answer that is," Mrs. Pollard said.

Shelley Raye handed the tomatoes toward Mrs. Pollard who refused to take possession of them.

"I don't see why you begrudge every little thing I do for him," Shelley Raye said. She withdrew the tomatoes and went quickly into the house.

Mrs. Pollard stood in the naked light shouting toward the screen door of the kitchen, "It's your good name I begrudge, sister. Your good name. I don't mind so much your cooking for him at a decent hour, nor washing his clothes, nor cleaning his house. Lord knows the man's had his troubles. But all at a decent hour. All in good season. Traipse over there all you want in the daylight, but at night...and Saturday. Well, I'll have no more to say about it. You'll soon be thirty years old and if you ain't learned already you like as not won't never. I've give you my last caution about it, but I won't have no disgrace fall on this house long as I can stand and dispute it. And the Lord knows my feet's been killing me."

The screen door opened. I heard Mr. Pollard's voice. "Will you come in the house and just shut up? Just shut up for once?"

"I know you," Mrs. Pollard said. "You don't think neither one of them would do no wrong if they was both stripped off naked at midnight in the Garden of Eden."

"Hush," he said.

She said something back to him but I was running away and did not hear it. As I turned the curve in the lane, almost at the edge of our yard, I saw the light in the kitchen window.

I entered the living room, placed my duffel bag quietly on the sofa, and inched my way toward the doorway leading into the kitchen.

There sat my father, between the table and the stove, in profile, in his underwear, his hair shining, the work-firm muscles moving in his great shoulders as his big hands fumbled to pull a sock over one lifted foot. A million years of time passed by me in both directions. A few months before I had won the poetry prize at the lycée for three poems, one of which was called "Pieces." I had translated the other two into English but not "Pieces." While I watched my father—who must have thought I was thousands of miles away— pull on his socks and lace his shoes, I began in my mind to translate:

> Love is yesterday, never tomorrow,
> Always time past,
> Spread like a patchwork quilt,
> A piece of time,
> Long ago and far away.
> And all we ever own is yesterday.
> A piece of time:
> The store, the sawmill,
> The gravestones, the locusts,
> And the men in their overalls
> And sweat-stained jumpers
> And the women who wait
> For the sound of steps along the porch.

All a piece of time,
Locked in the dark of the moon,
Fresh as the smell of honeysuckle
On a rainy afternoon,
Bright as April dogwood,
Clear as the crying of the locusts
That goes on and on forever,
Clear as the train whistle.
Love is the joy and sadness
That shaped my father's face.

My father leaned toward the stove, away from me, and spat into an old enamel wash pan. I knew he had a chew of snuff. He turned his back and took from the nearest chair a pair of freshly washed and ironed overalls. Slowly and awkwardly he managed to thrust each shoe-clad foot through the overall legs. I remembered how that order of things, donning his shoes first, had angered my mother. Standing with his legs wide apart, the bib of his overalls hanging like an apron, he put on a white shirt and carefully fastened his galluses. He sat down again, spat into the pan of ashes, reached for his watch and began to wind it. Above the faint sound of the winding I said, "Papa."

His head jerked upward slightly but he did not turn his face. For fully ten seconds he remained frozen, absolutely motionless, his fingers on the watch stem, his lips slightly parted. I think he was frightened. Then his face turned fully toward me and he rose slowly.

I cannot remember exactly what happened. We did hug each other and he pushed me an arm length away, gripping my shoulders, gazing at me. But somehow it was not quite what I expected. Gradually we became calmer, each of us retreating inside ourselves, moving away. The idea crossed my mind that this brief candle of excitement would soon burn out and we would be like strangers. Oddly enough the idea was not painful to me. I felt merely a tinge of sadness. My father began to ask some of the questions I expected: about school, Bordeaux, the trip, my grandfather. He did not mention my mother.

He helped me prepare a tub of bathwater. He arranged towels and soap while I brought my clean clothes into the kitchen. As I stripped for my bath the luxurious bathroom at Vingt-neuf Cour du Maréchal Foch flashed before me. Somehow, I knew my father could see those things working in my mind. We were strangers. We had to be strangers until that void of years could be filled with the old magic, or with something.

He sat a few feet away, staring at me with approval I thought. Occasionally he spat into the pan of ashes. A daring idea came to me, something I had wanted to ask him for years. I was no longer a child. I said, "Can I have a chew of snuff?"

At first there was hardly a sign that he had heard. Then he half smiled and said, "Hah." The word came out as if he spat neatly.

"I'm not a baby," I said.

"I can see that." He pointed down toward me, laughing. His face was beginning to turn red.

I sat down in the tub. "I've seen one a lot nicer," I said.

His face was a flaming red.

"I smell cabbage," I said.

"Hah," he said. He got up and went to the back door and spat all the way across the porch.

"I smell cabbage," I said again.

"Yeah." He was not looking at me.

"Did Shelley Raye cook them?"

"Yes."

"She stayed after dark," I said.

He turned and stared at me, and then he looked down at his soiled clothes that still hung on the back of a table chair. The strangest sensations imaginable were creeping over me. Courage and fear, cold and warmth, joy and sorrow. I had rarely, almost never used an ugly word before my father. He used plenty, when and where he wanted to, except in the presence of women. It thrilled me to hear him. But I knew that I was forbidden such words as surely as I was forbidden a pinch of his snuff. Nevertheless, I said, "Did you go to bed with her."

My father turned to absolute stone. Then I could see the goose pimples on his fingers. After a bit his eyes came back to life through the red sea that flooded his face.

"Marcus..."

I had never heard my name called, whispered, so strangely. He went to the doorway again and spat. The night was so still I could hear his spittal hit the ground. From the corner of my eye I could see he was leaning out the doorway, scanning the heavens. He spat again. I was suddenly very much ashamed and afraid I was going to cry. I felt I had terribly mistreated him and he had had enough mistreatment already. I jumped out of the tub and dried myself quickly, glad that his back was turned to me. I jerked on my clothes. When I dared look up his face was a terrible picture framed in the doorway and I could not imagine what he was thinking.

His voice was as calm as if we were bathing at the springs and he had asked me to reach him the soap. "I can't expect you to understand these things."

"Maybe I do understand," I said. He remained still, looking at me. After a while I said, "It's okay with me."

He went onto the back porch. I could hear him washing the snuff from his mouth. When he entered again his face seemed somewhat freer. "Do you want something to eat?"

"Yes sir," I said. I wanted to go and put my arms around him. But I could not, and worse still, I knew that something else was bound to come out of me.

He began to take things out of the warming closet. Cornbread and country-fried steak, cabbage, and stewed potatoes. We ate very slowly, as if we had already eaten somewhere else. It seemed as if I grew smaller and smaller and he grew larger and larger. That feeling had happened to me often, long before I was old enough to go to school. My father always fed me at the table. There was no high chair. I sat in his lap and he took the silver spoon that belonged to me and coaxed me again and again. He could get me to eat anything simply by pretending the spoon was the old dump truck that hauled away sawdust at the mill. He would make the sound of a racing motor: "Rrrmmmhhhhmmm. Rrrrmmmhhhmm...Here it comes. Here comes the old dump truck. Are you ready?" I remember how the spoon would inch toward me, and my father's face, larger and larger, would move farther and farther away until I felt he was feeding me from the very peak of Hammerhead Mountain.

The food, which Shelly Raye had cooked, was both wonderful and slightly nauseating. For some reason I thought of Aunt Bella's letters about the depression, how people were almost starving. Her letters were always to both of us, my mother and me. My father had continued to work, Aunt Bella had written, because nobody else knew half as much about the sawmill and lumber and timber. She gave no credit to Mr. Galloway.

"Is the depression still bad?" I said.

"Not quite as bad," my father said.

"Did you work all the time?"

"Yes, except when the mill closed two or three times."

"Did Aunt Bella lose most of her money?"

"Some. But things may come back."

"Didn't you pay for Mother's funeral?"

"Yes."

"Did my grandfather ask you to do it?"

"No, he didn't ask me. I asked him."

"Why did you do that? He's rich."

"I know he's rich. That has nothing to do with it."

"But you don't have any money."

"I made arrangements. I got it."

"How?"

"I signed a note. I promised to sell some timber."

"The cypress grove?"

"Yes."

"I don't see why you didn't let him do it. He's rich."

"She was my wife. Your mother was my wife."

"She wasn't coming back."

"I know that."

"Why wasn't she coming back?"

"Good reasons. To her."

"Because of Shelley Raye?"

"No. Nothing like that. Nothing like that happened before."

"Why did she go away?"

"I don't know. It can't be explained. It was nobody's fault I guess."

"Why did you let her take me away?"

"I don't know. It was not what I wanted."

"Why did you let her?"

He crumbled some cornbread into the cabbage soup in his plate and ate it with a spoon. "It seemed the right thing to do."

I had stopped eating. Everything inside me was churning. "For a long time I didn't know she wasn't coming back," I said. "But you knew. And you let me go away."

He kept scooping up the cornbread and cabbage soup. I got up and began to stack the dishes. "Leave them till morning," he said.

I went to the doorway and looked out into the night. "Why did you let me go away?" I said.

"Goddammit, I said it seemed the right thing to do. It wasn't her fault. It wasn't anybody's fault. It's just the way things happened and I don't want any prissy-assed snobbish questions. I know this was no world for her." He went out of the room.

I went onto the back porch and felt how suddenly the night had turned cool. I urinated. A whippoorwill cried deep in the woods toward Hammerhead Mountain.

I returned to the kitchen, turned off the light, and went into the living room. In the darkness I could see or imagine every piece of furniture as it always had been. I stood on the hearth feeling a warmth from the dead ashes. Then I sat down and waited. For a while I wished I had never come home, that I could be safe and sleeping in my big bed at Vingt-neuf Cour du Maréchal Foch. It was well past midnight there. My grandfather would send me the money, but I knew I did not want to go back. *Il pleut. Il pleut.*

After a while I went toward my room. As I passed my father's door he said very quietly, "I fixed your bed, but you can sleep in here if you druther."

Then I began to cry. I did not answer him. I entered the room, took off my clothes, and slipped into the bed beside him. I kissed him on the cheek and chin and lips and held him as tight as I could. My face was against his shoulders and I could smell the sharp lingering of soap. I could feel the firm flesh as if most of the power in the world had been caged beside. I felt his hand, rough, gentle, accusing and forgiving.

"Say something to me in French," he said.

"*Car Dieu a tant aimé le monde qu'il a donné son Fils unique, afin que quiconque croit en lui ne périsse point, mais qu'il ait la vie éternelle.*"

"What is that?"

"Don't you know? That's John 3:16. For God so loved the world..."

"Nice. Say something else."

"*Je t'aime...je t'aime,*" I said. "I love you more than anything else in the world."

4

BEFORE I BECAME fully awake there was a sudden and overpowering fright that I was alone, lost, and would never again be able to orient myself. Soft blue light came from somewhere and washed against the half-opened door of the big walnut wardrobe in the corner of the room. I thought I had seen the door swing open, but as I focused clearly everything seemed deathly still and I knew where I was.

My father was gone. Within a breath or two all the night-scattered pieces of my mind came together and I knew that my father had put on his khaki trousers and shirt and leather jacket and had gone to the church where he had gone every Sunday morning since I could remember to sweep and clean and arrange the chairs in the choir and the songbooks along the unpainted white oak pews. He seldom went to Sunday school and preaching but he cleaned the church every week for no pay. That always angered my mother.

My first impulse was to leap out of bed and go to help him, to be near him. Then I remembered it was something he liked to do by himself. It had never seemed strange to me before, his cleaning the church, but now I felt there was something odd and extravagant about it, something sad and depressing. Like Miss Malinda and Mr. Carmichel, both of whom might be dead now for all I knew. Miss Malinda lived in the biggest house in Hammerhead, larger than the Galloway house, a fading yellow three-storey affair partially shaded by giant pecan trees. There were no flowers in her yard. There was nothing in her yard but the pecan trees and two big ferocious dogs that came loping to the fence like tigers, bristling and snarling, the minute they sensed the presence of anything on two legs.

Mr. Carmichel lived in a little bungalow near the school grounds and his yard was covered with flowers the year around. In his black alpaca coat and tiny bowtie and silver visor he ran the bank for Mr. Galloway. He had been married when he was twenty and his wife had died a year or two later. Miss Malinda and Mr. Carmichel had courted each other for forty or more years. They had never married, people said, because she had promised her father she would never change her name from Malinda Marlowe. But every Sunday afternoon they walked through the town and down the road and past the sawmill to the cemetery and looked at his wife's grave. They were both Presbyterians. She always took her parasol and he always wore his black alpaca coat, usually with striped trousers. Sometimes he carried a handful of flowers. Obie and I used to watch them.

I jumped out of bed, thinking of Obie. I dressed quickly, found the kitchen table clear except for some cornflakes and a pitcher of milk. I ate as fast as I could and ran out of the house. Silvery waves of light pushed the blue in all directions. It was warm for October. The single cry of a guinea hen behind the Pollard barn made me realize how still and quiet the whole earth was.

There was wine in the air, mist in the valleys, for the sun had not yet showed itself. I rushed past the Pollard house and entered a path in the woods, a shortcut to Obie's house. Looking back I saw Mr. Pollard, barefooted, in his shirttail, come to his back porch and prepare to urinate. I remembered how my mother would scold my father for such a thing. How could she be dead now? How could anything beautiful die? Through the trees, across October, beyond the wide waters I saw her walking through the park between my grandfather and me toward the opera house, and much as I wanted to blame her for the last four years I could not. It is awful hard to blame people after they are dead. But I certainly would not blame my father either.

Although it was quite warm for an October morning there was a breeze all around me, as if a million noiseless and unseen birds beat their wings in a slow and peaceful cadence. I could hear my footsteps on the dry leaves like pages torn quickly from a calendar, and I had the feeling that the forest would never end. I was lost for a moment. To be lost at night is frightening enough but to be lost in early morning October light is more terrible, for every direction seems to lead to eventual darkness.

Such were my thoughts as I passed on hurriedly. I had thoughts like that very often. Sometimes I felt I was completely crazy. But anyway, the old black dog was not following me. The old black dog had first appeared one night, not long after we went to Bordeaux. I was coming from the river where I had gone to watch a light cruiser pass by. It was very dark and I was late although we never ate supper until nine o'clock. I was thinking: *Ab ovo...ab ovo... Ab ovo usque ad mala.* From the egg to the apples. It was something we had read in class that day. I reached the park running, looking ahead, trying to make out the great oval door of Vingt-neuf Cour du Maréchal Foch, expecting to see my mother outside, angry and squalling at me in a way my father never had and probably never would. I heard the loping and panting behind me. A monstrous black dog was chasing me. The burning eyes and bared white fangs and slobbery red tongue came nearer and nearer. In my fright and haste I stumbled against the corner of a park bench and crashed into sweet-smelling shrubbery. I looked back and there was no dog, only the deep dark shadows of streetlights and the damp, fermenting smell of the city. I could not remember where

I was. But that did not frighten me. I thought morning will come. I will find myself when morning comes no matter how dreary and rainy. *Il pleut.*

But the feeling of being lost in the woods that October morning, on my way to Obie's house, was different. Strange flashes of time moved about me like leaves, different shapes, different colors, different heights. I felt I had never gone away to France. My mother was not dead. Shelley Raye had never cooked anything for my father. My mother had a beautiful name: Alma Cara Tissot. Aunt Bella said "Almacora."

I ran out of the woods onto the field road that led down toward the Negro church and the Negro schoolhouse and led upward toward the Galloway house. In the brighter though still pale light I saw a tall thin figure, bundle under arm, coming up the road. With half a glance I knew it was Lizzie, who cooked for the Galloways. I had always loved her almost as much as I loved Sarah. She was so tall and straight and spoke perfectly in a beautiful voice. Her husband, Jonathan Thames, was the principal of the Negro school. He also spoke like a cultivated Englishman, which very much aggravated Mr. Galloway, and others too I suppose.

Lizzie did not see me and when I suddenly confronted her on the shoulder of the field road she screamed and her bundle flew into the weeds.

"Who are you ... who are you?" she cried.

"Oh, Lizzie, it's just me." I scrambled into the weeds to recover her bundle of Sunday clothes.

"Marcus? Is that Marcus Oday? Mr. Willard's boy?"

I brushed the dust from her bundle. "Of course it's me. I'm sorry, Lizzie, I didn't mean to frighten you. I'm back."

"You certainly are," she said. She took the bundle, her hands trembling.

"I sure didn't mean to scare you."

"Of course, you didn't. But you never know. So much meanness. It's got so you can't trust people. My, but you have grown. You have indeed. You're most tall as Mr. Willard."

"Not quite."

"No, but you will be."

"Do you think so?"

"Surely. How old are you now?"

"Fourteen. I'll be fifteen in two weeks."

"I'm sorry about your poor mother. She was a sweet person."

"She liked you too, Lizzie. She missed you."

"Miss Alma was a mighty sweet person."

"I think she liked you better than anybody here. You and Jonathan too."

"Oh, no."

"Yes. She did, I think."

We had started walking toward the Galloway house, the back of which we could see at the crest of the hill. I was thinking how Lizzie would cook breakfast, then dinner, then dress in her Sunday clothes for church because she would not have time to go home. Things hadn't changed very much.

"You haven't seen Obie yet?"

"No. I got home late yesterday. How is Jonathan?"

"Well enough. He keeps trying."

"Is he writing?"

"Yes. He's had a thing or two in magazines recently."

"I won the prize for poetry. In school."

"Did you?"

"Yes."

"In French?"

"Yes. Three poems. They don't translate very well into English. But I'll show them to you and Jonathan. They're sort of about my father and mother, in a way."

"I'd like to see them. I'm sure Jonathan would too."

We had reached the big screened back porch of the Galloway house. Even from the back the house was impressive. It was a lot like Aunt Bella's house, two-storey, white framed, rambling, with cypress shingles. It was much better kept than the Elms, neater, more orderly. There were no missing shingles or cracked windowpanes, no decaying weather boards, no rusty screens, no drooping rain spouts. Mrs. Galloway's father, Oscar Baron, had built it in the days when he owned the first sawmill in Hammerhead. Obie had told me lots of times that his father didn't like the house.

Lizzie went ahead of me into the back hall. She placed her bundle on the table beside the walnut staircase. I knew that Mrs. Galloway slept downstairs on the east side and Mr. Galloway slept downstairs on the west side, and Obie had the second floor all to himself.

"They're all still asleep," Lizzie whispered. "You can just run up and rouse him."

I knew the way well enough, but I climbed the stairs cautiously, as if it were the first time and I did not know where everything led. I knew every step, every corner, every chair, every picture, every curtain of the whole house. But there was a feeling of strangeness. It's all gone, I thought. It's all changed. Once, in spite of Mr. Galloway, I had loved that house more than any other spot on earth, unless it was the springs. I loved every color, every smell, every taste. Surely it could not have vanished entirely. In a minute it would all come back, the smell, the feeling, fresh and bright as my father's orchard in April.

The door to Obie's room was closed. I stood looking at the doorknob for a long time. The polished brass looked bluish in the gray light, hard and hot, as if the touch of it would singe my fingers. Always before it had seemed soft and inviting. I touched the metal tentatively, opened the door slowly, and stood inside.

He lay on the bed in a half curl, his face between the two pillows, one of which he clutched in his left hand. The covers had been kicked back so that I could see he slept in a polo shirt and shorts. Golden light seeped under the half-drawn window shade and set his features in sharp relief. He was much darker than me, with black hair, black eyes. His brow was wide and high and his nose was straight and a bit too long, but I thought he was strikingly handsome. I did not find much change in him, except his arms. They appeared to have doubled in size while his hands were the same as ever, giving the impression of being not quite clean nor noticeably dirty.

The room looked the same. It smelled the same too, like flowers in a vase rather than dew fresh on the bush. I thought we might take up where we had left off but I was not certain. Slowly I began to whisper:

> Rise and shine,
> Rise and shine,
> The king of England
> Is a friend of mine.
> If he comes over
> To borrow some lard,
> I want somebody
> To meet him in the yard.

It was something my father used to say to me. As I whispered, Obie tried to come awake. He turned his face away from the light and buried his nose in a pillow.

Then I said his name the way my mother used to say it. "Os-cair Bar-rone."

He bolted upright and screamed, "Samson!" He had the old fire in his eyes. "Damn you! Where did you come from?"

I stood laughing at him. He beat on a pillow and cried, "Samson . . . Samson, damn you."

It was a name he had given me long ago when I wore Samson-brand overalls instead of knickers. I wanted to grab him and hug him but I was afraid the time was not right.

"Sit down," he said.

I started toward the nearest chair.

"Not there. Here."

He shoved a pillow against the headboard and I crawled onto the bed. He seated himself in the middle of the mattress, his legs crossed and his feet tangled in the sheet.

"Your hair is too long," he said.

"I'll cut it if that's what you want."

"You would, wouldn't you. God, you shocked me. Is it really you?" He reached over and grasped my ankle, pulled my sock down and rubbed my shin. "It's you. I'd know you in the dark. I had no notion you were coming home. Have you just got here?"

"Last night."

"Do you think I'm retarded?"

"Retarded?"

"I flunked first-year algebra. I'm taking first and second this year. Now I'm flunking both. Sanford thinks I'm retarded."

"And you're trying hard not to undeceive him?"

"I'm not trying hard to do anything. Undeceive? Samson, you're a pink-ass genius. That's what you are. I've missed you. I never flunked anything when you were here. Why did you have to run off?"

"I didn't run off."

"What happened to your mother?"

"She had an accident."

"I know that. But what happened?"

"Do you know where Biarritz is?"

"Me? I'd have trouble finding France."

"Biarritz, from Bordeaux, is about like from here to Nashville. She ran off the road, off a cliff. There was a priest with her."

"A priest? A priest was with her? In the car?"

"No, not in the car. When she died. To give her the rites. She was coming from Biarritz. Sometimes she went there by herself. I didn't like Biarritz."

"I guess you don't want to talk about it."

"Sometimes I don't. Sometimes I do. They bury people on top of one another."

"In the same grave?"

"On top of one another. Things are not like they used to be, Obie. I don't know what it is. I've thought about you a lot. Things used to be easy. Remember?"

Obie did not say anything. He looked sad. He had funny ways on the outside, funny ways of talking, but deep inside he was guiltless. I got up and went to the window. The sun was coming up pure gold. Across the street Dr. Zender came out of his house and went along the sidewalk with his satchel. Aunt Bella called him Ziddie. He was not hurrying. He paused as if to go into his office which was beside his house. Then he went on, more quickly, along the sidewalk. "It's sure different," I said.

"What is?" Obie said.

"I don't know. The world, I guess."

"Is everything in France old?" he asked.

The question surprised me. I turned to look at him. Whatever was going on inside me was going on inside him too. "Old? No, everything there is not old."

That seemed to settle something.

"What time did you get home last night?"

"About dark."

"I wish you'd come by last night."

"I thought about it."

"I took Sanford's new log truck to the top of Hammerhead and came down. He'll kill me if he finds out. I wish you'd been with me. I could have killed myself."

"How did you get the keys?"

"He keeps his extra set hid under his chair cushion. In his office. Your dad's gonna drive it till Tony Carl gets well. Tony Carl broke his leg."

"How?"

"A boomer flipped and a log rolled on him. You want to go with me next week? We'll take her to the top one night."

I didn't say anything.

"Well, do you or don't you?"

I still didn't say anything. I thought he knew it was the sort of thing I would be afraid to do and he was laughing at me. I was afraid to do a lot of things he wanted to do.

"Okay, I'll get somebody else."

"Who went with you last night?" I asked.

"Nobody. If I don't get nobody I'll take her up again by myself and this time bring her down with the lights off. I don't need you to help me. I can do it without the continental kid. You're not my idol, you know."

All the sunlight had vanished from the room. I moved a few steps toward the door, then turned. "I came up here because I was . . . was . . . felt lost or something . . . and I thought you'd make me feel better. But you don't want to make anybody feel better. You just want to act foolish. I never thought I was anybody's idol and don't want to be."

By the time I reached the door he had grabbed my arm and twisted me around. "Are you crazy? I didn't mean to hurt your feelings. When have I ever hurt your feelings?"

I kept looking at him. He seemed like a stranger. He caught the pocket of my coat and tugged lightly. "When? When have I ever?"

"I don't guess you ever have. It's not that."

"What is it?"

"I don't know. I'm all...crazy likely. I only want to do what's sensible."

"About what?"

"My father. You. Everything. I don't want to be a Catholic. I don't want to be a Baptist. I don't want to hear anything about my father and mother. It's nobody's business. I don't know what's bothering me."

"You think nothing ever bothers me? Listen. You don't know how glad I am to see you. I guess that is why I was acting a fool."

"I didn't mean that, Obie. What I said."

"I don't care, long as you're not mad."

"I'm not mad."

"Well, sit down. Let's start over again."

"I have to go to Aunt Bella's after awhile."

"She can wait. She's probably not up yet. When it's ready I'll get Lizzie to bring us up some breakfast like she used to."

I sat down in a chair. Obie sprawled on the edge of the bed. "I want to tell you something," I said. "No matter what's happened, if the world started new again and I could choose my parents I'd sure want the same ones."

"I never thought about it," Obie said. His voice came from far back in the past, and the room grew brighter and warmer.

5

IT WAS ALMOST noon when I reached the Elms. The shade of the great walnuts and oaks and elms at the edge of the yard was inviting, for the sun though not directly above was sweltering the earth in the manner of the deepest dog days of August. I stopped in the shade to look at the house which Aunt Bella had more than once told me would one day be mine. Roses and verbena and cape jasmine lingered in isolated patches, reluctant to believe that winter was not far beyond Hammerhead Mountain. The house was old and dilapidated in many areas but no part of it seemed neglected or misused.

The room most alive to me was Aunt Bella's office at the back of the house, across from the big kitchen. It had more of the feeling of Aunt Bella than the rest of the house. All the other rooms with their pictures and old pieces of furniture and scatter rugs and doilies seemed to belong to the past, to somebody else in the long ago. The northwest upstairs room was somewhat different. It seemed to belong to my father. That was where I always slept and where my father had slept as a child. Some of his childhood toys and pictures were still there and Aunt Bella would not let them be removed from the room for any reason.

My father kept his rifle there. I don't know why. I think it might have been because of my mother who hated every kind of gun. I know that when we went hunting we left from the Elms and returned to the Elms, although my father made no secret about where we had been. It was an exceptional rifle. I could occasionally hit sycamore balls with it at fifty and sixty yards while my father rarely missed at any reasonable distance. The northwest room was my favorite room and Aunt Bella's office was my next favorite, probably because of her typewriter. The walls were lined with all sorts of school photographs and mottoes and needlework and certificates and awards. Prominent among the display were two framed copies of poems I had written when I was nine or ten.

Most prominent in the office was a large picture of Oliver Tolliver on a horse in front of the boardinghouse, called Corley's Den, where Aunt Bella lived when she taught in Old Town. My father said Oliver Tolliver had been Aunt Bella's beau in those days. I think she liked for my father to tease her about Oliver, who was a very strange character according to both my father and Aunt Bella. When I would do something awkward or strange or mildly aggravate my father, he would invariably call me Oliver Tolliver.

The first time I could remember staying in the house I was two years old. Aunt Bella taught me the alphabet, she taught me to read and to write. She let me peck away for endless hours on her old typewriter which nobody else was allowed to touch. By the time I was five I knew the names of a hundred Confederate heroes and the outcome of fifty battles, great or small: Vicksburg, Shiloh, Gettysburg, Iuka, Holly Springs, Brice's Crossroads. Long before my first day in school she opened her Civil War rosewood casket and read me all the letters her uncles had written home from the battlefields. In great detail, I heard Van Dorn and Beauregard and Longstreet praised, Jackson and Forrest and Pemberton glorified, Lee censured for invading the North, Joe Johnston damned for sitting idly in Canton, pouting and fretting, never once even feinting to relieve Pemberton at Vicksburg. She told and read and sang to me the whole southern history of the Civil War. When at last she had covered everything, had exhausted her resources, she began to invent in order to hold my interest. She combined, reshaped, transposed, embellished, all with the conviction that if the facts shifted like clouds in the wind, the truth remained as fixed as the stars. Her favorite story, and one of mine too, was about her uncle Elbert who sneaked through the enemy lines surrounding Vicksburg to bring back percussion caps from Canton. Uncle Elbert claimed to have talked with Grant's twelve-year-old son. The star-fixed truth in her mind was simply that the Dixons were glorious heroes and never backed down from anything.

I was still looking at the house when I saw Aunt Bella's old Buick touring car appear on the road leaving a little wake of dust. Brooks was driving, dressed in his chauffeur's jacket which he often wore to church. Beside him was my father. In the back seat was my trunk.

We had our homecoming on the front porch of the Elms. Aunt Bella in her bonnet and gray wrapper, tapping her cane every fourth word, took center stage. She kissed me no less than half a dozen times and kept whispering, "Poor Almacora...poor Alamacora." She ended each embrace by backing away and giving me a few love licks with her cane. Sarah left the scene twice to see after something in the kitchen. Brooks kept smiling during the whole reunion. He had the most winning smile I had ever seen on a human countenance, his perfect white teeth shining, his eyes gleaming a willingness to perform any favor. He kept saying to my father, "The great day done come." I don't remember my father saying anything until we were seated at the table, and out of the blue he asked, "How was Obie?"

I don't know why the question should have startled me. But it did, enough to make me slow in replying. "He's fine," I said.

"He may be fine," Aunt Bella said. "The child may be all right. I don't know any harm against him, and I don't hold with visiting the father's sins on the children. But I've got a presentiment that one of these times you, Willard Oday, are going to rue the day you ever had any dealings with Sanford Galloway."

My father seemed much more interested in the food that crowded the table than anything Aunt Bella had to say about Sanford Galloway from her chair of authority.

"He may have his shortcomings," my father said. "Most of us do."

"Shortcomings," Aunt Bella cried. The room shook with her voice. It was an enormous room, with the great dining area on one end and the kitchen area on the other. Except for the electric stove and the sink and a few minor changes, I imagined the room, with its cherry and maple hutches and built-in cabinets and fixtures, to be very little altered from the time when William Marcus Dixon sat at the head of the great walnut table.

"Shortcomings," Aunt Bella repeated more quietly. "I don't label his transgressions shortcomings. He's done more harm in the name of good than a dozen rabid Crusaders. He didn't hurt me when he abolished Latin, nor this child's poor mother when he in his infinite wisdom chose to delete French from the curriculum. No, he didn't hurt us. We could live. Thank God Grandpa and Grandma Dixon saw to that. But the poor fact-starved children. Do you think his infinite wisdom provided one nodding thought for the children? He did it for spite. Your wife could have been teaching French till doomsday for all he cared if she had not taken it on herself, from the goodness of her heart, to help a few poor little darkies, on Saturdays, Saturdays mind you, in their own little hovel of a schoolhouse. Don't tell me about Sanford Galloway's shortcomings. He's a spiteful, greedy, inconsiderate, goody-goody dough-faced humbug."

Brooks and Sarah, eating at the cook table in the corner of the kitchen, had stopped to listen. The tirade was not new to them nor to my father and me. Aunt Bella was not finished, though she paused to get a few bites down. My father continued to keep his interest on the skillet-fried chicken, the green beans, the early winter mustard, which he doused freely with hot pepper sauce, and the golden brown cornbread muffins.

"I don't know how such a man, sprouted from nothing, could get his hands so thoroughly on the very throat of this town. Because the Dixons are all dead I reckon—all but me—that's one reason. But some day somebody with the same blood type and temperament I was raised with will call that rooster's hand. I hope I'm living to see it. As for you, Willard Oday, you're too good natured for your own good. You let people run over you. That's how the bottom rail gets on top. He never would have wrangled that cypress timber out of me. He made you a loan for that sole purpose. That and that alone. I've never maligned his shrewdness. No. He has ways . . ."

At that moment Brooks leaped up and ran out of the kitchen. The others seemed to know what all the commotion was about but I did not. Sarah cried, "Git your gun, Mr. Will. It's coming."

Sarah and Aunt Bella gathered at the kitchen window, peering out toward the garden.

"Don't go out there," Sarah warned me. "You'll scare it away."

"What is it?" I asked.

"A chicken hawk big as a buzzard," Sarah said. "Pore little chickens. You hear 'em?"

I did hear the chickens squawking and found me a place by the corner window to watch.

My father was almost hidden in the weeping willow by the garden gate. The heat shimmered around him like summertime. He stood stone still, searching the cloudless blue sky. In his hand he held the rifle, a piece of magic to me.

It was a beautiful .22 Winchester with an octagon barrel of blue steel, a butt plate of black steel, and a walnut stock so carefully oiled and polished for years that I could almost identify my image on its surface. Once could. The feel of it was remarkable, not its perfect weight, but its uncanny balance which made the smallest and most distant target appear to be an easy mark.

My father continued to search the sky. I tried to look for the hawk too, but something about the garden held my attention. It wore the sadness of coming winter, with bean vines purple and brittle, cabbage leaves hanging yellow from their stalks, cucumbers gone soft and golden on dark vines. The only greenness was a patch of early winter mustard. The garden was like a house abandoned, a pasture without stock or cattle, a room without furniture save for a single piece of bright rug.

"I see him," Brooks cried from his nest in the shrubbery.

"Don't move," my father said.

The hawk flew straight up out of the woods, vivid as a Roman cannon fired in the darkness. It hung over the valley as if it might explode, and then it began a lazy circle, gliding lower and lower until it was lost behind the edge of the highest trees.

"You can't hit him with that rifle," Brooks said.

"We'll see," my father said. "He'll come back."

"Is he a chicken hawk?" Brooks said.

"A rabbit hawk I think," my father said.

"You'll never hit him with no rifle," Brooks said.

I lifted the window to get a better view. The only movement of my father was to caress the blue steel barrel gently.

I was almost tired of waiting when I heard Brooks cry, "See him? See him?"

"Hold still," my father said.

The hawk rose from the valley, climbed high above the giant oak in the pasture, circled twice, dropped slowly toward the roof of the barn, and then with a lightning dive flew toward the eerie, squawking sound of rushing chickens. The wings did not seem to move but rather appeared to be impaled against the hot blue sky.

My father fired. The brown speckled blot came on and on, bounced once, bounced twice in the dust of the chicken yard, soft as a seagull settling on a wave. Then it rose, twenty, thirty feet, sailed over the head of Cleo and crashed into the trunk of a tree. For a moment it hung against the tree like a brown knot, then settled to the earth slow as a handful of cloth.

Brooks burst from the shrubbery shouting, "Ain't nobody in the world coulda done that but Mr. Will. Nobody. You see him? You see him?"

The rest of us rushed out of the house to find Brooks holding up the hawk like a soiled garment and calling on us to witness the miraculous effort.

Sarah said, "You take that jennyman right now and put him in the ground with a shovel." More directly to the hawk she added, "You done had your last mess of chicken, you have, Mister Skythief."

"Don't gloat," Aunt Bella said. "Don't gloat. There may be others."

"Won't be no more others now," Brooks said. "After they seen this. Yawl see Mr. Will? Ain't nobody in the world coulda. You see him? I mean that thing was coming down like a bullet and Mr. Will done picked up his eye. Bet he shot him through the eye." He pretended to examine.

"You go on," Sarah said. "Put him away."

My father was calmly replacing the rifle in its case as if his feat was the most ordinary occurrence. He followed Aunt Bella and Sarah into the house.

I watched Brooks make his way to the toolshed and disappear beyond the barn with the hawk and the shovel. When my father came out of the house he had a towel over his shoulder and bar of soap in his hand. He gave me the slightest wink. We went down the hill together to the springs with my heart pounding wildly.

We did not once mention the hawk. The great stream of water roared from the earth and fell on the level floor of rock. We stripped and piled our clothes on the ground and crept under the cold, gushing stream. The water, falling from the height of a ceiling, struck our bodies like the weight of falling earth. We staggered and struggled against the force, yelling like children, our voices echoing down the valley.

I knew the ritual very well. I could not count the times. I grabbed the soap from the rock without being asked and vigorously soaped and rubbed my father's back. Then his shoulders, neck, chest. Then he took the soap and rubbed it roughly over my body, hair, forehead, neck and ears, armpits, chest and belly. His face was set, serious and determined, as if he worked on the pruning of his favorite apple tree. He rubbed harder and harder and I felt as if my soul was being cleansed. I wished the washing could go on forever.

We both moved under the roaring torrent, rinsing ourselves, darting and stretching, lifting our mouths from time to time to drink.

I came out of the water to the shelf of rock where I always dried myself. Rubbing the towel over my body I realized how much I had changed since our last trip to the springs. A great surge of something, a strange sense of power flowed through me. I stood naked on the rock and looked at my father, his eyes gleaming in the soft shadows, his body as motionless and beautiful as a savage. I sat down. My father began to soap and wash himself again. It seemed strange to me that he would wash so carefully and meticulously again. I had never thought of him as being dirty, not even when his hands were smeared with axle grease, his face caked by field dirt, his clothes sweat-drenched and circled with white patches of body salt. He kept on washing and I could not take my eyes from him.

The air was deathly still and somewhere in the woods above a mourning dove was crying. Time seemed to halt. There was no yesterday and no tomorrow and nothing moved in the world except my father. The big shoulders leaned under the water causing a spray of droplets that hung in the air like fog. Stamped in the mist I could see a rainbow so clear, so brilliant, it seemed to be touchable. My father moved and stood for a moment in the arc of the rainbow, looking in the distance, toward the hills, motionless, not smiling, yet seeming to laugh, to defy the rocky earth he stood on. And though his throat, his face and lips seemed not to move, a great yell, a triumphant cry escaped and echoed down the valley. In that moment of rainbow and sound I divided the world, rather, the universe into two parts: on the one hand a man, a god, sheltered by his rainbow; on the other hand, all the other mortals of the world, myself included, and all the land and forests and rivers and stars.

The rainbow was suddenly gone. A voice was speaking but I could not hear, could not bring the world into focus. I knew that the god standing before me, talking, laughing, was mortal, yet I had seen him one moment and forever in a timeless rainbow world, in the Garden, his father and his father's father and the others in the long line stretching back to the Tree. My blood was pounding. In my childish heart something was telling me that the god there, a mortal now drying himself with a towel, was stronger, cleaner, kinder, more perfect than all the others in that long line stretching back, and I would love him now and forever beyond anything else, man or woman or animal or object.

Suddenly something was flying at me like a great yellow bird, and I could not lift my hands to ward it off. The towel fell across my knees. I hid myself with it. My father was saying, "You wanta go up Hammerhead? We might find some early chestnuts." The voice was pure as the mourning dove still crying in the woods above us.

We started toward Hammerhead, passing along the west side of the cemetery. At the old road we turned toward cypress grove, which we sometimes called Cypress Swamps. It was actually a false swamp that meandered from the old cemetery road and ended abruptly against the rocky cliffs that hid Dixon Creek. The ground was dry and crusty as it usually was in the fall, and in certain bare spots the earth was cracked into squares like a giant checkerboard. Great cypresses, water-marked around the roots, rose as straight as flagpoles.

"Did you sell it to pay for my mother's funeral?" I asked.

"I sold it to meet my debts," my father said. "My honest debts."

"Did you have any other debts except her funeral?"

"No."

We began to hear the locusts.

He did not say so, but I knew my father had the muscadines in mind. We knew exactly where they were, near the cliffs, where the scrub oaks mingled with the cypress like cocklebur around corn stalks. The grove was cool, like a tomb, and quiet except for the locusts. From a distance we could see the clusters, clear and irregular as stars on a Christmas tree. Closer, we could see that no one had bothered this year's crop. The muscadine vines smothered the smaller oaks, crossed over a cypress limb and ran straight up the trunk of a mighty oak.

"The higher the fruit, the sweeter the taste," my father said, as if he stood in his orchard looking up one of his apple trees.

We satisfied ourselves with gathering only what was within easy reach. Then we went on, exploring the world, while the plaintive grind of the locust grew louder and louder.

We went to Hammerhead, to the very top, and did not come down until pitch darkness had settled in every valley. We had a wonderful supper of crackers and cold tomatoes and salmon straight from the can. I was almost asleep on my feet when I fell into bed, drunk with happiness.

My father put his arm lightly over me. "Are you asleep?" he said.

"Nossir."

"For your birthday . . . is it two weeks from today?"

"Yessir."

"I'm going to give you the rifle."

I went to sleep with my father's arm around me, feeling that peace had invaded every corner of the world and I would be happy forever. If I could have seen the road ahead I think I might have died that night.

6

THE RIPE GREEN of summer had long since lost itself in heat and dust. The full glory of autumn descended in waves and patches, until finally the hills in every direction blazed with all the colors of the spectrum and the skies were so still and blue and cloudless they appeared as unreal as stage canvas. Cool, crisp days came one after the other as if some omnipotent magician of weather strived for utter perfection.

I started to school. The cotton gin hummed night and day. The sawmill ran overtime except on Saturdays. The sounds of axe and saw, hammer and wedge, echoed in the woods. My father took the new red log truck to Hammerhead Mountain four and five and six times a day. He always told me how many trips he had made.

Long before the first crowing from the Pollard chicken yard my father would be in the kitchen. He would call me for breakfast and we would eat together. Then he would go off in his overalls and jumper, his lunch in a flour sack hanging over his shoulders. I always cleaned the kitchen before I left for school. At night we ate at Aunt Bella's.

My father seemed very happy. The only cross words I ever heard came from Sarah. She scolded everybody except my father. I rarely saw Shelley Raye but I knew she came almost daily to our house, because I would find something changed, or something cleaned, and always found my clothes and my father's clothes washed and ironed and neatly in the proper place.

At night was the best time. My father would sit for a while before the hearth, whether it was cool enough for a fire or not, his legs stretched out, his shoes off, his eyes only half closed, his chew of snuff swelling his jaw. I would usually be occupied with my own schoolwork, and sometimes with an assignment for someone else. Almost every night, without preface or warning, my father would tell me something about his own childhood, or something about his parents or grandparents, who were all dead before I was born. It was generally pleasant and sometimes very funny.

When he went to bed I put away my schoolwork immediately. He slept so peacefully I don't think my crawling under the covers would have disturbed him. But I did not risk it. Usually I lay awake long after he was sound asleep. Sometimes, lying warm beside him, I felt like I was guarding him against all the evils of the world.

There was nothing to mar my happiness. Yet, a dark oppressive cloud lurked in my mind. Some days, coming from school, I felt the old black dog following in the wine-bright stillness. I could hear the distant panting, the soft, ominous trot, could imagine the long drooling tongue, red as sumac, hanging from the skeleton face with its almost eyeless eyes. If the feeling was strong enough and the image clear enough I would turn and actually look. When I looked I saw all the colors of a blazing autumn, dramatic as a city on fire at night.

Sometimes, instead of the old black dog, I heard a warning in the sad rustling of frost-crisp leaves. It was more than a vague uneasiness, more than a nagging concern. I was convinced that something awful was about to happen, and I believed it to be something related to Aunt Bella. Perhaps she was not as well as she pretended, perhaps the doctor was wrong, or perhaps I had not been told the whole story. It would not be the first time the whole story had been withheld from me.

Then a totally strange transaction added to my uneasiness. It had to do with my mother's estate and some arrangements made by my grandfather. A trust fund was involved and a small checking account. Aunt Bella did most of the explaining, which simply meant to me that I could write a check for two dollars at any time on the Merchants and Farmers Bank of Koslo, a check for five dollars in emergencies, and anything else required permission of Aunt Bella or my father. Sarah and Brooks several times hinted that the trust fund was enormous. Aunt Bella told me without my asking that the amount was not to be discussed until it was settled. I asked my father if he would take the money so he would not have to sell the cypress grove. "It's already sold," my father said.

"But not paid for," Aunt Bella said.

"He has my word," my father said.

"Under duress," Aunt Bella said.

Nothing was done, and for a few days my uneasiness and anxiety related to my grandfather.

I did not concern myself whether I believed in presentiments. Yet, I found myself hugging Aunt Bella when we left at night, which was something I had not done often since my first school days.

A few days before Halloween there was a heavy frost. The leaves began to fall and much of the color disappeared from the hills. The bleakness, the feeling of winter's coming, fed my presentiments. For my birthday I had got the rifle. Aunt Bella gave me a new coat, a rich brown tweed. The day after Halloween, to lift my spirits, I wore it to school for the first time. I was not surprised when Obie failed to notice it. But later, at noon, I was somewhat jolted when he seemed completely out of humor, avoided me somewhat, and finally said with a touch of anger, "If you'd come by last night, I wouldn't be in trouble."

"Last night was Halloween. We went to Aunt Bella's," I said.

"Friends go where they're needed," he said.

I remembered the special problems Mr. Jarvis, who taught algebra II, had assigned to Obie and others who had flunked algebra I.

"I'll help you," I said. "You'll probably end up with a B."

"I'll probably end up with Sanford sending me to reform school," he said, and walked away. "Help her. I don't care."

I knew he was referring to the poem I had promised to write for Juanita Oldham. But that was not what bothered me. In my strange way I twisted things around and wondered if something awful might be closing in on Obie instead of Aunt Bella or my grandfather. The feeling was still there, somewhere in the back of my mind, when we entered algebra II.

Mr. Jarvis was copying an equation on the blackboard, making the chalk squeak as if he wrote with his fingernails.

"That gives me the shivers," Juanita Oldham said. She was a very pretty girl, thin and pale. I remembered her in fourth or fifth grade as plump and red. Her father, Harley Oldham, had worked with my father at the mill and in the logwoods for years. He claimed to be one-quarter Indian. She was sitting beside me because the class was arranged alphabetically. A few days before she had asked me to write her a poem for third-year English. I was taking second-year English, which was really a joke, because I knew more about English than the seniors.

"Have you got my poem?" she said.

Obie was trying to signal something from four chairs away. I supposed his message concerned the special problems, for Juanita had also flunked first-year algebra.

"Obie wants you," I said.

"Have you got my poem?" she repeated.

"Yes."

"Where is it?"

"In my pocket."

"Give it to me." Her tone irritated me. I didn't like her all that much. I did the poem mainly because her father worked with my father.

"Not now," I said. "Obie wants you."

Reluctantly she turned toward Obie, who liked her more than I did, but it was too late. Mr. Jarvis was already facing the class. He said, "Mr. Galloway, when you've finished with your pantomime, maybe you'd like to come to the board and solve this equation."

"Nossir," Obie said. "I'm not sure I can."

A voice from the corner of the room mocked, "Now, Obie, don't be modest."

Mr. Jarvis turned his attention to the heckler and said, "Why shouldn't he be modest? In algebra, Mr. Galloway has a great deal to be modest about."

There was a roar of laughter from the class. At that moment the classroom door opened without knock or ceremony and an eight- or nine-year-old boy stood in the doorway panting, unable to speak, evidently having run all the way from the grammar school. He continued to gasp and managed to say, "Miss Fairfield she... Miss Fairfield she..."

The class roared louder than ever. I was laughing too, until the boy finally delivered his message in three quick pieces. "She said tell you... they want Marcus... at the hospital."

Then I was smelling Juanita's hair and handing her my books and running out of the building, never seeing her face. I remembered the sound of my typing manual falling to the floor with a great explosion.

I ran ahead of the messenger boy toward the grammar school. When I reached the road I heard the sound of a horn behind me and looked back to see a taxi rolling slowly toward me across the schoolyard.

The taxi stopped before it reached me. The driver, an enormously fat man, took off his cap, wiped his forehead with his coat sleeve, and said, "Are you Marcus?" He looked down at a clipboard on the seat beside him. "Marcus Oday?"

"Yessir."

"Well, they want you at the hospital."

I did not get into the taxi immediately. I said, "What for?"

"I don't know, son. All I know is they got a call and they sent me."

I went around the car and got into the front seat. I heard the gravel spew and felt my back press against the seat. Tanner's Store seemed strange to me. Then we were on the highway.

"It's my aunt Bella," I said.

"Ya aunt been sick long?"

"Nossir. But last year she was. I wasn't here, but the doctors thought..." I did not want to say the word. We were passing a field of cotton. The leaves were gone and the rows seemed to run together in one solid white mass. In a far corner of the field four or five headless bodies moved in the bright sunlight. As the taxi passed, heads emerged from the white sea and gazed curiously.

"The doctors?" the driver said.

"Sir?"

"You said they thought something."

"They thought it was...cancer."

"Oh," the driver said.

"But then they said it wasn't. They treated her for her heart. Is my dad with her? At the hospital?"

"I don't know."

"Did he call you?"

"Don't know that either. I come in from the depot and they give me your name and said Hammerhead School. I figured it was the grammar school."

"I wish I knew who called you. I don't have any money."

"Well, I guess we can figure it out some way."

"I don't have a check blank either."

"You don't?"

"Nossir."

"You got money in the bank?"

"Yessir."

"Which bank is that?"

"Merchants and Farmers."

"Your dad a farmer?"

"He used to be."

"What's he do now?"

"He hauls logs."

"And you got a bank account?"

"Yessir."

"You a paper boy or something? Sell grit?"

"Nossir."

"How'd you git a bank account?"

"It was given to me. A trust fund."

"A trust fund? How does that work?"

"I'm not sure how it works."

We were passing through Old Town. The driver looked at me and smiled. "You wouldn't shit me, would you?"

"About what?"

"A big bank account."

"I didn't say it was big. My dad told me never to say how much it was, because I don't know. I don't know how much the trust fund is either. He'll have the money. If he's there."

"If he's not there, what we gonna do? It'll be a dollar."

"I knew something was going to happen to Aunt Bella. I had a presentiment."

We were crossing the railroad. The car squeaked like new harness.

"I say what we gonna do if your dad ain't there?"

"I don't know. I never do cash a check without asking my dad. Or Aunt Bella."

The driver turned onto Fillmore Street. "Lemme tell you something, sonny. Whenever'n you in a tight, jist always tell the truth and folks will hep you. I don't mind if it's free, ya aunt being sick and all. What I mind though is when a feller starts pissing on my leg and tells me it's raining." He turned the car angrily onto Waldron Street.

I was staring at the driver. "Stop here," I said.

"Naw, I'll take you all the way being's as I've already started this goose chase."

"Stop here. I want to stop at the bank," I cried.

He stopped the car. Before he could pull to the curb I jumped out and ran down the street. I looked back to see he had got out of the car and was staring at me as I turned the corner. A man was about to lock the bank doors, but he let me in. In a minute or two I had a blank, and the check written, and a teller gave me five new dollar bills. I asked for an extra blank and the teller gave me that too.

The driver saw me coming with the money in one hand and the blank check in the other. He got into the car and leaned over to hold the door open for me.

The driver didn't say anything for two blocks. Then he said, "I guess I owe you some kind of apology."

"That's all right," I said.

"I talked purty rough. I'd as soon you didn't tell ya daddy."

"He wouldn't care. He'd think it was funny. He's very good natured."

"Well, tag me Miss Agness and call me out," the driver said. We could see the hospital a block away. "Yessir, you never know. I was way off base and got my ass caught. I shore hope ya aunt gits better."

"I hope so too," I said. "I got this blank check if she needs something."

"Lord, Lord, you never know," the driver said. He pulled up to the hospital steps. I gave him a dollar. "Good luck, son."

"Yessir. Thank you," I said. I ran up the steps and into the lobby.

A woman in pink was behind the counter. "My aunt is here," I said to the woman. "And they called me to come."

"Your aunt?" the woman said.

"Yes ma'am. They called me from school. Her name is Miss Bella...Miss Buellah Dixon."

"Dixon? I don't think we have a Dixon."

"Are you sure?"

"I can't find a Dixon. What's your name?"

"My name is Marcus Oday."

"Oday? Yes...I know who you want. She's in the waiting room. Go into the hall. It's the fourth door on the right."

I entered the hall and the peculiar smell, like overripe muscadines, reached me. But I was feeling a certain relief. If I could see her so easily and she was in the waiting room it couldn't be anything awful. I counted the doors. I was a bit concerned that the sign on the fourth door read: EMERGENCY WAITING ROOM. Maybe she was waiting for the specialist, Dr. Davidson. I opened the door slowly. From the doorway I saw no one. I closed the door quietly and crept forward. Aunt Bella was standing in the far corner of the room looking out the window.

"Aunt Bella," I said.

She turned. She held a handkerchief to her lips. There was no walking cane.

"Aunt Bella, what happened to you?"

The tears began to come. She stood quite still. I could not remember when I had seen her cry. Maybe she had already seen the doctor and the awful word was true. I went to her and hugged her tightly. "What is it, Aunt Bella? How did you get here? Where's Brooks?"

"Wouldn't you know I sent him to Pickwick, of all days. Tony Carl brought me, bad leg and all. He's gone now to find Sanford Galloway somewhere." She tried to straighten her face with the handkerchief. "Your daddy...your daddy has had an awful..." Her voice broke into a terrible cry that I could barely hear. She turned away from me to the window.

I stood rooted to the floor. A great nausea commenced to rise, as if a living animal crawled upward in my body. I tried to speak and nothing formed on my tongue or in my mind. Everything was gray. The handkerchief and then Aunt Bella came into focus again. She was saying, "Don't you want to sit down?"

I shook my head. I could smell the sweet scent of her handkerchief. Her words were clear but strange. "He was coming down Hammerhead Mountain...and the brakes...loaded...and the brakes failed. Tony Carl said."

I felt the tears high in my nose. "Have you seen him?"

"No."

"Is it awful bad?"

She nodded. Then she said, wiping her eyes, "I don't know how bad it is. But they won't let me see him. He's still in the emergency room."

As if someone had commanded us we sat down on the sofa. I held her hand in both my hands and looked at the floor. She watched the door.

"Can't I see him?"

"No. He...They used him for everything. They couldn't run the place without him. Planer. Sawyer. Anything. They ran over him. But I'm not blaming anybody. It was nobody's fault. God will just have to take care of him. I didn't forget you. I was so unnerved.

Brooks gone. I didn't want to start disturbing the school if it wasn't bad. The nurse told me to send for you. They've got three doctors... in there. Dr. Davidson for one. That helps."

I could feel a calmness in her hand, could hear a calmness in her voice, and it made all the tides I had ever held back break loose. "Aunt Bella...if God will just let him live. Just let him live. I don't care if he's crippled or can't walk or what. If God will just let him live I'll take care of him...I'll take care of him every day as long as I live..." I could hear my own voice, loud, strange, not seeming to end. Slowly I collected myself and kept swallowing until I could hear a popping in my ears. I got up. I tried to smile. "I won't do that anymore," I said.

I went to the nearest window. Time seemed to shift in a curious way, as if today were tomorrow and tomorrows were time past. Through the glass pane the early tease of rain had now become more threatening. I thought of the poem I had written for Juanita's English assignment. I was glad I hadn't given it to her. I took the sheet from my pocket and unfolded it. The rattling of the page caused Aunt Bella to look at me.

"That's such a pretty coat," Aunt Bella said.

I read:

Oliver Tolliver

Oliver Tolliver dresses nice
And tells his private stories twice
As loud as other idle men
Drinking coffee in Corley's Den.

He brags about his close acquaintance
With the great and his maintenance
Of horses faster than the best
In one or another major test.

He tells of many mighty deeds
In progress, though he really needs
A little time to finally bring
The crowning touch to everything.

He gets extremely nervous when
One of the regular coffee men
Inquires about some slight detail
Of great ones Oliver knows so well,

Or when the uninvited take
A corner chair and boldly make
An unexpected move to learn
What Oliver's actually done.

Oliver Tolliver suddenly faced
With such specific questions placed
Upon the table deeply regrets
His loss of memory and sweats.

I stood by the window reading the poem over and over again, hearing the voice far away, "Watch it, Oliver."

"Is that some schoolwork?" Aunt Bella said.

"Yes ma'am."

I was folding the sheet and replacing it in my pocket when I saw the nurse in the doorway. As if calling the next patient she said, "The doctor wants to see you in the prayer room."

I felt a faint electric charge pass through my body. I walked toward Aunt Bella. She reached for my hand and rose. Her hands were trembling slightly, though her face was dry, almost tranquil.

"I know what it is," I said.

"Are you all right?" Aunt Bella said.

I nodded. "You know what the prayer room means?"

"Yes. I know," she said.

"I didn't even get to say goodbye."

"No," she answered calmly.

"Nobody will ever run over him again," I said.

"Don't feel that way," she said. "It was nobody's fault."

She held tightly to my hand as we passed through the doorway and entered the long hall.

7

AUNT BELLA SAID that almost every year after the typhoid epidemic the deacons had planned to close the old cemetery road in order to have more space for additional graves. But somehow an unclaimed plot was always found and the deacons, who were the trustees for the cemetery, put the matter away until the next death occurred.

The road itself was not very wide, and yet winding and stretching from the east gate to the west gate, it contained space enough for many graves on excellent ground.

They closed the west gate the day after my father died. And a day later they buried him near the new link of fence, in the center of the old cemetery road. It was a choice gravesite, as the deacons had explained to Aunt Bella, for the land rose higher at that point and drained westward toward the false indentation of Cypress Swamps. They chose the center of the road because that was halfway between the Tanners and the McClintocks.

A slow, autumnal rain fell during the afternoon funeral. The rain increased toward nightfall and grew still heavier during the night. Aunt Bella and I did not go back to the cemetery that day.

At first dark we made a fire in the living room at the Elms and sat before it, she with her crocheting and I, for some reason, with a copy of *The Hunchback of Notre Dame*.

First dark after the funeral is the worst time. Not while the casket is in the living room, nor when neighbors and friends come, nor when the final lowering begins, nor when the awful piling on of dirt commences. First dark after the funeral is the worst time. All the night sounds begin, locusts, whippoorwill, mourning dove, crickets, and you know he does not hear, will never hear them again. Can never hear you say "I love you," nor speak the words himself. And all you haven't done, and all you haven't said, can be forgotten.

I didn't cry when the people came to the Elms, not when Obie came, not when Shelley Raye came. I didn't cry at the church or the graveside. But Aunt Bella knew I could not go on forever. She stopped her crocheting for a bit and said, "We showed Hammerhead how to put on a funeral. The kind your daddy would approve. You paid for it, because everything I've got is yours anyway. We gave him the best to be had and it's all over now. If you want to cry till it puts out the fire, go ahead."

I did. It did not last long but when it was finished I felt I had emerged from the springs with my father.

Aunt Bella said, "I wanted Brother Willburn to read one of your poems but I guess it was best not to. The eulogy was nice enough. Not too long. I don't know Brother Willburn very well. He came here while you were gone. I like him though. I may pay him a call some Sunday morning. But I guess it was best not to use one of your poems. That last one kept crossing my mind. 'Pieces.' I thought about it. Something like that." Suddenly she began to laugh. "But the one your daddy would have liked wouldn't do at a funeral. Run and get 'Never Say Hello' and bring old 'Humbolt Chambers.'"

I went to her office and brought the two framed copies. She held both in her lap and with the hem of her dress wiped at dust I could not see. "You couldn't have been ten years old when you wrote these." She looked from one to the other.

Never Say Hello

Never say hello to sadness,
Nor dare give her a smile,
For she is sure to stop
And stay a while.

And happiness watching
From the corner of one eye
Is apt to mend her pace
In passing by.

Humbolt Chambers

Humbolt Chambers had a dog
Who chased a bear into a log.
A word from Hum, the dog went in
Never to come out again.
Ho hum, ho hum,
Rotten log,
Rotten log.
That's how Humbolt Chambers
Lost his dog,
In a log.

Humbolt Chamgers had a wife
Who swore one night she'd take his life
If ever he got drunk again,
And out he went to get more gin.
Ho hum, ho hum,
Butcher knife,
Butcher knife.
That's how Humbolt Chambers
Lost his life,
Angry wife.

She waved the frame of "Humbolt Chambers" and laughed until tears rolled down her face. Very soon I was laughing too. "Sometimes I would hear him laughing," she said. "Hear him laughing all over the house. And you know where I would find him? Standing there in my office reading old 'Humbolt Chambers.' Law, law, he was so good natured."

She went back to her crocheting. After a while she said, "I don't know how you feel about it, but I think, in your place, I think I'd politely put on my clothes in the morning and go to school. I know you're repeating things you've learned twice over, but it won't hurt. Whatever you think. Tomorrow's Friday. You could wait till Monday."

"In the morning is all right," I said.

Early the next morning I went to the cemetery. I had intended merely to look and go on to school. But I lingered. After a while I set about straightening and rearranging the rain-washed flowers. Then I began to wander about the cemetery, looking at the headstone, trying to decide which type my father should have. An hour went by before I returned along the old cemetery road, picked up my books from a nearby Tanner stone, and stood looking at the grave again. For the first time, I understood the merits of the site, which the deacons had tried so hard to explain to Aunt Bella. I saw the slight rise in the land and how the heavy rains of the night had moved off toward the false swamps. I rearranged one last flower and went back to the Elms. It was not yet ten o'clock.

I went to the kitchen because that seemed to me the only place in the world where things were under the control of mortal hands. I scattered my books on the table.

"Where is Aunt Bella?"

"Upstairs," Sarah said.

I waited for her to ask why I was back. She continued her chores, as if nothing in the universe touched her mind save the washing of a greasy skillet.

"Folks say don't wash a skillet. Been told that all my life, don't wash a skillet. Say it'll make them stick. Been washing skillets since I couldn't hardly touch an apron string. Not had one stick yet. People all time want to tell you something. People can't tell you nothing you don't know already. You got to know first. Some folks is born knowing and some folks never will know. If you one of the folks born knowing, then maybe folks can remind you. That's all."

"What's Aunt Bella doing upstairs?"

"New quilt. She know to keep her hands busy. And you better."

"You telling me? Or reminding me?"

Sarah didn't answer. I stacked my books neatly, my typing manual on the bottom and my algebra on top. Suddenly I wondered how my books had got home. I had not been in the schoolhouse since the fatal day, which was Tuesday.

"Who brought my books home?"

"Your girlfriend."

"I don't have a girlfriend."

"Well, I remind you she was somebody nice and she acted and talked like a friend. How come you ain't in school?"

I didn't answer.

"You going Monday?"

"Maybe."

"That ain't no more answer than the wind blowing."

"Maybe. Maybe not."

"You better."

"You telling me? Or reminding me?"

"Just suffering for you. That's all."

The next morning I went to the cemetery again. As I approached the south fence I could hear the loggers in the Cypress Swamps, the sound of the saws and the axes and the mule teams. I climbed over the fence and entered where the cemetery was thick with gravestones bearing the Perkins name. I heard the loggers again and stopped beside a mossy Woodman of the World stone. Leaning against the monument, taller than my head, I could not see the loggers. I saw instead my father in his overalls and jumper. In my imagination, real as life had ever been, I pictured every inch of his overalls. The stout cloth, the watch pocket, the bib pocket where he kept his pocket book, the Tuf-Nut label, the indentation of every button, the red stitch of every seam. And one twisted gallus. Only once in my life could I remember seeing my father with a twisted gallus. We were undressing to bathe at the springs. I saw it and laughed and my father's face turned red, as if he had said something vulgar in the presence of women.

The vision went away and I walked on, hearing the loggers. Thin clouds moved overhead in low patches. I came within a few yards of my father's grave and suddenly stopped. The blood rushed to my head. I saw something so revolting, grotesque and scandalous to me that I thought I was walking in my sleep. The new link of fence had been set aside. Deep log-wagon ruts marked the old cemetery road and passed directly over my father's grave. The flowers which I had carefully rearranged the day before were scattered in all directions. Deep prints of mule hooves appeared like postholes in the fresh mound of red clay.

I ran. I leaped over the south fence and ran all the way to the Elms.

Returning to the cemetery, I did not run. But I walked swiftly and steadily, carrying the rifle, sometimes gripping it with both hands, as if I might drop it.

I waited by the grave. Very soon I heard the wagon creaking toward me from the cypress grove, invisible among the trees and undergrowth. The wagon stopped. I heard the panting of the mules. The wagon started again.

Then I saw the bridle of the first mule, then the team, then the wagon. The ends of three logs made a triangle: two on the bolster, one in the groove. The driver straddled the top log, crouched so that I could not tell whether he sat or stood. The handle of the boomer seemed to stick up out of his hip pocket.

The driver was someone whose face I could place in my childhood but I could not call his name. The wagon moved on slowly toward me, the mules straining, the driver flicking the checklines and urging them on without using the long snake-whip that hung over his shoulder.

He saw me and stopped the mules a few yards short of the fence. He gave out a curious laugh, knowing something was wrong. With a quick motion he wiped his face with the back of his hand and looked up at the low-flying clouds.

"Reckon it's more rain?" he said.

I did not answer. I stood by the grave, holding the rifle with both hands.

The driver seated himself, twisted uneasily as if to find a more comfortable perch on the log. Tiny clouds of vapor shot from the nostrils of the panting mules.

"Well," he said, "I better mosey along. Ain't made but two loads yet."

"Not this way," I said.

The driver commenced a laugh, then stifled it. "Why, son, I knowed your daddy real well. They ain't no other way." He looked back, nodding his head. "Can't go off that ten-foot bank." Looking around toward me, he added, "Can't go around. Git one inch off that road where you standing and these logs would take her to the axle. They ain't no other way."

"Not this way," I said. I raised the rifle a few inches.

"What you aim to do? Shoot the mules?"

"The mules will go where you drive them."

"Look here. It ain't me doing this." The driver pointed toward the mill. "It's his orders. He's down there. Go tell him."

"I don't care whether he's told or not." I said. "Nobody is driving over this grave ... alive."

The driver put the lines aside. He laid the whip carefully across the logs and climbed down to the doubletree. He patted the rump of the lead mule, looked at me and back at the mule. He turned and put his hands on the logs as though he intended to climb up again. Then he suddenly jumped to the ground, fell to his knees, stumbled up and started toward the mill without looking at me. He passed the corner of the cemetery, climbed down the steep bank into the road, passed the tangled heap of Himalaya vines that grew on the other side of the road and disappeared beyond the great stacks of lumber and crossties.

Hours seemed to pass. I saw Mr. Galloway appear behind the lumber stacks. He came at a moderate gait, neither slow nor quick, giving no indication that he was disturbed at all. He looked the same as always in his leather jacket and khaki and brogans except that his gray Stetson tilted upward more than usual on his forehead. The driver followed six or eight steps behind. Both of them stopped at the patch of Himalaya vines and looked at each other. They were nearer to me than they were to the log wagon.

"Well, well," Mr. Galloway said. "You didn't make it up." He knew that I could hear him. Perhaps he wanted me to hear. He slapped two or three times at his neck as if a gnat or mosquito buzzed around him.

"I told you," the driver said. "Standing there with a rifle."

Mr. Galloway laughed. "Which one scared you? Him or the rifle?"

"He's mad," the driver said.

"It ain't the first feller you ever saw mad, is it?" Mr. Galloway said. "There's mad and then there's downright mad. I think he's just peeved a little. I don't think he means a thing. Just his feelings is hurt. Them wagon ruts looks worse cause it's wet. Which is why we got to git them out of there. If it rains much more we can't. Hop on up there and let's go."

"I ain't driving through," the driver said. "Not and him standing there with a rifle."

"Well, goddammit, I'll do it myself," Mr. Galloway said, but he made no move toward the wagon. He kept looking at the driver.

"I'm surprised the deacons let you take that fence down," the driver said.

"I didn't ask the goddammed deacons. That's a government order." He looked back toward the mill. "I guess Obie jist ain't coming. He wouldn't do nothing to Obie. They're good friends. That boy has eat at my table no telling how many times. He wouldn't harm nobody, me or you neither. His feelings is hurt. That's all. Best thing is just climb on the wagon, by god, and don't say a word to him." Mr. Galloway looked toward the wagon.

"I already told you I ain't driving through," the driver said.

"Goddammit, I said I'd do it. Why'd you stop anyway?"

"Why?"

"Yes. Why the hell did you stop in the first place?"

"The mules had to blow, I got three big logs on and after the rain..."

Mr. Galloway brushed past the driver who turned and started toward the mill.

"Where you going?" Mr. Galloway said.

"I'm walking away from this," the driver said.

"Well, you keep on walking, goddammit," Mr. Galloway said. "You just keep on walking, you hear? Don't stop at the office and don't come back Monday, or Monday week neither. And don't be telling me this winter about doctor bills and ya wife's sick. By god, if a man can't do what I tell him to do he can go to hell..." Mr. Galloway was talking long after the driver had disappeared.

He climbed the steep bank at the corner of the cemetery. He never even looked toward the grave where I stood. And the only word he spoke was to the mules, quietly. He stepped onto the doubletree and climbed up slowly. He never used the whip. He never took the whip into his hands at all. He held the lines in one hand. He won't do it, he won't do it, I thought. He's going to say something to me. He's going to argue with me and I'm not going to answer. But he won't do it. If he was going to do it he would hold the lines in both hands. Then the one hand moved. He spoke to the mules, louder now, and his voice seemed to ring all over the earth. The creak of the harness exploded in the silence. The mules were moving. They came on and on. I lifted the rifle. Still, he seemed not to see me. I held it forever, pointed into the face far, far away, tiny and round, no larger than a sycamore ball. When the first mule stumbled slightly in the soft red earth I pulled the trigger. The spot on his forehead looked like an age-old wart.

I dropped to my knees. In the soft red clay, with the rifle butt, I scratched the sign of the cross and could not have told why nor reasoned why to save my soul from a million years of agony.

8

I WAS NOT cold in the jail, not once. More often, I was hot. The weather continued to be unusually warm and the jail had steam heat. Aunt Bella sent me two quilts, some books, and a goose-necked table lamp. There was no table but I set the lamp on the radiator and had ample light for reading and writing. The only things that really bothered me were the flies and the smell of urine.

Stella, the Negro woman who cooked for the prisoners, gave my cell a special scrubbing that helped immensely. She was a graduate of Tougaloo College and once taught at a one-teacher school on the edge of Old Town before the school was abolished. She was very neat and methodical and quite cool to me in the beginning, before I mentioned Jonathan and Lizzie. Usually she brought me my meals, though occasionally they were brought by Miss Daisy. Most of the prisoners ate in the Back Room downstairs but Miss Daisy said the sheriff said I was not to be one of them. I didn't want to eat in the Back Room anyway.

I was in the special wing on the second floor, in the King's Cell, reserved for capital cases. Most of the time it seemed to me nobody else was in the building. The jail was a gray three-storey building at the very edge of the railroad tracks. From my window I could look across the railroad to court square and the Confederate monument and the big clock and the pigeons and the whittlers packed on the benches with their knives and pieces of cedar. The pigeons and the courthouse chimes and the whittlers kept me from feeling alone when the building was too quiet.

For the first week I never saw anybody other than Stella and Miss Daisy and Mr. Molock, the lawyer. Miss Daisy and her husband, Neal Fancher, lived in the jail. He was the official jailor but Miss Daisy carried the keys. She was a stout, dark, peculiarly cheerful woman, very energetic for a sixty-year-old. They had been farmers in the Antioch community until their neighbor, eight or ten years before, was elected sheriff. Mr. Fancher had been jailor since that time and everybody knew he had TB. Miss Daisy told them.

Aunt Bella sent notes by Brooks every week but it was almost a month before she came herself, without the walking cane. Miss Daisy took me down to the living room, which she called a parlor, where Aunt Bella waited. It was a long, narrow room with chairs and sofa and a used rectangular wood-burning stove at one end of the area and a round dining table covered with a red-checkered oilcloth, four cane-bottomed chairs, and a huge, oaken, rolltop desk at the other end. Aunt Bella was sitting at the table.

"Set where you like," Miss Daisy said. "I've got to go see about Neal. I guess you know he's got TB."

Aunt Bella looked as if she did not know.

"He's been worried about my Christmas shopping. I told him, Lord, not to worry. I didn't tell him Christmas ain't no more to me now than a train passing through. If we could all be well that would be Christmas enough for me. Neal's going down fast. I give him till the sap rises."

Aunt Bella put one hand over her lips and the other hand fumbled for the walking cane which was not there. Miss Daisy struggled to wedge the great mass of keys into her apron pocket while she continued talking. "This place ain't no great big pleasant help to him. We've still got our little farm out at Antioch to fall back on where he could have hot sweetmilk straight from the cow's tits morning and night. But he won't have it. Won't think of leaving. He's got it in his blood after all these years, this place I mean, and you couldn't prize him loose. They'll just back up the hearse. When I know for a settled fact what warm sweetmilk straight from a cow's tits can do. Done it for a cousin of mine who got to where she couldn't talk above a whisper, now singing in the choir. Not at Antioch. Over at Farmington. Yawl just make yourself at home. If the sheriff comes in you tell him I'm running this place. This boy don't give me one lick of trouble. He's just quiet as a mole. I never hear a word out of him less I speak first. He just props hisself up in one of them quilts you sent him and works algebra problems or something all day or all night. Reads. I don't cut the lights out no matter what the sheriff says, less there's a lot of racket. Maybe Saturday night. Sheriff usually comes by more on Saturday night. I tell you Neal's been so porely a few nights lately, with Stella gone, I've had to unlock and call on a feller or two. You may be the next one I call on, young man. I can tell. I know who'll do and who won't do. Yessir. Yawl make yourself at home and don't feel bashful."

After Miss Daisy was gone Aunt Bella sat looking at me for a full minute. We both began to laugh quietly.

"Give me a hug," Aunt Bella said.

I hugged her and kissed her and stood behind her chair for a while with my face against her hair. Then I sat down and held her hand.

"Have you been all right?" I said.

"Yes. That's not what kept me away. I wanted to think about it. Let it simmer a while. I thought it would be good for us both to let time bring it into focus. Oh, I've been over it from every angle. From scheme to skillet." She paused to look about the room.

"I could get you out of this place. Out of this country. I've got the money to do it with and there's your granddaddy too. But deep down in this old worn-out heart I know it's not what I want to do. It's not right. You know it's not right. Or would know. I suppose it never entered your mind."

"No," I said.

"No," she said. "Because you've had some advantages that few people in the world ever have. Love. Plain love, child. Deep, overwhelming, honest love. From more than one. It's not to your discredit that it blinded you for a moment, although blinded is not the right word. If you have to pay something for what you've had then just look at it that nothing comes free."

We sat for a long while holding hands before she started to talk again. "I loved once. A roamer. A braggart. A ne'er-do-well. A dreamer. Your father didn't tease me for naught. There was a lot of smoke. But fire too. Fire. Yes. I loved once. With open eyes. I knew everything about him. Knew, heard, saw. Love isn't blind. It isn't blind at all. It's all-forgiving. That's the answer to the riddle. It knows and forgives. Hears and forgives. Sees and forgives. Even smells and forgives. If it's a one-way street, that's sad, but it's still paved with gold and beats by far all the old ordinary, gravelled roads. If it's a two-way street, like yours, and something goes wrong—well, sometimes we just can't manage it."

She withdrew her hand as if to go, and again unconsciously reached for her cane. "I've talked to Christian Molock several times. And, child, I can't advise you. I don't presume to advise you, but I can't see the wrong in holding your head as high as your heart will allow. You'll have to work out your own salvation and I'm going to rest perfectly assured that you can be trusted to do it." Then she stood up. "If it's any comfort to you, I haven't yet— and I've waited long enough—I haven't yet been able to blame you one iota."

The next day Mr. Molock came again. I had already noticed that when he stood beside Miss Daisy he looked old and stooped and slightly disagreeable. Beside Stella he looked younger, straighter, more pleasant. Half of his scalp was totally bald but beginning above his big ears was a mound of thick white hair that rose inches above his head, bulged to either side, and hung down well below his coat collar. All his features were sharp and angular. His hands looked like triangles.

Miss Daisy was with him—I could hear—which meant it would take him three or four minutes to get from the top of the stairway to the chair beside my bed. I was sitting on a folded quilt with my back to the radiator. I put my books and papers beneath the pillow and waited on the edge of the bed.

"Yawl can go down to the parlor if you prefer," Miss Daisy said.

"No need," Mr. Molock said. "I don't want the sheriff on my neck."

"Sheriff go to the blazes," she said. "And have his conniption fits too. I'll run it to suit myself long as I'm here. I didn't tell you about the cake."

"No," Mr. Molock said.

"I baked this big coconut cake this morning. Put it there on the table in the parlor, and he comes down, the sheriff, snooping around and walks out with it, me being occupied with Neal having one of his spells. Tells Stella the board of supervisors is not paying for cake to convicts no more. I politely called him up and said you better have that cake back before it's good and cold or I'm calling the newspaper and name ever whiskey still in this county. Which I can do. They tell me all about it. He had a conniption fit right there on the phone but back comes that groundhog of a deputy with the cake and I didn't so much as offer him a smell. Try some when you come down. Stella will git you some coffee."

"Thanks anyway," Mr. Molock said. "I have to hurry back to the office."

They had reached my door. She handed the mass of keys to him, selecting the one he would need. "You know how to lock it back. Leave 'em with Stella if Neal's got me tied up."

Mr. Molock left the door open. He sat down in the only chair and put his briefcase on the corner of the bed. Neither of us spoke for almost a minute. A fly buzzed frantically somewhere, as if caught in a puddle of urine.

"Are you going to give me the note?" Mr. Molock said.

"Nossir."

"You always minded your parents, didn't you?"

"Yessir."

"You don't have to say sir to me. If your aunt asked you, would you give me the note?"

"No."

"Don't you know it could help you?"

I looked away toward the window.

"Do you want to be punished?"

My throat moved in tiny swallows.

"I don't mean reformatory school. They could send you to the penitentiary for life. The electric chair. You're going to be tried as if you were my age. Do you realize that? Just as if you were my age. Do you know how old I am?"

"No."

"I'm fifty-nine. Almost sixty years old. I've been before the jury with capital cases more times than you've seen Sundays. Faced a lot of jurors. I doubt I've seen twelve good and true in the whole lot, much less twelve in one box. There won't be any women. There won't be any blacks. I'm looking for a straw. Just a straw floating out there that you can grasp. Or that I can grasp for you. And you won't give me the note?"

"No."

"I know what's in it."

"I didn't tell you."

"Miss Daisy told me. Wasn't this it? 'I can't come to see you. I tried to tell him how much you loved your dad and you would do it. But he wouldn't listen to me. Someday I will tell you something about the whole business that will make your blood curdle. I still love you.' Wasn't that about it?"

"I'm not going to talk about it."

"And a postscript. A postscript asking you not to show it to anyone. What did he mean by 'something about the whole business that will make your blood curdle'?"

"I don't know."

"You sure?"

"Yes."

"Can you imagine what it might be?"

"I'm not going to talk about it."

"You've got some idea, haven't you?"

"Yes."

"What is it?"

"I don't want to think about it."

"Is it that bad?"

"Yes."

"What is it?"

"I think he might have started to drive the wagon himself. I think his father asked him to."

Mr. Molock seemed disappointed. "That's not much," he said. "You sure it wasn't something else?"

"I'm not sure of anything."

"But listen. 'Someday I will tell you something about the whole business that will make your blood curdle.' That sounds like a matter that didn't have anything to do with Obie, don't you think?"

"I've told you what I thought."

"All right. Suppose...just suppose it had been Obie. What would you have done?"

"He wouldn't have."

"Suppose he had."

"He wouldn't have."

"Dammit, suppose. Suppose he had."

"Leave me alone."

"You hired me."

"I didn't hire you. My aunt did."

"All right. All right. I'm just trying to help you. Will you give me the note?"

"No."

"Why? There's nothing to be ashamed of. Nothing embarrassing. Nothing dishonest. Nothing to conceal. You know I could call Obie as a witness. I could make him testify." He went to the window and looked out. I suppose he was letting the matter sink in on me. He came back to the chair and sat down. "You know that, don't you?"

"I hope you won't," I said.

"Why?"

"I've done enough to him."

"Yes, I suppose you have. His forgiveness is very important to you I imagine."

"Yes."

"But he never said he forgave you. He said he loved you. That's not the same thing."

"It might be. And I have to be worthy of it. I can start by not giving you his note."

"You don't really believe I can save you, do you?"

"I don't believe the note can save me."

Mr. Molock went to the window again. "Probably not. It's probably not important at all," he said, quietly. "It might look as if we planned it, might even hurt you."

He waited a long time before looking back at me. Then his eyes lighted, as if some new inspiration had come to him. "I always know how a case will end. Almost always. I work hard. I dig it out. I put it together piece by piece. I surprise if I can. I prepare for surprises if possible. But in your case there are no surprises, no pieces, and very little to dig out. There is only one straw to hang on to. He is sorry. He is deeply sorry. You've got to say that and make the world feel it, believe it. Oh, I know how you feel. But consider these factors. You're a bright, bright young fellow. You're an honor student. You've lived in Europe. You speak French, you're half French. You've had a lot of advantages. The deceased employed your father. He employed a lot of people. He was a successful and outstanding man. His son was your friend. Your aunt is rich. Do you think any of that is going to help you? No. You've got to say you're sorry and make the world feel and believe it. You've got to say..." A train whistle sounded and interrupted him. "You've got to say you're sorry."

"I won't say it," I said.

"What are you leaving me with? I could say he cursed you, but he didn't, did he?"

"No."

"I could say he lashed you with the whip. He had a whip, didn't he?"

"Yes."

"Did he strike you with it? Attempt to strike?"

"No. He didn't even hit the mules."

"The truth is you never thought of who was doing it. You didn't care whose face it was. He just goddammit was not going to drive over your daddy's grave. Is that correct?" His voice had reached a high pitch.

"Yes."

"And the purest truth of all, pure as cold spring water, you'd do the same damn thing again."

Something made me get up. I had to rise. I had to stand up and say what was in me. My voice commenced quietly and rose stronger and stronger. "He could have built a road in an hour. Found another way out. He didn't have to come that way. He owned the whole world, and he ran over people. He mistreated my aunt. He mistreated my mother. He took advantage of my father and then he couldn't even respect his grave. Yes, I'd do it again, and I won't say I'm sorry to you or the judge or anybody else." I sank back on the bed, surprisingly calm after my outburst. "They built a new road. Aunt Bella told me. They've put the fence back. Nobody else will run over him."

"No," Mr. Molock said. "I don't imagine they will."

On the second Tuesday in January I was arraigned before the presiding judge in open court. That day there were no more than five or six spectators in the gloomy, shadowy courtroom. The judge asked the district attorney to read the charge. I heard: "Comes now the grand jury, duly impaneled and sworn, and on its oath charges that William Marcus Oday, on or about November 5 of the calendar year past did willfully and unlawfully and feloniously and with malice aforethought kill and murder one Sanford Bush Galloway, a human being, contrary to the laws and against the peace and dignity of this state."

I heard more or less what I had expected to hear. But I saw that Mr. Molock, beside me, had turned very pale and his face was twitching. Suddenly he cried out, "My God, man, you're charging him with first degree. You're charging this child with first degree murder."

"The jury can decide," the district attorney said.

"But you led me to believe..." Mr. Molock turned to the judge. "Manslaughter, your honor. He certainly led me to believe manslaughter."

"Your honor," the district attorney said. "I did expect manslaughter. But I am not the conscience of the grand jury. The world well knows that the victim was a leading citizen of the western part of this county. Of the whole county for that matter. It distresses me too."

"What distresses you is the loss of a political supporter," Mr. Molock said.

"Your honor, your honor," the district attorney cried. "This is too much. This is a brutal attack on my..."

"Gentlemen," the judge said. "Gentlemen..."

Mr. Molock and the district attorney were glaring at each other as if they might come to blows.

"How do you plead?" the judge said.

"Not guilty," Mr. Molock said, very weakly.

The trial commenced two days later. It took a long time to select a jury, but the trial itself was brief. Every face in the jury box seemed hostile to me. The swivel seats reminded me of the state's portable electric chair. In the middle of the trial, after a joint motion of the prosecution and the defense, the judge accepted a reduced charge of manslaughter.

The sentence was fifteen years, a year for every year I had lived. "The court," the judge said, "is painfully aware of the fact that the defendant has shown no sign of remorse whatever."

Mr. Molock was stunned. His voice trembling, he said, "Your honor, I ask permission of the court to file for reconsideration of the sentence." He whispered to me that he expected the motion to be granted, taken under advisement, and he would have time to prepare his statement.

Hardly a minute later, the judge said, "The motion is granted. If you have something to say, the court will hear it now."

Mr. Molock walked toward the nearest window. I knew he was stalling for time. I could see that he felt miserably unprepared. But as he returned slowly, his head bowed slightly, a great change came over his face. "Your honor, granted the defendant has refused to make a statement, does silence mean he is not remorseful? May I respectfully refer to the record of many honorable and courageous men who fought for this country, as did the defendant's father, in the late Great War? Honorable men who killed human beings because they felt they were defending this country. They destroyed human lives. Would we ask them to repent? Should they be remorseful for having served their country, as you, your honor, served, with great distinction, the recipient of many battlefield decorations? Can not the actions of this child be placed somewhat in that category? He was defending his castle, the final resting place of the one he loved most in this world. The action was brought to him, your honor. I submit that his silence, his refusal to make a statement of contrition, has nothing whatsoever to do with remorse. Your honor . . . your honor . . . many times in the dark hours of the night the image of this child has come to me, like a brave soldier on guard, and the tears come to my eyes because I wonder . . . I wonder if I would have the courage to so defend the one I loved. And if I should . . . I think, your honor . . . I think I would not say I was sorry."

Mr. Molock sat down. The tears were visible on his face.

"Thank you," the judge said. "I will rule on your motion tomorrow at ten o'clock."

The sentence was reduced to five years.

II

Olanberg

9

A DEEP GRAY hush lay over the road and the countryside, filled the car, and seemed to hold everything, even the small town through which we passed, motionless.

In the backseat of the car I slumped, my eyes partially closed as if I were asleep. Something was flowing through my mind like the cool clear water of the springs. God, I thought, all I ask for now is no smell of urine and no flies. My mind was not drifting back, it was fighting back, clutching, seizing, trying to hold onto a moment somewhere in time and space, flesh and blood clothed in a rainbow.

I was free for a while, free of the flies and the odor. Night after night I had dreamed of being in a barnyard far from home, sleeping there, unable to move while the chickens walked by and left their prints in the soft, urinated earth. Chickens walking at night.

"Boy!"

I sat erect quickly and looked straight ahead at the two men in the front seat.

"Just wanted to know you was still on the ball," the sheriff said.

I smiled, for no understandable reason at that moment. Then I remembered, still looking straight ahead at the two. It was their heads. I leaned forward slightly, my gaze fixed on the shoulders, the necks, the hair, and how the ears were attached. The deputy, the driver, was round in the body and big and soft, and his head was square as a shoebox. The sheriff was tall, so that the front seat cramped him considerably, and he was thin and hard. Reddish hair, like corn silks, grew all the way down to his shoulders which were large and thick for a man so tall and thin. His head was rather well shaped but his ears looked like ashtrays. That was really it in both cases. Their ears.

I reached up and felt my own ear and wondered fleetingly how my own head appeared from behind. I began to feel my hair at the back of my neck, and tried to imagine how much longer my father's hair would be now.

The deputy took his eyes from the road and adjusted the rearview mirror. "What you doing back there?" he said. "You making me nervous."

The sheriff turned, raised his left hand and brushed the back of the deputy's head. "He's looking at your dander," the sheriff said. "God, you got dander awful, Wooley. Don't you never wash it?"

"Wash it?" the deputy said. "My wife does."

"I'd use a vacuum cleaner. The trouble with you, Wooley, you ain't got no imagination." The sheriff turned to me. "You don't have no trouble with dander, do you?"

"No," I said.

"Can't you say sir?" the deputy said.

The sheriff looked quickly at the deputy. "Dammit, Wooley. Me and him's having the conversation. This boy's daddy voted for me. You worrying about his grammar when you best be concerned about your goddam dander. Might turn into cancer or something. You ever thought about that? No. You don't never think about nothing. You wouldn't know how to use a piece of baling wire if the hame string broke." Then the sheriff whirled around to me. "You know what a hame string is?"

"Yessir."

"Ya daddy used to farm, didn't he?"

"Yessir."

"And you went back with ya mammy to France?"

"Yessir."

"How's the wimmen in France?" the deputy said.

"Oh, goddam, Wooley, shut up," the sheriff said. "How you think the wimmen in France is? I don't like jokes about wimmen."

We rode on in silence, the deputy's eyes straight ahead. The sheriff looked out across the gray level stretch we were entering.

"Your school record looked pretty good," the sheriff said. "Mighty good, in fact."

"You good in grammar?" the deputy said.

"There you go again," the sheriff said. He looked hard at the deputy. "Grammar is a mighty serious thing," he said. "It's just . . . it's so . . ." Whatever he reached for was too large, too out of place, like a huge freight train sidetracked in a town too small for a railroad in the first place. Finally he said, "This country's flat as piss on a board."

Again we rode in silence. I sank back in my seat, deep in the blue-gray haze of memory. It seemed a year ago since we had left the jail. The car was moving toward sundown, or where sundown would have been without the deep gray mist.

I thought of Aunt Bella. What would she do now without Sarah? Not that Sarah would ever think of leaving. Sometimes in my dreams I would get Aunt Bella and Sarah confused. Sarah would be speaking such beautiful English. Once in a dream Sarah and I carried on a long conversation in French. And once I dreamed that Sarah was my mother. There was one thing for certain, she would take care of Aunt Bella, sick or well.

The last goodbye had not been so bad, not half as awful as I had expected. Aunt Bella had laughed several times and had only the one brief spell of crying. I might not have noticed it except for her handkerchief. When she was ready to leave she said, "I want you to remember one thing, and keep on remembering it. No matter what the world thinks, your daddy would never blame you. I'm proud there's a lot of Dixon in you. Just keep your head as high as your heart will allow." I understood her words to mean that I didn't have to say I was sorry.

I lay farther back in the seat, closed my eyes, and tried to imagine that the car was going in the opposite direction. After a while I succeeded. I felt the car was speeding backward toward the Elms. It was a trick I had learned by lying down in Mr. Pollard's wagon bed and looking straight up into the sky. It was easier to do in Mr. Pollard's wagon than in ours because his had higher side planks. You could manage it in a car because of the motion being so much smoother and swifter than a wagon. Shelley Ray once told me it would give me worms to do such a thing, the same as spinning around very fast, until you're drunk and want to vomit. Lots of people have told me that old tale about spinning around. If it is a tale.

Anyway, I kept on speeding backward toward home until I dropped off to sleep.

I awoke with the sound of the deputy belching. Night was coming quickly over the endless level stretches of barren cotton stalks.

"Turn your lights on before we end up in a cotton patch," the sheriff said. "We oughta started earlier. Only I didn't want to miss church."

"You coulda handcuffed him and you wouldn'ta had to come," the deputy said.

"I wouldn'ta got paid neither."

"You ain't gonna git mileage no way. That's where the money is," the deputy said.

"I ain't?"

"Ain't supposed to."

"You watch. I'm gonna pay you. That comes outa one fund. The supervisors gonna pay me. That comes out of another fund," the sheriff said.

"That's paying twice," the deputy said.

"That ain't twice. It's once for you and once for me. You want me to come for nothing?"

"You gonna ask for mileage?" the deputy said.

"I ain't walking, am I?"

I had almost no idea, no conception of what the prison would look like close up. Fences, gates, buildings I could well imagine, but the details inside were not there, and until now I had not allowed myself to think about it. Looking ahead, visualizing, imagining, had always been a favorite game with me. How a teacher would look, the size and furnishings of a classroom. When I actually saw them they were never the way I had imagined. But the fun was in the reaching out, the going beyond, always believing that someday, somehow, it would all be exactly as I had imagined.

And another favorite was thinking back and back until existence was nonexistent and nothing was understandable. Exactly when I had commenced that game I was not certain, but my first distinct memory of it was in our cotton field, before my father started working at the sawmill: I lay between the cotton rows, late in the afternoon, looking into the sun and wondering what was behind the round blazing mass, what was beyond. I had heard my father's voice in the orchard and my mind began to say, "Before me was my daddy and before him was his daddy and before him and before him and before him was God and before God was something because nothing could be always, not even God." I had never once thought: Before me was my mother and before her was her mother...

For no reason that I could see, the sheriff suddenly turned in his seat and said to me, "Your aunt's gonna be all right, ain't she?"

I was slow in answering and the deputy said, "She ought to be all right. Inherited all that stuff from old man Dixon. I went to school to Miss Beullah."

The sheriff glared at the deputy. "His aunt is a sick woman. That's what I'm talking about. Can't I have one decent conversation today without you buttin' in?"

"I wasn't buttin' in," the deputy said. "Miss Beullah was a fine teacher."

"That's where you learned so much, I guess," the sheriff said.

"Old Town," the deputy said. "Mental arithmetic."

"You?" the sheriff said.

"Yeah," the deputy said. "I could do mental arithmetic."

"You couldn't do mental three-little-pigs." The sheriff turned back to me. "Maybe she'll be all right. I sent all your papers to Olanberg a week, ten days ago. I done all I could. Your daddy always voted for me. Aunt Bella too, far as I know. Which I know she did if ya daddy did." He turned and looked straight ahead again.

It would not be long now. I began to imagine the walls. Fences. A monstrous plexus with barbs interwoven and electricity hidden. Long, low buildings. Narrow caged windows. God, I thought, if only there would be no smell of urine, no flies.

I opened my eyes to see that the rain had commenced. The two men in front seemed not to know they had another passenger. They looked straight ahead at the rain like two children at a window.

I thought I could smell urine.

The sheriff looked hard at the deputy and said, "If you fart one more time in this automobile, Wooley, I'm going to fire your ass. You ain't got no manners a tall. If it was where I could, I'd leave you at Olanberg and take this boy back home. Am I gonna have to tell you to turn on the goddam windshield wipers?"

"They don't work," the deputy said.

"Ain't you got nothing that works? Besides your tongue? And your bowels? If I was to strike a match right now this whole car would blow up."

10

I WALKED AHEAD of the guard, hearing his steps but not my own. Each step seemed to ignite, explode, and scatter across the rain-swept night. The pounding of the heels seemed deliberate, as if to let the world know the position of the walker at the end of every stride.

In all directions powerful searchlights hung in the air, obscured by the night and rain and fog until they appeared like hideous one-eyed birds. The walking of the guard produced a curious echo, like the vague lingering of a poem. I was trying to remember the poem. The lines were coming back to me, not all at once, but a word, a sentence, a stanza, gathering like a flock of Aunt Bella's hens when she scattered corn on the ground. I had written the poem for Miss Fairfield's class when I was in the fifth grade. She was my all-time favorite teacher. It was about Obie that Halloween. All that week the weather had been weird: cool, then blazing hot, then a frost killing some of Mr. Galloway's winter peas, then warm and rainy. Halloween night Obie bet me a dollar he would slip out the window stark naked and bring a bucketful of sawdust from the mill yard. He did, and took all my ninety cents and the promise of a dime.

I tried to say the lines in cadence with the heavy stamping of the guard, but everything was totally wrong, there was no way of matching the rhythms:

> Killing frost and mortal fever,
> Spring or summer, autumn, winter.
> Peas dry up and clover wilts,
> June nights call for extra quilts.
> Two gone mad, quite insane,
> One walks naked in the rain...

"Move on," the guard said. "Nothing ahead of you."

Directly, as if to atone for something, the guard beamed his flashlight ahead of me, revealing thin pools of water on the tar-smeared slag.

We turned onto a walk that led to a square building which looked much taller than the others. A window was lighted on the left side downstairs and on the right side upstairs. The guard moved ahead of me as we mounted the steps. He rapped on the door and entered the dark hallway without waiting for an answer. The door to the right was labelled WARDEN, the door to the left was labelled SANCTUARY.

"Mr. Craig," the guard called. He pounded the sign again and called, "Mr. Craig."

The door moved slowly, with faint little squeals, like a mouse caught in a trap. The strip of light grew wider and wider and the great form of a uniformed man took shape. He wore raincoat, rain hat, and laced boots. Strings of yellow wet hair hung down over his forehead. His immense and clean-shaven face was yellow in the light, except for the bright scar on the side of his nose which looked like a dime pressed into the flesh skin deep. His big hands were almost as white as the scar. He probably wore gloves, I thought.

"Oh," the guard said. "Captain Burt."

"What's the trouble?" Captain Burt said.

"Why, they turned him over to me at the Main Gate," the guard said. "Receiving is closed."

"Who signed for him?"

"I don't know. They just turned him over to me and said bring him to the Sanctuary. To Mr. Craig."

"Goddammit, I don't know why they keep sending 'em on Sunday. At night too," Captain Burt said. He pointed to me. "Come on in here. I'll see if I can find the Chaplain."

"Are you relieving me, sir?" the guard said.

"Yes. You're relieved." The Captain stepped back from the doorway, staring as I entered. "My God, how old are you?"

"Fifteen," I said.

The Captain went to the doorway, looked down the hall, looked back at me. "I'll be goddamned if I know what a sheriff means coming in this time of night. Just set down there. I'll get the Chaplain."

I sat down in an oaken high-backed chair near the desk. The Captain went into the hallway, closing the door behind him.

I glanced about the room. The vast space was partitioned with files and cabinets and furniture into what appeared to be not one but four separate rooms—an office, a library, a kitchen, and a small chapel. It seemed to me very odd that I should be brought first to the Chaplain. I shaped the words in my mind: "I'm sure as hell not going to tell them I'm sorry, if that's what they want."

My eyes began to inspect more carefully the items nearest me—the leather sofa, which looked very old; the stacks of papers and magazines on the desk, which looked as if they had been there a long time; the glass ashtrays with corners nicked; the black leather chair, which had a greasy indentation at the top of its narrow headrest. The bronze nameplate bore no name but the lower slot carried the identification: DEPUTY WARDEN. There was no smell of urine, no sound of flies. There was the smell of food in the room, something like boiled cabbage or fried collards. For all its lack of neatness the room seemed to have some definite order. I was beginning to feel warm and dry and a rush of hope flooded my heart, dispelling some of the rumors and horrors I had heard about Olanberg. My hands moved over the top of the oaken desk touching old ink spots and scratches. The desk could easily be sanded and polished into something very attractive, I thought. I had half risen intending to look at the books in the library section when I heard footsteps in the hallway. I sank quickly into the chair again.

A very short man, certainly not fifty years old, with jet-black curly hair and deep green eyes, entered. All his prominent features, the wide forehead, the Roman nose, the square chin and peculiar mouth, had a marble-like appearance, grayish and shiny. What astonished me was the cigar set firmly in one square jaw, for I assumed the man was the Chaplain.

I got up while the man moved briskly to the black chair, sat down, and pedalled forward until one button of his dark blue coat scraped against the edge of the desk. He put his cigar in an ashtray. "Go ahead and sit down," he said.

He pulled from the top drawer a folder and opened it. "I've had your papers a week or more." He read for a few seconds. "Well, I haven't, but Receiving has. I got them two, three, maybe four days ago. I rather thought it would be tomorrow. But I might as well do this part now. I'm the Deputy Warden as well as the Chaplain." He began to laugh. "I have to solemnly swear, make an affidavit, duly notarized . . . can you spell duly?"

"Yessir."

"Can you spell affidavit?"

"Yessir."

"How you spell duly?"

"D-U-L-Y."

"They got it down here D-U-E-L-Y. And how you spell affidavit?"

"A-F-F-I-D-A-V-I-T."

"They got that right then. Anyway, I have to make an affidavit that you are who you are and not an imposter. Now. How...how do I know...so that I can solemnly swear...?" He looked down at the papers. "How do I know you're William Marcus Oday? We can start with a driver's license."

"I don't have one," I said.

"Oh," the Chaplain said. "I guess not." He turned over a number of pages. He settled on a page and read it carefully. "Your father's name was Willard?"

"Yessir."

"You're not named after him?"

"Nossir. I was named after...my aunt's grandfather."

"Your great-grandfather?"

"She was my great-aunt, my father's aunt," I said. I felt that something foolish was occurring over which neither he nor I had control.

The Chaplain turned from his reading and looked up. "When did it happen?"

"You mean my father's accident...or the other?"

"The other."

"Last November."

"It's pretty up there in November, isn't it?"

"Yessir."

"I can imagine. I've been to Gatlinburg twice. Before I was Deputy Warden. Of course, you're not nearly that far up. That's Tennessee. But you do have those rugged hills and springs."

The electric current I had been expecting struck my bloodstream. The Chaplain noticed the change in me. "Don't you have springs?" he said.

"Yes," I said. "We have springs. I'm going to be sick."

"Bend over," he said. "Bend way over and put your head between your knees."

I felt the Chaplain's hand on my head. The weight of the hand went away. I raised my head slowly and the blurring was gone. The Chaplain was seated again. Everything was in focus. I saw the Chaplain smile. "What you need is a glass of good spring water."

I suddenly cried out, "Why do you have to talk about the damned old springs?"

"Oh," the Chaplain said. His lips quivered and grew very still.

"I'm terribly sorry," I said.

"Do you talk that way very often?"

"Nossir."

"How about your father? Did he?"

"He said whatever he wanted to."

"Did he go to church?"

"To the services? Not much."

"Do you?"

"Sometimes."

"You never found anything in church?"

"Found what?"

"Are you a church member?"

"Nossir."

"Did you fight very much in school?"

"I never fought at all."

"Never?"

"No."

"Did your mother and father quarrel often?"

"No."

"You had a happy home life?"

"Yes."

"What went wrong?"

"You mean about my father and mother?"

"No, I didn't mean that. But tell me about your mother and father. Were they separated?"

"She went back to France."

"And left your father?"

"Well, she went back to France. Her father was sick."

"You went with her?"

"Yes."

"How long did you stay in France?"

"Four years."

"Did you like it?"

"No."

"Do you think it'll be hard for you here?"

"Yessir."

"Do you realize that the law in a capital case makes absolutely no distinction between you and a person my age?"

"Yes."

"Does that seem unfair to you?"

"Nossir."

"You don't think you should have preferential treatment because of your age?"

"Nossir. I did it."

"Are you very sorry you did it?"

"Nossir."

"Not at all?"

I flared again. "I won't say I'm sorry! I wouldn't tell the judge! I wouldn't tell the lawyer! I won't tell you! I won't tell anybody!"

"You won't?"

"No. I won't say I'm sorry."

"Do you like to hurt people?"

"No. But I won't say I'm sorry."

"And you don't like to hurt people?"

"Certainly not."

"Why didn't you shoot to scare the man? Maybe he would have stopped."

"I only had one cartridge."

"Only one?"

"Just one."

"What if you had missed?"

"I guess I wouldn't be here."

"No. Probably not. Have you been searched?"

"Yessir."

"Do you ever pray?"

"Sometimes."

"For what?"

"For my aunt. She's sick, sort of."

"Anything else?"

"That my father will understand why I did it. If he knows."

"Do you think he knows?"

"Sometimes I do and sometimes I don't."

"Have you got any money?"

"You mean with me, or in the bank?"

"Both."

"I have twenty dollars with me. In the bank I have a checking account and a trust fund."

"A trust fund?"

"Yes."

"How much?"

"I don't know exactly. It's not settled."

"Is it a little or a lot?"

"I don't know."

"Like five thousand. Or more?"

"More."

"Can you spend what you like?"

"Not without my aunt's approval. Until I'm eighteen."

"You're some case. I don't know what I'm going to do with you."

"Have I proved to you who I am?"

"There wasn't much doubt. But the precaution is not altogether foolish. We've had cases of people doing time for others. Anyway, not too many people coming here can spell *duly* and *affidavit*. Which gives me an idea. I'll think on it tonight and tomorrow. You'll go through Receiving tomorrow. Tonight I'll send you to Piccadilly."

He went to the hallway and called for Captain Burt. He remained in the doorway, waiting, half turned toward me. "When you finish, I want you to come here to the Sanctuary. No matter what your papers say, you come here."

Captain Burt appeared in the hallway.

"Is Loman still in the Infirmary?" the Chaplain said.

"He hurt his arm pretty bad..."

"Is he still in the Infirmary?" the Chaplain cut in sharply.

"Yessir," Captain Burt said.

"Take this boy to Piccadilly. Give him Loman's place tonight."

"Loman will more'n likely be out tomorrow."

"Captain, I'll worry about that when the time comes," the Chaplain said, his marble face growing red.

"Yessir," Captain Burt said.

11

PICCADILLY WAS NO more than two hundred yards from the
Sanctuary door. It was a long one-storey brick building with a
beacon tower on the front of its roof. In the fog and drizzle I thought
it looked somewhat like a submarine half submerged with periscope
fully extended. I had several questions to ask Captain Burt but
I sensed that he was not in a very good humor.

I was surprised when he suddenly said, "This gonna freeze.
Gonna be zero by tomarr'. Maybe below."

I tried to think of a suitable answer but my attention was
focused on the powerful searchlights a hundred yards to the right
of Piccadilly, four of them forming a square, and in the center of
the square a gate so enormous and monstrous that the Main Gate
seemed like the barnyard entrance at Deer Forks. "What is that?"
I said.

"That? That's the Second Gate," Captain Burt said.

Then I saw the great fence and the guard station, emerging as a
gigantic picture in a gigantic dark room.

The big door to Piccadilly was unlocked. Once inside, Captain
Burt took a clipboard that hung on the wall and turned its
pages, searching. Voices came from the end of the hallway, lively,
nothing angry. For some strange reason the noise reminded me of
the backstage commotion at the Bordeaux Opera House when my

mother had led me behind the curtain one night to meet an old acquaintance of hers. I remembered the smell backstage more than anything else. The man and the woman looked very much alike in their dance costumes. Only after I was in my bed at Vingt-neuf Cour du Maréchal Foch did I realize the man and not the woman was my mother's friend.

"Come on," Captain Burt growled. He was already several steps down the hallway. I hurried to catch up. We entered a large rectangular room that stretched across the width of the building. I looked about and tried to count the number of men quickly, two dozen or more. The smell of smoke struck me sharply. The whole area became quieter but not silent. Bunks were spaced along one side and one end of the room. The showers and toilets were at the other end of the room. At various spots were long black tables with short backless benches. A number of men sat at the tables. Others lounged on or stood around the bunks. No one seemed to notice me in particular, yet I felt they were all aware of my presence.

"Hawthorne," Captain Burt called.

A man rose from one of the tables and came toward us. He was tall and stout. He moved with that unmistakable ease of the athlete, and with a confidence that would have appeared as arrogance in a younger face.

"You have the bunk next to Loman, don't you?" Captain Burt said.

"Yessir," Hawthorne said.

"Take care of this boy. He can use Loman's bunk tonight."

"Yessir," Hawthorne said.

Captain Burt left, and Hawthorne led me to the bunks in the far corner of the room. Once he was there, Hawthorne was suddenly confused as to what more he was expected to do. "That's Loman's next to the wall. This one is mine." He opened the cabinet and pulled out a towel. "This is clean if you want to wash up or something."

I took the towel and sat on Loman's bunk. Hawthorne was prompted to a quick, embarrassed laugh. "That's about it, unless you want to play cards or something."

"No, thanks," I said. "You go ahead."

"I'm through," Hawthorne said. "It's about time for lights out anyways."

I noticed that Hawthorne, and about half the other men, did not wear stripes. He wore some sort of blue denim. "Are you a guard?" I said.

"No. Everybody in here is a trusty or a free trusty."

"Is that why the doors aren't locked?"

"Yes. I reckon." Hawthorne sat down on his bunk.

"What's the difference between a trusty and a free trusty?"

"Clothes mostly. A free trusty don't have to wear stripes. And he can go to the store and things."

"What do you do?"

"We're sort of like guards. Most of us are on a swing shift. Laundry, barn, store, maintenance...wherever Captain Burt says. He's captain of the trusties. I drive a lot. Sometimes I work behind and sometimes up front. If you want to wash up, you better go before it gits crowded."

I went to the toilet. While I stood before the mirror carefully washing my face and hands, I could hear the patches of laughter and quarrelling at the tables: "You knocked it off." "It fell." "Fell, my ass. You knocked it off a purpose." "Whata we do now? Horsefly knocked the widder off." "Redeal." "I'm a sonofabitch if I redeal." "You wasn't fixin' to shoot the moon, was you?" "Don't step on 'em you clumsy bastard, you already knocked 'em off already."

I could also hear another voice: "Well, Oliver Tolliver, looks like you've played hell."

The toilet had a faint Lysol smell. I took a long time in washing my face and neck and ears. I could hear the flush of a toilet bowl and beyond the toilets a shower running. Outside, in the main room, the noise of the men grew louder and louder. Sarah said people who worried a lot got cancer. The wail of a siren startled me. I thought it shook the mirror. The man behind me flushed the toilet. The sound of the shower ceased. I dried my face hurriedly and started out of the toilet as five or six men entered around me.

I made my way through moving figures toward my bunk. Two men were arguing over a deck of cards. The smaller man grabbed for the cards and missed. His swinging elbow struck me in the side. The man laughed. I laughed back.

I undressed and got into my bunk. I watched Hawthorne undress, then stand tinkering with something in the cabinet. The room was growing quieter. A whistle sounded in the hallway outside. Everything went black. After a minute I could see the form of Hawthorne crawling into his bunk. I kept breathing deeply, glad of the darkness.

Finally I could hear only the occasional sounds of turning, adjusting covers, deep breaths, coughs. Then I began to hear the sound of my heart throbbing, as if some ocean of time above me was falling into my ear drop by drop.

I heard snoring far away, painful and labored, and then a quieter, easier snoring beside me, four feet away, not actually a snoring, but a deep and steady vibration from Hawthorne.

For a while I was all right. Then a slightly burning weakness, a faint nausea, began to possess me. I closed my eyes tighter and tried to visualize the room and its objects. Could I ever find my way to the toilet if I had to urinate or vomit? I heard the rain outside beating against the wall. The snores grew sharper. They seemed to take shape, like little hump-backed worms, move toward me, reach my bunk, infiltrate the covers, and crawl over my body. I tried to smell the urine, to hear the flies. That would help, I thought. I began to tremble.

I turned in the bunk and drew myself into a tight ball. My forehead touched my knees. The trembling quieted to a shiver. My mind grew clearer. I thought about the acorns. For a week now my mind had been playing tricks. There would be the feeling of ease, a strange calmness, and suddenly a sense of terror would strike. That was when I would play the game of acorns. I played it now. I could see them falling through the golden leaves, hear them strike the earth, taste their bitter kernels, smell their broken crowns. But the snoring did not cease. The trembling commenced again. I was shaking. I could hear my bed move.

"Damn them, damn them," I cried to myself. "I will not say I'm sorry." I turned onto my back and stretched out. I was hot now. I pushed back the covers, allowing the coolness to flood about me. I thought: "I'll die before I'll say I'm sorry."

Suddenly my body grew still. I pulled the covers up tight. For the first time it occurred to me that I was sleeping between rough sheets where someone else had slept. But it did not matter. I grew warmer. I could hardly hear the snoring. I felt my body moving through timeless and undefined space, though I knew the reality of where I was anchored. It was like that moment in a bad dream when the mind knows it is dreaming, struggles to return to the real world of old familiar objects, yet the knowing and the dreaming and the struggle continue together.

I fell asleep.

The clouds parted and I heard the trumpet blow. Standing on a dark cloud, dark as a mountain rock, was Gabriel without wings, with his horn in his hand, naked and sexless, tiny white hairs glistening on his body. The dead began to rise, not quietly but with a great clamoring and stomping of feet, yelling and cursing, mingling.

The strained, pale, worn faces struggled feverishly in the gloomy, almost foggy atmosphere of the room.

I realized I was awake. I sat up in my bunk quickly. Hawthorne stood at the foot of his bunk, in his underwear and sock feet, holding a towel. The tiny white hairs glistened on his thighs. His large brown eyes were like searchlights.

"Hey, old top," Hawthorne said.

"Hey," I said. Past Hawthorne I could see the frail spindling legs of other prisoners, and their ugly kneecaps, moving in a stampede toward the toilets. The only strong and sturdy legs I saw were those of Hawthorne.

"If you want to take a shower," Hawthorne said, "wait till it clears out some. You got plenty of time." He sat down on the foot of my bunk, as if standing guard.

I slipped from the covers and put my feet on the cold floor. Four bunks away a man stood with his back to me, stripped to his shorts. Across his right shoulder blade were four or five bright streaks as if a thin paintbrush had left its marks. He turned and pulled a T-shirt over his head. His face seemed to have no life at all, emerging through the hole like the dead, waxed shape of a mannequin.

"I'll show you how to make your bunk," Hawthorne said.

Very quickly the bunk was in perfect order, the blanket stretched and tucked smoothly over the bolster.

I showered quickly. I was in a hurry to get back to Hawthorne, like a soldier who feels somewhat safer at his usual battle station. That was an idea that came from my father, something he said once about the war. I dressed quickly. My rich brown birthday coat seemed heavy across my shoulders. Hawthorne now sat on the foot of his own bunk, his back as straight as the post of a cane-bottomed chair. The room had become oppressively quiet. I thought of Sarah. "Old blue Monday," I could hear her say.

We went across the hall to the dining room. It was a very large room, larger than the sleeping quarters, with only four long tables. At one end was the cafeteria line, at the other end were crates and boxes of supplies somewhat like a miniature wholesale warehouse. In one corner a hundred or more folding chairs were stacked around a small platform on which stood a lectern and a large Bible. Behind the cafeteria line swinging doors opened into the kitchen.

Breakfast consisted of powdered scrambled eggs, battered fried fatback, sawmill gravy, grits, thick cottony biscuits and strong coffee. I was careful to stay near Hawthorne. At the table I sat between Hawthorne and a very old man in stripes who seemed not to notice me at all. I was surprised that the food was so good.

Halfway through the meal there was a general stir at all the tables. Word went around like the passing of salt and pepper shakers—"Apple Ass is outside."

Faces kept turning between bites toward the doorway. "The Warden," Hawthorne whispered to me. A minute or two later a huge man entered the room. Beside him was Captain Burt carrying a clipboard from which a pencil, secured by a string, dangled. The tables became silent but no one stood.

The Warden was of medium height and so heavy, I thought, nothing smaller than the scales of a cotton gin could weigh him. He came to the edge of the first table, stared at the men as if they were engaged in an activity totally foreign to him. His eyes were all but hidden with fat and brows. Thick folds of iron-gray hair spilled from one side of his overly large black cowboy hat. Everything about him seemed out of proportion. His nose and eyes were too small, his hands and ears too large. His face was too dark and his hands too white. His head, with not one inch of neck visible, sat like a little round ball on shoulders grotesquely thick and wide. He wore a dark suit and vest, begrimed with food and drink.

His shabby woolen topcoat flopped open and back as if he had commenced to remove it and forgotten. Across the vest, which strained to hold the belly intact, stretched an enormous golden watch chain. Over one shoulder hung a soiled navy-blue scarf. He turned to Captain Burt and said, "Where's Hossfly?" His turning buttocks bulged as if a basketball lay in each hip pocket.

"Right here, sir," Horsefly said and rose. He was a gangling, sharp-featured young man.

"What happened to that mule, suh?" the Warden said.

"I don't know, Mr. Hull. Looks like he'd been kicked. It kept swelling Friday. Got worse on Saturday. We put him in a swing," Horsefly said.

"I know that. I saw him. I want to know what happened to him, suh?" the Warden said.

"Like I say, I think he got kicked."

"Which one, goddammit? Which one kicked him?" the Warden said.

"I don't know," Horsefly said. "Musta been Thursday night. They was all there together. Six of 'em in that north stall."

"Can't you tell which one's the mean 'un? The kickuh?"

"Nossir."

"By God, suh, I could. If I was 'round 'em much as you. When I have a kickuh at Little Egypt I trade him. Keep yo' eyes open. See can you spot the kickuh. Come plow time we can't 'fode no mules with busted shoulders." The Warden's eyes jerked around to a corner of the room. "Yawl have church yestiddy?"

"Nossir," Captain Burt said. "It's only once a month now."

"By whose ordahs?" the Warden said.

"The Chaplain," Captain Burt said.

"The Chaplain? I'm the wahdon of this prison."

"Yessir," Captain Burt said, "but the men voted for once a month."

"Yawl? Yawl done that?" the Warden said. "And yawl the trusties? The leadahs? I ain't missed a Sunday in church in fifteen year. I don't like it, Captain."

"You can't make men go to church, sir," the Captain said.

"You can make men do anything, suh." The Warden surveyed the men more closely. "Yawl wanta go back behind the Second Gate?"

The men sat in silence, staring. There seemed to be no special concern or worry in their faces though the Warden's gaze was covering us one by one.

"What's that little feller doing in heah?" the Warden said.

"He come in last night," Captain Burt said.

"Last night? Sunday?"

"Yessir," Captain Burt said.

"I'm a son-of-a-bitch if them local sheriffs can't screw up a funeral. Git this boy outa heah and git him some decent clothes."

"Receiving is closed now," the Captain said.

"Goddammit, he can knock on the do'. He can set on the steps till they open."

"Hawthorne," the Captain said. He came and leaned over Hawthorne, with his back to the Warden, and said quietly, "Get him on out of here. Take him on now. Find Mitch. He'll let you in early."

Outside, the damp cold air struck my face like the sudden sting of ants. It had turned much colder in the night. Ice was beginning to form in the scattered puddles. We hurried across the yard. In the twilight the heavy gray clouds almost touched the beacons.

"The Warden sounds like a mean old bastard," I said.

"Apple Ass?" Hawthorne said, and laughed. His breath was like a tiny lost piece of cloud.

We had gone halfway across the yard when Hawthorne added, "He's not mean a tall. Nobody's afraid of him. Besides, he's just

Warden in name. The Chaplain's the man. Talks nice and soft and will bust your ass before a cat can lick his tail. No, the Warden's not mean. He's just old and crazy. Not here half the time. Always Mondays. Sometimes Tuesdays. And tries to surprise us the rest of the time. His plantation's up the road a piece, where they gin all the prison cotton. Who knows how much toll he gets? Who cares? I don't. Oh, he gives some trouble now and then when he gits in a cranky mood. But the Chaplain is the man around here. Yessir, old Perch Mouth is the real cheese."

I recalled the Chaplain's unusual mouth, and his marble complexion. "Is he mean?"

"The Chaplain? Not to me. It's the captains give you hell. The captains behind the Second Gate. I had three year of it. Lord knows I'd have to feel for anybody going back there."

I 2

THE DOOR WAS not locked, but the space was like a death cell to me while I waited in the windowless quarantine room of the Infirmary. Receiving had been rather pleasant, a rambling, dark, disorderly warehouse that smelled of new denim and old leather. Hawthorne had left me in Receiving early that morning with a jolly little fat man in overalls who tried earnestly to find items that would fit me: striped gray shirt and trousers, blue cap and jacket and overcoat, black shoes. I had also received a toilet kit and an extra set of clothing in a purple straw-handled satchel. Then a yellow slip for the Infirmary, where an elderly woman led me to the quarantine room. It was the lack of a window that made the room so depressing.

I waited for blood samples, which a young woman took. I waited for urine samples, which a young man took. I waited for vaccinations, some by the young man and some by the young woman. Somewhere in the midst of waiting the young woman brought me a hospital tray of food. I ate a few bites and flushed the remainder down a toilet bowl. I was frightened when the roll did not disappear. I reached into the water, crumbled the roll and flushed the pieces. The young man returned for another urine sample and said the doctor would be there sooner or later.

I waited. I knew the room was not locked and yet I felt it would be a great violation to open the door and poke my head into the hallway. The room was too small, too hot, too dark, too quiet, too ghostly. It was like a coffin, a grave. More than once I thought of Hawthorne and wished the young woman would return for another blood sample, anything to interrupt the painful and unbearable stagnation of the windowless place.

I had lost all track of time but I felt it was surely night outside. Finally the doctor arrived, a thoroughly bald, middle-aged man, slow, quiet, patient. "If you'll fill these out, please." The doctor spoke so quietly I could hardly hear him. He handed me a pencil and four pages and disappeared.

The waiting became more unbearable than ever. I smelled urine. I heard flies. I would not dare open the door though it seemed to me one peep into the hallway would be a great relief.

The doctor finally returned. He glanced at the pages. "You're to report to Mr. Craig at the Sanctuary," he said. "You know where the Sanctuary is?"

"Yessir," I said.

"You like snow?" he said, quickly and as if he did not expect an answer.

What a question, what a crazy man, I thought. I wanted to run through the doorway, which the doctor had left open. "Now, do I go now?" I said.

"Any old time," he said, reading the pages I had filled out so carefully.

I grabbed my satchel and topcoat and hurried out of the quarantine room and down the long hallway with the sudden hope the Chaplain would send me back to Piccadilly and Hawthorne. What a pleasure it would be to see Hawthorne and talk to him.

When I reached the outside steps of the Infirmary a whole new world dashed up against my face. For a moment I thought my mind had come unhinged. Through the weird gray twilight I saw a vast expanse of whiteness. Then I realized it was snowing. I put on my topcoat. The flakes, mixed with tiny slivers of sleet, were roiling down in an angry hiss as if determined to hide the road and fences and buildings and guard stations as soon as possible. I stood for a moment looking toward the Sanctuary which was almost obscured. Distant buildings appeared more clearly. I was faintly aware of separating everything this side of the Second Gate from everything beyond. The Infirmary, the Administration Building, the Sanctuary, Piccadilly appeared to me as home ground, and everything beyond the central guard station was foreign. Beyond the Second Gate I could see the barest sketches of the camps like tiny blots in the mad sea of whiteness.

I tucked my satchel under my arm and stepped into the snow. I walked for a way in the powdery whiteness and then looked back at my dark tracks. I stood looking until the dark imprints turned to white again. Then I went on toward the Sanctuary, glancing up at the flat-topped two-storey building where an unmanned search-light appeared in the whirling snow like an old scarecrow.

I climbed the steps of the Sanctuary, cleaned my feet carefully on the porch mat, entered, and again cleaned my feet on the inside mat. I turned toward the sign SANCTUARY and entered without knocking. The room seemed as familiar to me as the living room at the Elms. I placed my satchel beside the leather sofa and took off my coat. Though no one was visible I could hear steps in the kitchen and the sound of running water.

"Oday?"

"Yessir."

The sound of the water stopped.

"Come here."

I moved past the row of tall filing cabinets. The Chaplain was standing before the sink, drying his hands with a dish towel, look-ing out the window. Smoke floated about his head. He turned, holding his cigar firmly in his jaw, and stared at my clothes rather than me. He took the cigar from his mouth and laid it on the edge of the sink. There was a slight hiss as the ashes dropped into the water. On the small table was a single plate with two ham-and-cheese sandwiches and a glass of milk.

"I fixed that for you," he said. "Sit down and help yourself. I want to watch you eat."

I sat down and began to eat. It was some time before the Chaplain said anything.

"You can tell a lot by watching a person eat," he said. "Do you know what it is to be really hungry? Hungry because you don't have it and can't get it?"

"Nossir."

"Are you sorry for somebody in that shape?"

"Yessir."

"I am too. I've been in that shape. Or close to it. But you can satisfy hunger. That's about the easiest problem in the world to solve. You want to know what's the hardest?"

"Yessir."

"Selfishness. Do you like books?"

"Yessir."

"I do too. I've managed to get the board of corrections to put a library in every camp. And I managed to get a mattress factory too. We've got a lot of books and a lot of mattresses we didn't used to have. But the books seem important to me. Because a book can sometimes take us outside ourselves. And when we're outside ourselves we're not as selfish. When we're not selfish we can be trusted. Do you know how many camps we've got here?"

"Nossir."

"Nine. For some reason they're numbered two through fourteen. Number Two is bad enough. Number Fourteen is living hell. Do you know what those stripes you're wearing mean?"

"Nossir."

"They're the stripes of a trusty. An ordinary trusty. The badge you have to have to live on this side of the Second Gate. You can wear them on the other side too, but you've got to have them to stay on this side. You've made a tolerably good impression on me. I like just about everything...except one thing. You are stubborn. Do you realize that? Not obdurate but stubborn. You haven't noticed that in yourself?"

"Nossir."

"God will save the vilest sinner if...if he repents. He would not save the grandest saint who was not contrite. Could not. You understand the word contrite?"

"I think so."

"Fully understand it?"

"I'm not sure."

"In the religious sense it means deep sorrow for sin. I'm not trying to make it religious. I'm not asking you to come to the altar... for a public profession and that sort of thing...which is too often nothing. But if I'm to help you, to save you from God knows what... I think you owe me some word of repentance, some assurance that you would be worthy of trust. I've read your record, remember? Those clothes fit you better than you expected, don't they?"

"They're okay."

"Could there be something symbolic about it?"

"Symbolic?"

"Maybe you deserve to be here."

"I never said I didn't deserve to be here."

"Here! This side," the Chaplain almost shouted, then became calmer. "I don't think you understand yet." He moved toward the back door. "Come with me. I want to show you something."

We went outside. The Chaplain led the way across a concrete stoop at the back of the building and began to climb an outside stairway that zigzagged to the flat roof. Halfway up the snow-covered steps he looked back to see that I was following. The snowing had almost stopped.

At the top of the guardrail he turned and indicated for me to turn and look. In the twilight the vast layout of buildings and barns and sheds and fences and fields was remarkably delineated by the snow. He pointed to a row of houses. "That's the Circle of the Guards, where most of the personnel live. Not just guards, but clerks, secretaries, nurses, the doctor, myself, my wife when she's here. We're fenced in too, but I don't worry when I lie down at night. Do you know why? Because everybody on this side of the big fence, this side of the Second Gate, is trusted. Piccadilly isn't locked. See that little cabin by the dog kennels? It isn't locked. See that old gin building to the right of the barn, off the edge of the circle? That's the Lumber Yard. Upstairs is a shop and living quarters. It's not locked. Get a good look at it. It's on this side. Now look over to the left, on the other side. Behind the Second Gate. What do you think that is?"

"Men working."

"Yes. And one, two, three, four, five, six mounted guards. That's Camp Four. About ninety men in that bunch, with hickory axe handles knocking down old cotton stalks. They've been out there since early this morning. Except for lunch, of course. They'll go in when the Captain tells them to go in. Or when I tell the Captain. But I don't interfere with a captain very often. He's got some reason for keeping them so late. In the snow. If I ask him, he'll have a reason. We all have our reasons, don't we?"

I could see he did not expect an answer from me. He started down the steps quickly.

In the Sanctuary kitchen he took his cigar from the edge of the sink and lighted it. He smoked while I stood beside the table. "Well," the Chaplain said, "what is it? This side or the other side?"

"You want me to say I'm sorry?" I said.

"Yes."

"I won't say it."

The marble in the Chaplain's face turned purple. "Damn you, Oday. You're a child. You don't know what you're doing. Do you want to be punished? Is that what you want? Do you want to see what it's like behind there?"

"Nossir."

"What in the hell is it? I'll be damned if I'll have a trusty I can't trust. I'll be that stubborn myself." He went around the cabinets to the telephone. I heard: "Get me Captain Burt. Well, where is he? No, don't tell him anything. Never mind."

He kept looking into the library section when he came from behind the cabinets. He no longer had his cigar. "Come here," he said.

We stood six feet apart gazing at each other.

"What kind of person are you?" he said.

"I don't know."

"Aren't you afraid of anything?"

"Yessir."

"What in the hell is it?"

"You."

"I'm not going to hurt you. There's plenty back there that will."

"You're going to put me in a camp."

"I sure as hell am. If you don't change your tune. But tonight . . . tonight I'm sending you to the Lumber Yard. A man named Mims is there. He's upstairs in the Lumber Yard, that old gin building. There's an extra place there." He started toward the desk, then stopped beside the sofa.

I went around the cabinets and picked up my topcoat and satchel. "You might as well send me to a camp tonight. Because I'll never, never say I'm sorry."

"Damn you," the Chaplain said quietly. He sank onto the sofa and lowered his forehead against one clenched fist. "Damn you and the whole rotten mess. Why I ever came here myself is God's own secret. I told you where to go. Get out of here."

Before I had reached the door he called, "Oday?"

"Yessir."

He sat and stared at me. He did have a mouth like a perch. He said, "Maybe you're right. Maybe you shouldn't be sorry. I'm not God, even if I do enjoy pretending. You find Mims where I said. He'll show you how to muster in the morning. Then you come here. At least you can spell."

"Thank you," I said.

"You're welcome."

"And thank you for the food."

"You're most welcome."

The snow was falling again but I could still see a considerable distance. The whirling flakes gathered the fading twilight into weird patches that illuminated the buildings and the bodies that moved slowly and ghost-like from the central guard station toward Piccadilly. Beyond the Second Gate the ninety men drew closer and closer to a long narrow building as if the wind blew them along the ice.

Fifty yards from the central guard station I turned into the road that led to the Circle of the Guards. When I had gone a few steps the sound of a whistle jerked me around as if some invisible hand had snatched at my arm. A dark-coated figure came flying at me waving a clipboard and yelling, "Where the hell you going?"

"Mr. Craig, the Chaplain," I cried, trying to explain and failing miserably. My words seemed to fly straight up, hardly reaching the figure I recognized as Captain Burt. The bright scar on his nose looked like one huge, indestructible snowflake.

"You what?" Captain Burt said, the whistle still in his mouth as the words flew out. "You know where Piccadilly is." His big hand grabbed my free arm and slung me toward Piccadilly.

I stumbled for several feet and fell sliding into the snow, never letting go of my satchel. I got up slowly.

"Mr. Craig told me to go to the Lumber Yard," I said.

Captain Burt removed the whistle and wiped it on his coat sleeve. "Oh, hell," he said. He studied his clipboard in the fading light. "Why can't they make up they goddam mind?" He waved me on in the direction of the Lumber Yard.

Halfway along the circle the road branched off toward the barns and toolsheds. Although the snow was more than two inches deep I could tell the narrow road was unpaved. I passed the first barn, two sheds, then turned uneasily toward what I thought was the Lumber Yard, for I had somewhat lost my sense of direction. Directly ahead of me was an old two-storey building with hip roof, and beyond the corner of the building were stacks of rough weathered lumber. The nearer side of the building, along the first storey, was torn away and the cellar-like space was full of bright new planed lumber. I began to hurry toward the ominous form rising like a rock in the sea. Then suddenly I stopped, while the snow rushed down more heavily than ever, clinging to my hands, my satchel, my clothes. In the dark gaping wound of the building I saw some figure, a real figure, slowly climbing the stairs. The tricks of my mind made me imagine the figure to be my mother, the real and the unreal appearing as identical as goldfish. The figure disappeared and for one fleeting moment the old gin building had the shape of the Bordeaux Opera House.

I ran into the cellar-like space with the feeling of entering a dark and unfamiliar cave. All about me were various and irregular stacks of finished lumber and the smells of oak, maple, pine and the overwhelming odor of cedar. The long, mournful howl of a dog came shattering through the snow, near or far off, I could not quickly tell. I looked out toward the second barn. The snow was now so heavy the barn and sheds appeared only dimly, like something on a Christmas card.

The howl came again, a little less mournful, a little different. There was some small satisfaction in knowing the second sound belonged to a second dog. After a moment I heard a third and different howl. Then a fourth. Then all was so quiet I could hear nothing more than the wind moving the loosened squares of tin roof. I began to climb the very wide and unrailed angular stairway.

13

AT THE TOP of the stairs I halted as if something had exploded in my path. Before me was a shop so neatly arranged that not one item seemed out of place. I had expected nothing of the sort, and my first glance was like seeing a museum of fine woodwork with each division carefully separated and precisely arranged. I estimated the loft to be seventy or eighty feet long and at least forty feet wide. The east side was covered with shoulder-high stacks of dressed cedar, maple, cherry, walnut, oak and hickory. Along the middle of the shop were work tables and tools which appeared immaculate and clinical in the pale light. On the west side were the finished products—cabinets, chairs, tables, unnamable pieces—stretched out in a grand display. In the northeast corner of the loft a section, perhaps twenty by thirty feet, was partitioned off into a separate room.

As I stood at the head of the south stairs, awed by the established order of the whole area, a man came out of the corner room and disappeared down the north stairway. He seemed to be carrying an armload of old clothes.

I made my way quickly past the work tables to the north end of the loft. I put my satchel down at the stair head and looked out the window. The snow was continuing heavily. Again surprised, I saw a small garden and an orchard of twenty or more trees.

The man I had seen a moment before was laying tow sacks over a row of collard plants. His face was partially obscured by the snow but it appeared to be coarse and unpleasant. When the collards were covered the man waded through the snow toward a small, triangular area set apart in the corner of the garden with chicken wire. I could see then that he was tall, with a heavily built body, a large head, large hands. He wore a blue three-quarter-length prison coat and an oilcloth rain hat that all but covered his ears. The legs of his tan corduroy trousers were stuffed into his high-topped overshoes. He entered the chicken yard, opened the door to the small, slant-roofed shed, and turned on a light. Then he carefully refastened the door. He knelt, the methodical kneel of a farmer, and filled the two square portholes with the remaining tow sacks. At the gate he looked back for a moment to survey his work, and then came on slowly toward the open stairway. He looked up into the night just before he disappeared into the building. I continued to gaze through the window, wondering about the garden and orchard.

When I looked around, the man had reached the landing of the stairs, was bending over removing his overshoes which gave him some difficulty. He backed against the wall, finished with his overshoes, removed his dripping hat and slapped it sharply against his thigh. He had not yet seen me.

"Mims," I said.

He looked up slowly. He was neither startled nor surprised. "Ah," he said. "You're Marcus."

"The Chaplain sent me," I said.

The face did not appear so coarse now. There was a large scar over the right eye, a lesser scar on the left cheek point, and a tiny sunken scar no larger than a field pea on the left corner of the chin. The scars did not disfigure the face at all but rather seemed to give it balance and strength and a certain attractiveness.

"I thought he said tomarr'," Mims said. He began taking off his coat.

I watched the way the big shoulders emerged, as if that slight effort would break the seams. When the coat was removed, Mims appeared much taller in his tan mackinaw and his arms seemed exceptionally long. He wiped at his neck where the snow had fallen, pushing the collar away, revealing around the powerful neck a white ring that faded upward into dark brown flesh and into a mound of rich brown hair. The nose, though large, was a bit too narrow for the wide, quiet face. The eyes were firm and steady, gray and huge.

"Come on in," Mims said. He opened the door to the room and waited for me to pick up my satchel and enter ahead.

The room was not warm, although it felt warm to me when I first entered. I stood holding my satchel and looking at the stove, a low, long cast-iron shoebox with bluish pipes that rose almost to the ceiling then elbowed into the brick flue on the north wall. As I glanced around I saw the room was filled with new-looking furniture: a cherry dresser with an oval mirror; two walnut double beds, one made and covered with a patchwork quilt, the other covered with a guano-sack sheet still bearing the faded mark of V. C. fertilizer; a large chest of oaken drawers; a halltree near the dresser; two rockers and a straight chair; a small round table. Behind the table was the kitchen section with a sink, a hot plate of two eyes, an old refrigerator. Hanging from the ceiling in the center of the room was a tiny wagon-wheel chandelier of polished oak. Beside the rocker, on an end table sat a radio, and between the end table and the wood box was a cedar bucket of ashes. The entire floor from wall to wall was covered with a pale milky linoleum. In spite of the haphazard arrangement of items everything looked amazingly clean and smelled of soap.

"Radio said below zero," Mims said.

I dropped my satchel and turned to see Mims hanging his big coat on the halltree. I then saw on the dresser a comb, a hairbrush, a flat silver snuffbox, a large Bible, and a clock. I removed my own topcoat, hesitated, holding it until Mims took the coat and hung it on the halltree.

"I don't know why I thought he said tomarr'. Belikes, I didn't listen," Mims said. "I don't listen good as I used to, with nobody around."

"Have you been by yourself here?"

"Ever since I come to the Shop I have. Two year ago," he said. He went to one of the rockers and sat down and motioned for me to sit. We sat with the rockers angled toward each other, both looking at the stove. Mims lifted one foot to the apron of the stove and immediately the shoe, which bore the signs of regularly applied tallow, began to steam. "Got 'em wet before I could find my overshoes," he said. He moved his foot to one side of the apron. "Better dry yourn. I think I'm gonna lose my collards. The Chaplain likes collards."

I placed my feet on the apron. My shoes, being new and untallowed, did not steam as readily as those of Mims.

"You like Amos and Andy?" he said.

"Yes," I said with enthusiasm. Which was not the truth. Why had I said it? I wondered. I neither liked nor disliked Amos and Andy. But it was true that I wished to please Mims. And therefore, I had not lied. I added, "I'd like to hear them." It was a fine distinction, but I reasoned: I'd like to hear them because of Mims. And yet I felt a certain guilt for having given a curious shape to truth, for having done something which I felt Mims would not have done. Mims would have been totally honest. To relieve the vague annoyance that nibbled at my conscience, I said, "I've never listened to them much." Still I was not satisfied. Something in the face of Mims appealed to me deeply, made me ashamed of being careless with the truth, however trivially. "When I said yes, I meant I'd like to hear anything you like."

"They'll be on dreckly," Mims said. He changed his other foot to the apron.

We sat in silence, hearing only the wind against the tin shingles and the ticking of the clock on the dresser. Now and then the wind choked the flue and whiffs of smoke escaped from the pipes and the stove eyes. Gradually there was a lull in the wind and we could hear a faint peppering, like birdshot dropped on a table.

"Sleet," Mims said. He turned and for the first time looked carefully at me. "He didn't tell me you was so young."

"The Chaplain?" I said.

"He said a young feller. Belikes, I had you older."

I waited to be asked my age. But I could see no sign of a question in his big gray eyes. I saw instead the glimmer of a smile mingled with a sad sort of expression that died away.

"Did he tell you about me?" I said.

"Some," Mims said.

Again I waited for a question, wished for one. I wanted Mims to know. No question came.

"I thought it was tomarr'," Mims said. "I thought you was going to Piccadilly tonight."

"I came in last night," I said. "Late."

Again I waited for the question about my age, my father, my mother, my home, the crime itself, anything personal. If Mims would ask first, then I would be free to ask all sorts of things I wanted to know about him. I was a little aggravated with his silence though I saw more clearly than ever that the face was not the least bit coarse or unpleasant. Also, there was nothing meddlesome in the face, no disposition to inquire. If he were a doctor, I thought, he would place you on an elevated seat, listen to his stethoscope, examine your eyes and tongue, and write his prescription with a few grunts and without a single question. I caught the soft stare of the gray eyes again, the almost smile, and knew that he was no more likely to ask a personal question of me than to reach over and pull my nose.

"I stayed in Piccadilly last night," I said.

"Maybe that's what he said, Piccadilly last night. I git things confused. Ain't the brightest feller in the world."

I surveyed the room. "Did you make all these things?"

"Mostly," he said.

"That seems pretty bright to me."

"Oh, I done that with my hands. I don't have no trouble with my hands. I can figure pretty well. But readin' and writin'...I git worse and worse. And never was too good. I forgot. Ain't you hungry? I'll fix you something 'fore Amos and Andy comes on."

"The Chaplain gave me something to eat."

"I got plenty such as it is. It's cold though. I could warm you up some ham. I got milk."

"I'm not hungry at all," I said. "What do you do with all those things you make?"

"The ones we don't use here the Chaplain sells 'em. In town and all over."

"Who gets the money?"

"He buys books mostly. The Chaplain does."

"Don't you get any of the money?"

"I git credit at the store."

"Is that all?"

"It's all I need. I git clothes too."

"You wear what you want to?"

"Now I'm a free trusty I can. The Chaplain made me a free trusty."

"You like the Chaplain?"

The big face tightened into a frown and then relaxed. "Well, if you'd been in Camp Four and he put you here, you'd be a right smart apt to give him some credit."

The sound of the bloodhounds floated out on the wind, as if the kennels were miles away. The sleet commenced again, overhead and against the windowpanes. Mims pushed the stove lid sideways and heaped the fire with more wood, remnants of oak from the Shop. "We ain't fixed for zero weather," he said. He brushed his hands, wiped them on his prison handkerchief, and turned on the radio.

He went to the dresser, picked up the flat silver snuffbox and returned to his rocker. He sat down, took off his shoes, pulled the cedar ash bucket beside him and put a large pinch of snuff into his jaw. The maneuver thrilled me. I wondered how long it would be before Mims would have to lean over and spit into the ash bucket. Here was an unusual man. A body that would be at home in overalls. Hands that could shape the scrollwork on a cabinet with the ease of Sarah moulding butter. A kindred soul now. Higher than that. A high priest, more precious because he was unlettered and inarticulate and not curious. I wanted more than ever to ask about his life, home, his children. Most of all, how could such a man have found his way to Olanberg? I ached to know but I would not dare ask.

Mims leaned back in his rocker, his feet crossed one above the other on the stove apron. The voice on the radio was announcing the Amos and Andy show. He half closed his eyes and smiled.

I watched so intently that I was hardly aware of what was happening with Amos and Andy. I saw the big arms relaxed across the faintly rising and falling chest, the slight upward curving of the corners of the mouth, the motionless eyelids, all the face a bright expression of ease and pure pleasure. Again I wondered how long it would be before he would have to lean over and spit into the ash bucket. It seemed to me that a face so peaceful and strong, wholesome and earthy, had to be innocent. For one fleeting moment I wished I could be deeply sorry for all I had done. But the moment passed quickly with the sound of the bloodhounds on the wind. Amos and Andy carried on. Mims stirred, leaned over and spat into the ash bucket. I breathed a sigh of relief and laughed. He glanced at me, gave me a brief, good-humored smile and sank into his rocker again. His face, all his body, was unnaturally still.

I continued to stare at nothing but Mims. He was so utterly at peace. Certainly there seemed to be some drastic mistake concerning him. I had the greatest urge to interrupt Amos and Andy and the peacefulness with a definite question, "Look, Mims, what have you done to be here?"

Aunt Bella would be awfully surprised to know how peaceful everything was, at least at the moment. As I had once tried to imagine the face of an unknown teacher, I now tried to imagine the face of Mims's father, mother, wife, children. Mims was not nearly as old as he had appeared to be in the garden. He's not as old as my own father, I thought. Not quite. Or maybe he was. The face was so unusual.

The overwhelming sense of peacefulness made me drowsy. I closed my eyes and leaned back in the rocker. I could no longer hear the radio but I could hear the sleet, faintly. I was not warm but I was comfortable. Time changed, strange worlds drifted into my mind. I was in the kitchen, sitting on the bench, and my father, in overalls and jumper, was holding out a tray to Aunt Bella who sat on the woodbox. "You have to eat, you know," my father was saying. "You'll be skin and bones." My father bent over her and she pushed the edge of the jumper away from the food. With the touch of her hand my father suddenly wore khaki and I knew that could not be. And there was no bench in the kitchen. My father wore neither overalls nor khaki now. He was in a dark suit and his hair was growing and music was playing. I tried to wake up, felt my arms and thighs jerk. I saw the stove, then Mims, standing in his shirtsleeves, looking at me.

He moved to switch off the radio. The music went on a full second after the click. "You went sound to sleep," he said.

"I guess," I said.

"Won't be no more collards after this," he said. He went to his bed. "You can set up as long as you want to. Won't bother me none."

I got up. I saw that the patchwork quilt was now on the other bed. Each bed had one pillow.

Mims sat on the foot of his bed to remove his clothes. "It's a shower in there but the hot water's froze."

I put my satchel at the foot of my bed, dug in for my toilet articles and went into the bathroom. I did not know whether to close the bathroom door or not. I decided to leave it open, and brushed my teeth for a long time.

"It's a clean towel on the left there," Mims called.

When I came out of the bathroom I found Mims, in long underwear, still sitting on the foot of his bed. His clothes were piled on the end of a cedar chest. He still wore his socks. I removed my clothes and placed them at the other end of the chest.

"Ain't you got some long handles?" Mims said.

"No. They didn't give me any."

"Why, you need some long handles. You gonna freeze. Ain't you used to wearing long handles?"

"Sometimes."

"Belikes, they'll swallow you, but I got another pair."

"I'll be all right," I said.

Mims went to the dresser, wound the clock, and turned out the lights. We got into our beds. Mims still wore his socks. The room was not very dark. An eerie, uneven light crept through the half-shaded north and east windows. The wind had not quieted but the sound of sleet had almost disappeared.

"Maybe that quilt will be a little heavier," Mims said. "I'll git some more blankets tomarr'."

The wind rattled the roof, shook the windows, crept through every crack in the walls and floor and ceiling. I turned to one side and then the other. I tucked the quilt tight about my shoulders, pulled it close against my nose. My feet felt numb. The clock sounded louder and louder above the sporadic breathing of Mims.

I heard Mims turn restlessly, and wondered where the patchwork quilt had come from. The cold seemed to rise through the thin cotton mattress, which, I remembered from last night or today or somewhere, was made in one of the prison camps. Yes. The Chaplain had told me. Perch Mouth can kiss my royal ass, I thought. I won't say I'm sorry. For him or anybody. Mims wouldn't ask me to, wouldn't even expect me to. He would have done the same thing. Mims would. I don't think I like the Chaplain. But he did send me here. Pretty considerate of him. Not as considerate as Mims, certainly not, nor the same kind of man. He asked too many questions. The sandwiches were good enough though. One now might help to drive away the cold. I'm going to do the best I can to please him. Watch every step. I don't want to give him any trouble, nor Mims either. Mims has enough trouble. His collards are dead.

My body shivered. My feet felt totally numb and my teeth chattered. I drew myself into a ball but it did not stop the trembling. I could hear the bed shake. It gave me the feeling of committing some serious violation.

"If you wanta bring your quilt over here and us double up, I don't mind," Mims said.

I sat up quickly. I tried to speak but nothing happened except that my face shook. I scrambled onto the floor and dragged the quilt after me. In the darkness I felt Mims's hand pulling at the quilt.

"Git your pillow," Mims said.

I reached back for my pillow. It was cold as snow. I climbed across the foot of the bed, across Mims's legs, and settled myself under the covers on the side next to the wall. Mims was spreading the quilt.

"I was gonna give you this side," Mims said. "This side might be a little warmer."

"I'm fine," I said.

"Wind coming through that wall. This side would be warmer."

"I like this side," I said. "I'm okay."

"Never seen it this cold," he said. He turned away from the wall and reached back to see that the quilt and blanket covered me.

One long final tremor shook me from head to foot. Then I managed to lie still, feeling the great warmth of Mims, and staring at the ceiling. As I grew warmer I could hear the ticking of the clock more clearly.

"That better?" Mims said.

"Yessir," I said with the faintest tremble.

"Scrooch up close if you want to. It won't bother me none."

I lay for another minute on my back. Then I turned on my side, moved closer to Mims, and wrapped my arm around the big warm body. I was no longer cold at all, nor was I sorry about anything. I could never remember being so comfortable, so happy. I pressed closer and closer against Mims. I went to sleep quickly and easily with the vague unwordable feeling that if the world did not forgive me, Mims most certainly would.

14

THERE WAS THE sound of a rooster crowing and the smell of something pleasant. There was a flaming red streak, like the tail of a comet, fastened against pale blue light. None of it seemed real. I had slept so well it was difficult to get my eyes opened and adjusted. But finally I realized the red streak was a red-hot stovepipe and the smell was of boiling coffee and something frying. Soft light poured into the room as if pushed by the wind. The rooster crowed again. The ancient tin roof crackled. Icicles broke from the eaves and crashed. Mims was in the kitchen nook spooning something into a hot skillet. The sight of his clothes, the absence of stripes, reminded me of early morning at Deer Forks and made me hungry. Mims did not look around but he seemed to know that I was struggling to brave the cold linoleum floor.

"Git your socks on quick," he said.

As I commenced dressing he started to the bathroom with a stewer of boiling water.

"This is fer you," he said. "And it's boiling hot. Better watch it."

"I could wash in cold water," I said.

"I can too, but I like it warm when everything's froze up tight as Dick's hatband."

"You always get up happy?" I said.

Mims took the water into the bathroom and returned.

"Yeah, I like to git up early," he said.

"Why didn't you wake me? I can cook."

"Ah, it ain't no more trouble for two than one."

"You sure are good natured," I said. I went into the bathroom and washed quickly. I was very glad of the warm water and I was very hungry.

The small table was covered with a plate of fried eggs, a plate of fried mackerel patties, a bowl of sawmill gravy, a pie pan stacked with toast, and a coffee pot. We ate ravenously.

"My dad sometimes had fried mackerel for breakfast," I said. "You like it a lot?"

"Belikes, it's my favor-rite dish," Mims said. "It sticks to the ribs."

"I never liked it much before. But this is good. Real, real good."

"Sometimes I don't eat dinner," he said. He covered another mackerel pattie with sawmill gravy. "Or can't."

"Why can't you?"

"Oh, nobody bothers me. I could stop. Only if I'm in the middle of something I don't like to."

Mims took another egg, another pattie, more gravy. He scooped with his fork and sopped with his bread. But I didn't mind at all. I enjoyed watching him eat. There was something safe and secure and very wholesome about it.

"Did I kick you last night?"

Mims stopped eating. "Kick me?"

"Dad used to say I kicked in my sleep."

"No. You're a right good bedfeller. I didn't notice you kick. I slept good. Better'n I have in no tellin' when."

"I did too," I said. "The Chaplain said you'd show me how to muster."

"Yeah. They ain't much to it. We'll straighten things up here first."

Mims got up quickly, a cheerfulness in his face, as if some great pleasure awaited him. Within a few minutes the room was quite neat and orderly. We put on our heavy coats and went out. As we turned the corner of the building the cold air struck like a sudden dash of water. There was a blinding whiteness, a bitter wind, though nothing about us seemed to move. The frozen snow and sleet beneath our feet sounded like gravel. Our breath came out like smoke and hung in the air. "It shore Lord ain't moderated none," Mims said. "This oughta give the boll weevils a scare."

"You gonna get us some more blankets?" I said.

Mims stopped and pushed his cap back on his head. A great mass of hair covered his forehead. His big gray eyes seemed no more affected by the bitter wind than if it had been a summer breeze. "Why, ain't I a good bedfeller?"

"Yes. I didn't mean that. I just don't want to be any trouble to you. And I appreciate everything."

"I appreciate you too," Mims said.

When we had passed the barn we could see scores of men in the fields flailing at the dead cotton stalks as if each man had discovered a snake at his feet.

At the guard station a group of trusties and free trusties hovered and shivered while Captain Burt called the roll and checked the names on his clipboard.

"Ferguson?"

"Laundry," Ferguson answered.

"Okay."

"Porterfield?"

"Mule barn."

"Okay."

"Hammond?"

"Dairy."

"Okay."

"Leatherwood?"

"Mule barn."

"No. Make that the feed mill, Leatherwood."

"Yessir," Leatherwood said.

"Hawthorne?"

"Messenger."

"Okay."

The crowd was disappearing. Only a half dozen remained. "Yawl other just wait a minute," Captain Burt said. He ran down his list and made several checks on the sheet. I waited for my own name to be called, hoping that Captain Burt was in a better humor than last night. He continued to study the sheet and make check marks. The pencil was awkward in his gloved hand. He looked up toward Mims. Clear drops of water dripped from his nose. "I got you," he said to Mims.

Mims nodded toward me. "You got him?"

"Him?" Captain Burt said. He looked at the sheet. "Sanctuary." He made a mark on the sheet, and looked at me, almost a friendly stare. "Yeah, I got you." With the thumb of a glove he wiped the water from his nose.

Mims walked away and I followed him to the spot where our paths would divide. He stopped and winked at me and then went on his way. I watched for a moment before I turned toward the Sanctuary. All the wind seemed to be directly in my face. The Main Gate, which I could see at the end of the road, appeared to be miles away. I could hear the crunch of Mims's shoes going away on the frozen snow. I looked back and felt how much happier I would be if I could only stay close to Mims. Then I began to make my way again over the slippery surface looking back several times until Mims was out of sight. I was distinctly aware of two worlds now, one with Mims and one without him.

The Sanctuary was very warm. All the lights were burning inside, even the goose-necked desk light. But no one was inside. I moved about in the office in order to see into each of the other areas, the library, the kitchen, the chapel. There was no one. I removed my coat, laid it on the couch, and took a seat in the chair beside the desk. The goose-necked light was focused onto three stacks of papers which were not there the night before. I had a great desire to look through the papers, especially the stack which appeared to be letters. But I folded my arms with determination and looked above the desk into the chapel. Without moving I could have read the top letter, or parts of it. Instead, I continued to stare into the chapel and when I finally shifted my gaze I was careful to keep my eyes well above the surface of the desk.

I leaned back in my chair and closed my eyes, thinking of Mims and knowing the Shop would not be as warm as the Sanctuary. The Shop would probably be terribly cold. But if I could get back to Mims and smell the cedar the whole world would be in focus and perfectly acceptable. I thought of Aunt Bella who always had to sleep by herself. At this very moment she was probably in the kitchen with Sarah, and a little later would be upstairs busy with a patchwork quilt which she did not need and would never use. I could see her hands cutting the tiny square blocks, piecing them together, like days into a year, as if that would give her some command over time. I might write her for two quilts, if that was allowed, though perhaps it would be better to trust to Mims's blankets, for the quilts would be such a reminder. I thought I heard someone at the kitchen door. I got up and looked and finding the kitchen empty decided it was nothing more than the wind rattling the door.

I seated myself in the chair again and noticed with some surprise there was a clock on the wall, behind the desk and above the tallest filing cabinet. The big red second hand moved like a cloud shadow across a pond. It was five minutes past eight o'clock. I was worried. I quickly recalled my instructions. No doubt I was in the right place. Certainly the Chaplain had said come to the Sanctuary. Captain Burt had clearly said Sanctuary. But there was always the chance of losing one's mind. My cheeks burned. How did one check one's sanity? By the clock? By the room? By people? Whether I'm sane or insane it's seven minutes after eight. It's afternoon in Bordeaux and probably raining. *Il pleut.* I'd like to be in Bordeaux with Mims. I closed my eyes and tried to estimate the exact length of a minute. My mind's eye visualized the red second hand moving past three, past six, past nine, approaching twelve. Now! I looked up quickly. I was fourteen seconds too early.

I tried again. I waited and waited, my eyes closed tight. Surely the minute was up, and yet I waited. Now! I looked up. I was eight seconds too early. I tried again. I was seven seconds too early. How could a minute be so long? I started to try again but my attention was drawn to a great lumbering and stamping and angry voices at the back door.

"I had no such orders from you." It was the Chaplain's voice.

"I'm not talking about my awdahs," the second voice growled. I knew it was the Warden. The voices were now in the kitchen. "It's the presumption. Here and there and evahwhere I turn. Somebody presuming, suh. Always presuming. I don't want no presumptions. I will not submit to it. No, suh!"

"Order them back again," the Chaplain said.

"I'm not talking about my awduhs. Yours. What was in yo' mind, suh?"

"The Infirmary full of pneumonia cases. Order them back out there. You have the authority. I don't mind being contradicted. It's your authority. Exercise it."

"What was you exercising, suh?"

"My judgment. Not my authority. My judgment. In your absence."

"Well, now suh, that does make a difference. You was exercising yo' judgment. It's yo' best judgment then?"

"Certainly. If you order them back out I'll send them immediately. But if you ask my opinion, my judgment and recommendation is send them in."

"Both camps?"

"Yes, sir. I sent both camps back in."

"How's that mule?"

"What mule?"

"The one got kicked."

"Oh, he's in a swing."

"I know that, suh. How is he?"

"Can't tell for a few days."

"This cold. Ain't this cold bad on him?"

"He's in a stall."

"How you waterin' him?"

"In a tub."

"Make sho' it don't freeze. It's terrible cold. I know that. But I tell you what I've done in my day, suh, with no awdahs pushing me. I've waded swamps above my knees and cut logs and cleared land when the weather was so cold yo' naked hand would stick to a crosscut saw till the hide come off. Yes, suh. I've seen it that cold and me in water up above the knee holes in my britches. Yes, suh, maybe we cut a tree and broke the ice and you don't have no choice but to wade in. No, suh, I wasn't in no steam-heated schoolroom behind a warm desk. I was right alongside my daddy from the time I was twelve and we built Little Egypt plantation that-a-way. Cut it out and dug it out of the swamps with our own bare hands and mule scoops and fresnoes. I never sassed my daddy long as he lived and after he died nobody ever sassed me. No, suh. Not my wife, nor the chill-ren, nor the niggers. Not at Little Egypt. I was the boss. Yes, suh, I was the boss. You got some coffee on that stove?"

"Plenty," the Chaplain said.

I heard the rattle of cups and the pouring of coffee. I got up, thinking perhaps I should show myself, but the deep Delta, growling voice in the kitchen roared again and held me quite motionless. I sat down.

"Ahhh! I'll tell you, suh, many's the day I've pulled a crosscut saw in weather worse than this and come home to nothing but collards and cornpone and buttermilk and thought myself well off. Yes, suh. Many's the day. And slept in a log cabin which didn't have a wall I couldn't throw a cat through. Me and my daddy. That big house standing on Little Egypt today didn't grow outa the ground. No, suh, it didn't. And not till it was built did my mama and the gulls, my sisters, come down. They stayed up there in Carroll County for fo' year, in the red clay hills, never saw a foot of Little Egypt till the land was cleared and the swamps was drained and the house was built. Why, the fo'th crop was up before they ever laid eyes on it, on Little Egypt. My daddy was right proud of that place and he was the boss, from bread tray to hoss trough. After him I was. I been bossing folks almost all my life. I know how it's done. They ain't but one way to handle folks, white or black or in between, kinfolks or strangers, ain't but one way. Say it and don't look back. No, suh. Don't look back. Once you look back you done made the same old mistake Lot made. Gonna git yo'self turned into a pillar of salt. You ought to be familiar with that story, are you not?"

"Very familiar with the story of Lot. And his wife too."

"Sho' you are. It applies to womenfolks too. Say it and don't look back. You think I can go around having my awdahs changed, my authority questioned?"

"Never."

"Nevah, suh! I will not be a pillar of salt. I will not be a laughingstock. No, suh, I will not submit to it. I want you to understand it, ever'body to understand it. Ever prisoner, ever guard, ever trusty, ever nurse, ever orderly, ever horse, ever mule . . . What you think about puttin' a blanket on that mule? Standin' up in that swing he ain't gonna be as warm as layin' down. You know that don't you?"

"That's right."

"Well, put a blanket on him tonight. It ain't gonna be winter forevah around heah. Come spring we need mules."

"I'll have it done," the Chaplain said.

There was a scraping of chairs and the sound of steps. I jumped up. I saw the gigantic figure enter the library area, appearing exactly as he had in Piccadilly, except that he now held the black cowboy hat in one hand and the iron-gray hair looked like a monstrous wig. The begrimed suit, the shabby topcoat, the golden watch chain, the soiled scarf were all unchanged.

"Who is this?" the Warden thundered.

The Chaplain appeared immediately beside the mountain of flesh. "That's the youngster I told you about."

"What youngster?"

"From Woodall County. You remember."

"What's he doing heah, suh? I don't remember you speakin' to me of Woodall County. How old are you, boy?"

"Fifteen," I said.

The Warden turned to the Chaplain. "Woodall County? Didn't I say send him to Camp Fo'?"

"You mentioned Camp Four."

"Why's he not in Camp Fo'?"

"We're in the process . . ."

"You always in the process. Usually the process of changing my awduhs." He turned to me. "What you doing with a trusty's suit?"

I remained speechless, weak with astonishment and fear. The Shop was vanishing. The whole world was crumbling. I might not see Mims again for months.

"I asked you a question, suh."

The Chaplain interceded. "Why, I did that to keep him outside, until I knew exactly what you wanted."

"Didn't I say Camp Fo'?"

"You said you imagined it ought to be Camp Four."

"Imagined? I never imagined nothing in my life."

"Perhaps it was a different word you used. Anyway, I was uncertain. I didn't want to bother you at Little Egypt. So I put him in Piccadilly first."

"Why, yes. I saw you in Piccadilly. When was it?" He turned to the Chaplain. "Why was he in Piccadilly?"

"As I said, I was holding him in abeyance."

"Abeyance? For my instructions?"

"That's right, Mr. Hull. The board will be asking about this youngster. I wanted your explicit orders. In fact, I would like a memo."

"A memo? Goddam a memo!" He turned back to me. "How old are you, suh?"

The Chaplain nodded as if signalling to me to humor the man at all cost. "Fifteen," I said.

"Do you know who I am?"

"Yessir."

"I'm Samuel Hull, the wahdon of this place. When I say froggie I expect people to hop. Is that not right, Mr. Craig?"

"Absolutely," the Chaplain said.

The Warden smiled, looking halfway between the Chaplain and me. Then he set his eyes on me. "Are you a capital?"

For a second I had difficulty in understanding.

"Yes. He is," the Chaplain said. "You remember the account of William Marcus Oday? His father? The grave? The man killed in the cemetery?"

"They was digging up his daddy's grave and he shot a man. Was that it?" He did not wait for an answer. "Well, by God they wouldn't dig up my daddy's grave neither. It was washed up during the flood and I liked to a whopped a man's ass because he didn't fix it back right. What did I say do with this boy? Did I say Camp Fo'? Put him in Camp Two. That ain't too bad."

"I'll need a memo."

"Memo my ass. For what?"

"For the board."

The Warden glared at the Chaplain.

"Of course," the Chaplain said, "we could put him in the Lumber Yard without anything. You mentioned the Lumber Yard."

"I did?"

"Once."

"Well, goddammit put him in the Lumber Yard. The board'll like that. Son-of-a-bitch shoulda been shot with Iuka gravel, tinkering with a grave. Now what else have you got fer me? I'm going back to Little Egypt till this snow's over. That's my plantation, son. Six thousand acres. I got more niggers workin' fer me than they got prisoners here. Yes, suh. And two boys which I don't know where they are, more'n three or fo' times a year. They won't never go to jail worryin' 'bout my grave. But that's all right. The Lawd's been good to me in a worldly way. A course He won't fill yo' hand 'less you open it and take a holt. Samuel Hull don't need nothing they got heah, son. I'm wahdon of this place practically fer charity. Yes, suh. Practically fer charity. I say, what else you got fer me, Mr. Craig?"

"Nothing else that I know of."

"Take care of this boy."

"Yessir."

"And take care of that mule."

"Without fail," the Chaplain said.

"Where's my car? In the back or the front?"

"In the back. It's in the back," the Chaplain said.

The Warden moved toward the back door. "If you need me, don't say I'm not here. Just call, and I'll be here in eight minutes. Jules waitin' in the car?"

"Yessir."

"Where's my scarf? What did I do with my scarf? It's cold out there." He placed his hat firmly on his head and continued to look for his scarf.

The Chaplain took the scarf from the Warden's shoulders and handed it to him. The Warden wrapped it carefully about his neck. "About them stalk cutters, if you think it's dangerous cold tomarr', leave 'em in."

"Yessir," the Chaplain said. He opened the door and closed it quietly after the Warden was gone. He stood for a few seconds holding the door. Then he came to the center of the library area, drew in a deep breath and smiled at me as he might have smiled to a board member. "Well, now, you don't know whether I told a little fib for you or not, do you?"

"Nossir," I said.

"What do you think?"

"You're religious. I'm sure you have a proper respect for the truth."

"What is truth?"

"Sir?"

"What is truth? Is it sincerity? Genuineness? Agreement with that which is represented? Conformity to fact? Do the stars shine brighter by day or by night? Which? Day or night?"

"By night I guess."

"Think. The stars shine by day and by night with equal intensity. What we see is something else. What we see is altered by where we are. And where we are is altered by several things. You say I am religious. What is religion? The past is every man's religion, the future is every man's home. The truth is where all knowledge of the past meets all knowledge of the future. Therefore, truth is not available to the human mind. Are you following me?"

"Not exactly."

"Are you trying?"

"Yessir."

"That's all I ask. Try. Just try. Effort is the greatest of all miracles. And most people don't make it. No miracles for the average man because he just won't make the effort."

The Chaplain was trying to impress me, I thought, and he was not succeeding very well. In a vague way, lurking deep inside my mind, was the conviction that Mims, inarticulate and unschooled, might know more about the universe than the Chaplain.

The smile on the Chaplain's face was gradually replaced with a growing expression of resignation, almost hopelessness, like a lone worker with his hoe surveying a vast field of grassy cotton.

"Ah, well," the Chaplain said, "maybe things will run a little smoother now, with Apple Ass satisfied."

15

THE DAY DID not run smoothly for me. My mind was focused on the Shop and Mims. At the end of each task assigned I thought the Chaplain might dismiss me and send me to the Shop. But the day wore on with one assignment after another. I typed four letters, filed a number of papers, rearranged a shelf of books, answered the telephone while the Chaplain was away, made a fresh pot of coffee, posted the letters in the mail room at Administration, delivered a package to Captain Burt's office in Piccadilly.

A few minutes before noon the Chaplain put on his topcoat and hat, ordered me to do the same and follow him. We went out the back way and got into the Chaplain's jeep. It was an old National Guard vehicle with a blue striped flag attached to the left wind-shield post. As we swerved and skidded along the icy roadway toward the central guard station the flag unfurled itself, revealing a white circle and the lettering DEPUTY WARDEN.

The guards at the Second Gate came to strict attention and gave a smart salute with gloved hands. The big gate swung open slowly so that the Chaplain had to slow the jeep but did not stop. Two guards, with rifles, remained at rigid attention, their breath visible, as if they had that moment discarded cigarettes. Other vehicles had marked the roadway which was otherwise totally obscure. The road ran parallel to the gigantic fence that stood twelve or fifteen feet high and stretched as far as I could see across the shimmering white levelness. Beyond the fence the vast acreage of dead and frozen cotton stalks, almost shoulder high, appeared like a great sea of fingers groping helplessly and hopelessly for something.

We first passed a long dingy one-storey flat-roofed building squatting off the roadway a hundred yards and enclosed by a fence six or seven feet high. Beside the long building was a tin-topped bungalow, painted green. Several men were passing from the bungalow into the long building.

"Tag Shop. Where we make car tags," the Chaplain said.

A few hundred yards farther on was Camp Two which was very much like the Tag Shop, though the building was somewhat larger and newer. "That's a farm camp," the Chaplain said.

A laundry stood beside Camp Three, which was another few hundred yards along the road. "Now you wouldn't think it," the Chaplain said, "but the laundry, that's the laundry, causes less trouble than any camp we've got. I don't know whether it's Captain Daniels, he's in charge and a good organizer, or whether it's maybe that it's all so simple. The men know exactly what they're doing. Things come in dirty in the morning and they come out clean in the evening. Maybe they feel they're doing something worthwhile. And they can see the results in one day's time. I don't know."

There was a large field gate at Camp Four and on the field side of the gate was a huge toolshed, with plows, cultivators, harrows, planters, hoes, and items I did not recognize.

"You know what a middle buster is?" the Chaplain said.

"Sure," I said, feeling quite friendly with the Chaplain.

He turned off the road and drove toward the camp building, which was two or three times larger than the ones we had passed. There were several new additions to the original structure causing the whole to appear very haphazard and ill arranged. Inside the fenced area was a quadrangle where a basketball court and a softball diamond overlapped. Half a dozen men moved around one of the basketball goals, tossing and dribbling the ball like children on a frozen pond.

The Chaplain stopped the jeep beside two cars at the gate. A guard with his rifle stood stamping his feet in the snow and blowing on his free hand. The Chaplain looked at the cars, one of which had a white flag mounted on its top, the other a red flag. "Captain Parker inside?" the Chaplain asked.

"Yessir," the guard said. "He's waiting for you."

"Where's your gloves?" the Chaplain said.

"I thought they was in my car when I left home. I was in a hurry. Everything froze up." He opened the gate.

Captain Parker was waiting in his office. He got up at sight of the Chaplain and came into the hallway. He was a tall, portly figure, with the stamp of many outdoor summers on his hands and face. He wore a tan leather jacket, a plaid shirt, corduroy trousers, and high laced boots. The top of a gray sweatshirt showed about his neck. "Poke chops today," he said.

"You had pork chops the last time," the Chaplain said.

"That's what they like," the Captain said.

"And what you like," the Chaplain said.

"Why sho' I do. Ain't no meat got the taste to me like poke. Country-fried steak, which is the only way I like it, ain't as good as poke." He was leading us down the hallway. He paid no attention to me. "What did the old man say?"

"The usual," the Chaplain said.

"What about tomarr'?"

"Leave them in."

"He still here?"

"No. He went back."

"Well, you know I got more trouble bringing 'em in than leaving 'em out. But we was sho' headed for fifteen, twenty cases of pneumonia. They'll be a few fights tonight. But I'm gonna stay later than usual. I tole 'em when I brought 'em in, I tole 'em all, the first ruckus that's started I ain't gonna ask who's guilty, both parties gonna git ten strokes of Black Annie acrost they naked ass." He turned down another hallway. "We got yams too."

"And peas?" the Chaplain asked. "You got peas too?"

"That's right. They crowder. They ain't whooperwill. I'd soon have birdshot as whooperwill. Ain't nothing you can do to hep whooperwills. Onions, pepper sauce. Nothing. But they can't complain when they got poke chops, yams, crowders, and yeller cornbread."

"Yellow?" the Chaplain said.

"Sho'," the Captain said.

"Where'd you get yellow cornmeal?"

"Olanberg. Pott's Grist Mill. He's got plenty of yeller cone. He'll swap you. Bushel and a half of white for a bushel of yeller. You want some?"

"I might," the Chaplain said. "Goes good with collards."

"Man alive," the Captain said.

We had reached the dining hall. "Here," the Captain said. "Let me take yo' coat."

But the Chaplain refused. He removed his coat and hat and placed them on a chair near the door. I removed my coat and cap and dropped them on the floor beside the chair.

I hesitated inside the door, watching the Chaplain and Captain move toward a corner of the hall where the Captain's round table was located. The noise of utensils and the shuffle of bodies struck me as sharply as the cold wind outside. There were perhaps ninety or a hundred men at the tables which seated two hundred or more. With one glace I saw the desperate resignation on their faces, the reckless and frantic way they attacked the food. I smelled the odor of hot grease. The belching and swearing and clamoring seemed to grow louder and louder in my ears. A few men went past me, having finished their eating, and it seemed to me in the dismal light that the horror and terror in their eyes looked above me and below me and beyond me but never directly at me. All this I saw in less than a minute and a great nausea rose in my throat. I was finally aware that the Chaplain had come back to me and was telling me to go down the line and get my food.

I stifled the sickness in my throat and found myself in line holding out my tin tray for helpings. I chose the end of a table which was now vacant and did my best to push down three or four bites of the yams. It would be awful not to eat, and yet I was afraid I was going to vomit.

I dared to glance about myself cautiously, but no one seemed to pay me any attention. They would, of course, if I did not eat. Three or four minutes later I was somewhat relieved to see that half the men who had been in the room when I entered were now gone. I lifted my coffee cup and turned my head enough to see the Captain's table in the far corner of the hall. A cook was serving the Captain and the Chaplain. When I had swallowed the coffee my throat began to clear and I could feel the pulsebeats in my temples. I sipped again and again, stalling.

Before me and to my left were empty trays. Little by little, between sips of coffee, I pulled the empty trays nearer to my own. Then I cut the greasy pork chop in half. As I nibbled at the yams with my fork my left hand stole food from my own tray and passed it on to the empty trays. At last my tray was almost empty. I was certain I had not been discovered and I felt a great relief. I almost felt like eating. I finished all the coffee.

There were no more than a dozen men now left at the tables. I got up and stood looking at my tray, and then I saw for the first time there was a napkin holder on the table. I could not remember seeing anyone use a napkin. I pulled and two napkins came out. I looked about to see whether anyone had noticed. I wiped my hands carefully, leaving the napkins on my tray in such a way that they covered the remaining food. Then I made my way beside the row of benches, past the Captain's table, and waited in the hallway.

Within a few minutes the Captain and Chaplain came out of the dining hall. I followed them, almost unnoticed, to the Captain's office and again waited in the hallway. After a minute or two the Chaplain came out with a notebook and pen and led me into a small room which was crowded with large bookcases, four small tables, half a dozen chairs, and an old desk on which lay a number of pencils, a calendar and a pencil sharpener. Above each table a shaded light hung from the ceiling.

The Chaplain turned on all the lights and placed the pen and notebook on one of the tables. "I want you to take all these books and put them in alphabetical order according to authors," the Chaplain said. "Then, copy each title and author into this notebook. Like this." He tore the first sheet from the notebook and wrote an example. "Skip a couple of spaces between each one. You understand?"

"Yessir."

On the cover of the notebook the Chaplain printed in a very heavy but handsome hand:

BOOKS
CAMP FOUR

"Take your time. Write as neatly as you can. I don't know how many are here. About two hundred I imagine. It'll take a while. You figure out the best way to do it."

"Wouldn't it be best to..."

The Chaplain interrupted curtly. "You figure it out." He left the room.

I stared after him. The sudden and rudely concise manner disturbed me immensely. I went to the doorway and saw that the Chaplain did not enter the Captain's office again but went directly out of the building.

A heavy cloud of doubt and despondency floated into the room and settled on me. Perhaps the Chaplain was telling me that I would be left at Camp Four forever. That would be unbearable. I had seen too much of Camp Four already. Not the food alone. Everything. I didn't really trust the Chaplain. There might be a mean and vicious streak behind the deep green eyes and the wide forehead.

I suddenly heard noises and strange commotions down the hallway which I had not heard before, yet I knew, somehow, the sounds had been there all the time. The nausea rose in my throat. If he thinks I'm going to say I'm sorry, I said to myself, he's got another thought coming.

I went to a bookcase and fingered three or four of the books. I had no interest in what they were. Wild and frantic thoughts raced through my mind. If I was left at Camp Four I would starve myself...I would run away...I would tie a sheet around my neck...

But the Chaplain had not been terribly short, I reasoned. He had not been angry. He was probably in a hurry. There were lots of things a warden had to worry about. The best thing...the very best solution was to do the job well...and quickly. I could print the titles and names. Very neatly. The Chaplain would be pleased if not astonished and tonight I would be safely with Mims.

I grabbed an armful of books and put them on the nearest table. I reflected for a minute, counting on my fingers. The thing to do was put A through G on the first table, H through N on the second,

O through T on the third, U through Z on the fourth. I wondered for a moment whether the genius of authorship was more or less evenly divided along the alphabet. I supposed it was. Two hundred might not be a fair sampling. But if one table got overcrowded I would have to make some adjustments.

I set to work feverishly. Within an hour I had all the books grouped on the tables. Then I began to replace them alphabetically into the shelves. H through N had the largest number of books. I discovered error after error and my pace became slower and slower. When I had replaced about half the books I turned to find a tiny old man standing by one of the tables. I was startled by the sudden presence of the curious old figure in trusty stripes and peacoat, with a strange blue card dangling from one of the peacoat buttons. The man was hardly five feet tall. His face though dark and hardened had the strange appearance of a feverish child. His tiny, burning eyes were set far back in his head. His hands, closed and clenched, were like two dark doorknobs.

The old man began a wide toothless grin. I remained quite still, gazing at the ghostly figure.

"How old you think I air," he said.

"I don't know," I said. All the horrors of remaining at Camp Four pressed down on me.

"Air you gonna guess?"

I continued to gaze.

"Hit don't matter. I ain't never used eyeglasses. I read a dozen of them books. Two last year."

"Which ones did you read?"

"Last year?"

"Yes."

"I read Robbie Crusoe agin. And I fergit which one else. Maybe it was Lora Doone. Wasn't that the one about the robbers?"

"I don't know."

"You never read Lora Doone?"

"No."

"They didn't have no books when I was here the fust time."

"You've been here twice?"

"Three time. Only the fust time I was in Camp Eight. Lordy, but Eight was a booger."

"Worse than here?"

"I'll say. I was a mooney."

"A mooney?"

"Yeah. Still am. Only they started me off here the last two time. 'Bout all the moonies start here ever time."

"What's a mooney?"

"Why, moonshine. Up in Garland County I was. You ever heered of the Dan Doby Hills? That's where. They said I shot at a revenooer this last time. Got me ten. Them other times was only five. I didn't shoot at nobody. Never have. Why, I got a dozen dogs at my house but I don't never hardly ever hunt with a gun. They lied on me. Which wouldn'ta made no difference only it was ten instid of five. I could allus see my way through five. Ten's more tetchy. What air you doin' with them things? Takin' 'em away?"

"I'm making a list for the Chaplain. Placing them in alphabetical order."

"You air?"

I nodded. "Did you want a book?"

"Oh, you can't take 'em outa here 'less the Captain signs you up. Or the Chaplain. Chaplain got mine last year. I ain't here no more. Air you long?"

I was puzzled. I didn't know whether the question referred to my work with the books or to my sentence. I picked up an armful of books.

"I hope not," the old man said. He turned and went out. For a second I had the urge to call him back, to tell him how long my sentence was. But the urge quickly faded and I hurried to the shelf with my armload of books, wondering what time it was.

I finished stacking the books into the shelves, counted them and rechecked their alphabetical order. Then I commenced the list by taking six at a time to the desk where I could write more easily and neatly. The listing went more slowly than I had expected, for I was printing with meticulous care. My arm began to grow tired and ached but I was very proud of my legibility and orderliness. When I was on the final shelf with no more than a dozen books to be listed I rose from the desk to find the little old man standing in the room again.

"Air you 'bout finished now?" he said. "Maybe I come too soon."

I was again startled. He was holding out a blue card to me.

"What is this?"

"Ya pass. Fer the Second Gate. Perch Mouth, he sent me to git you. The Chaplain."

"Oh," I said and took the card as if it was a pardon. A sense of ease and well-being flooded the room.

"I keep the dogs," the old man said. "Been keepin' 'em three year. Only now, now that I'm a trusty I got that little crib-house by the kennels. Log. I ain't here no more." He moved to the window. "Come 'ere," he said.

I followed him to the window, where he pointed toward the gate outside and to a gray pickup with a wired cage built on its bed.

"When you air done, I'll be in that pickup." He grinned and started out of the room. In the hall he turned and came back to the doorway. "Leo. Leo Perry," he said.

16

IN MY EYES the list was a remarkable piece of penmanship. Not only was it beautifully printed but it was accurate, uniform, well spaced, a work of art. To my delight the Chaplain was pleased and after a brief glance through the pages he dismissed me with warm praise.

I hurried along the icy road toward the Lumber Yard with the image of Mims etched in my mind. Yet, in spite of the Chaplain's praise, a cloud lurked in my sky of happiness, a sense of fear that something would destroy my position of favor, cancel my good marks, undo my tranquility. The Chaplain might suddenly overtake me and send me to Camp Four. Captain Burt might appear abruptly ahead and drag me off to Piccadilly. The bitter cold was a dangerous omen. The mere howling of the dogs might bring on some sort of disaster.

The Lumber Yard rose ahead, the building looming before me like a temple of safety. To my left was the stark outline of the kennels and the small shack over which a thin cloud of smoke hovered though there was no sign of a chimney.

With every step I expected to hear the moaning of the bloodhounds and was preparing myself to resist it. When the cry came, the single sad moaning of one hound, I quickened my pace over the slippery surface and was almost running as I turned the corner of the building and entered the cellar-like area. On the first steps of the stairway I heard something uttered in the darkness behind me, a call, a grunt, a whine. Flooded again with the sense of having my world shattered, I stopped suddenly. The sound came again, nearer, more urgent, and with it the cry of the bloodhound. I was about to rush on upstairs to the safety of Mims when a small figure, bearing an armload of something, emerged from the dark recesses of lumber.

"Hey," the old man said.

I recognized Leo at once carrying a heavy load of very short planks.

"Air you with Mims?" Leo said.

I nodded.

"I coulda rode you over," he said.

There was something about the old man which made me sense again that fear of change, and I felt again the urge to run up the stairway. Or perhaps it was the howling of the dogs. The whole kennel seemed to be aroused now. I began to speak quickly, nervously, as if my words would keep the old man at a distance. "I had to go over the list with the Chaplain."

"I coulda waited," he said.

"The Chaplain liked it," I said. "He thought the list was perfect."

"Sho' now," Leo said. He looked down at the load he carried. "Farwood," he said. "You best come with me fer a minute."

"Now?" I said.

Leo nodded and jerked his head toward the kennels. The dogs were howling louder than ever. I did not budge. Leo walked away. He looked back and jerked his head again. I intended not to move an inch but I found myself following, frightened and uneasy and thinking: Maybe he has some authority over me; he can't hurt me, small as he is; what does he want? I followed at a distance.

Leo had entered the cabin and come out again by the time I reached the kennels. In his frail arms and doorknob hands he carried two folded blankets. He held them out to me. They smelled of dogs.

Leo smiled. "You don't have to be afeered of me. Them's for Mims. Or maybe fer you."

"Yes. They're for me," I said. I was sorry I had mistrusted the old man. "Thank you."

"Yours. Air you gonna stay with Mims?"

"I think so."

"Cut it, cut it," he whispered to the dogs. "Tell him they's more if he needs 'em." He nodded toward the house. "In my cabin. Which it ain't a cabin. An old crib. I got blankets all over the walls, if you needs more."

"Thanks," I said.

"Jist a neighbor. I allus tried to be a good neighbor. Anybody lived close to me could git what's mine whether he brung it back or not. Which Mims is too. A good neighbor. He'll do to go to town with air day of the week."

"Thanks again."

"Yours." The old voice was almost drowned by the moaning hounds.

I moved to go but the old eyes held me, almost pleading for a bit more time. Leo reached down, formed a little snowball and tossed it toward the dogs. "Cut it, cut it," he said, not very loud.

The whole place was suddenly quite still. Leo looked at me and grinned. Then his face became serious, almost sad. "One of my dogs is puny. This 'un here." He put his hand through the fence and patted the dog gently. It was a black-and-tan male. "Pet him," Leo said.

"Me?"

"It's all right. He knows you with me. Reach through there. They the gent'lest things a tall."

As if hypnotized, though still with a sense of fear, I reached through the fence and touched the dog. The skin felt thin and extremely loose. I rubbed the shoulders and then the head, which was pressed against the fence and turned up toward me with a solemn, dignified expression. I studied the dog carefully. His height appeared to be a little more than two feet and his weight near a hundred. There was a great shyness about the dog. The head, with its deep-set hazel eyes, was long and narrow, tapering slightly from temples to muzzle. I felt the ears. They were thin and soft to the touch, monstrously long, and fell in folds like a curtain. The nostrils were large and open. The neck was long, shoulders muscular and sloping. Suddenly the other dogs crowded around and I withdrew my hand.

"They jealous," Leo said. "I'd show you something but I can't whistle. How they mind. I'll show you some Sunday."

"Do they mind better on Sunday?"

"Naw, they don't mind no better on Sunday. But that's the onliest time I wear my teeth. Usually."

"Oh," I said. "I better go." I started away with the blankets.

After a few steps, Leo called, "Say?"

I stopped. Leo pointed to the ailing dog. "I'm gonna take me a coop and put him in the cabin so's maybe he won't git no worse and the others won't ketch it."

"Yes," I said and started away again.

"Say?" Leo called.

Again I stopped.

"You never tole me how old you think I air?"

"About sixty," I said.

Leo laughed heartily and finally allowed himself to adjust to his familiar toothless grin. "I were near that old when I come here the fust time."

After a moment I said, "Good night."

"Sho' now," Leo said.

I hurried toward the Shop and ran up the stairway. All the way I could smell the odor of dogs in the blankets. When I rushed into the room I saw no sign of Mims and for the fraction of a second was terribly disappointed. But I saw that the fire was going in the stove and there was food waiting in the kitchen nook. Then the bathroom door opened and Mims came out naked, shielding himself with a towel. A smile broke across his face. "You got 'em," he said. "I asked Leo this morning and forgot about it."

I placed the blankets on the floor beside the door facing. "They smell like dogs," I said. "And I bet they've got all kinds of fleas."

"Lord," Mims said. "I druther be cold."

"I can't stand fleas or flies," I said. My eyes fell on the patch-work quilt. It was as beautiful as any Aunt Bella ever had. "Where did you get that quilt?"

"I brung it from home. My mammy give it to me fer my wedding gift. They kep it in Receiving till I come here."

I looked down at the blankets. "These blankets stink," I said.

"Well, put 'em outside and I'll take 'em to the laundry tomarr'. We done all right last night."

With my foot I pushed the blankets outside and faced Mims again, who stood tall and naked, racing the towel across his shoulders. "Could I take a shower now?"

"Yeah, if you can stand the cold water. But hurry. We don't want to miss Amos and Andy."

"I'll hurry," I said. I began to shed my clothes. I hurried through the ice-cold shower and ran back into the room, shivering as I dressed. "I believe it's colder than last night," I said.

"We'll just have to scrooch up a little closer," Mims said.

The table was covered with fried ham, pork and beans, turnips, winter onions, and hoecakes. I was so hungry I ate faster than Mims. "I never had anything that tasted so good," I said.

We ate for a while before I began to recount the events of my day. Mims often stopped eating and looked up to show his interest in the accounts of the Warden, the Chaplain, Camp Four, Leo, the dogs.

When the meal was finished and the dishes were cleared, we settled ourselves beside the stove, and the magic of the night before commenced to work again. Mims took his pinch of snuff, leaned back in his rocker, propped his feet on the stove apron, half closed his eyes, and lost himself in the world of Amos and Andy.

Hypnotized I lay quietly in my rocker, watchful as an owl. I did not miss the slightest movement of Mims, nor the faintest grunt, nor the single time he leaned over and spat expertly into the cedar ash bucket. The stovepipes were blue and red with heat. Soft shadows made the room seem warmer. The wind growled around the eaves and corners of the building and shook the loosened shingles as if a litter of cats leaped about on the roof. Occasionally the cry of the bloodhounds overrode the wind, sounding sometimes near and sometimes far away. Now the hounds did not bother me at all. I felt that nothing threatened me as long as I was in the presence of Mims. We sat in silence for some time after the radio was quiet.

Abruptly a thought came to me and I delivered it before I realized I was speaking. "I bet you're not afraid of anything."

Mims opened his eyes. "Afraid?"

"Yes. You're not afraid of anything."

"Huh. Belikes, I'm afraid of lots of things."

"What?"

"What?"

"What, for example?" I said.

"Why, I'm afraid of God. Not afraid exactly. But I try to be mindful."

"That's what I thought. Nothing on earth. You're not afraid of anything on earth. I can tell."

"I wouldn't wanta tackle a bear," he said. He grinned and closed his eyes again.

I moved slightly to see the face more clearly. The whole man was so peaceful, so strong, so certainly a creature of some other world, different and far away, that I had to like him. The feeling was so easy and innocent that it was altogether like coming out of the darkest spot in cypress grove into the brightest sunlight. I kept staring at Mims like Aunt Bella threading a needle.

"I can't imagine why you're here," I said.

"I'm here because they sent me."

"I can't imagine why."

"They thought they had good enough reason. They had a trial."

"Did they?" I said.

"Did they what?"

"Have a good reason?"

"Belikes, you ask ever'body here, trusties and all, and lots would say no."

"What do you think?"

"It don't matter much what I think, does it?"

"No, I suppose not," I said. I was not at all satisfied but I was afraid to continue my probing, for the deep enchantment was so new and young and fragile that I had some fleeting sense it might quickly be destroyed. And anyway, my feelings would be the same no matter what Mims had done. I changed my line of questions abruptly and deliberately. "Did you know that every woman wants her first child to be a boy?"

"No. I didn't know that."

"They do. And most men do too. But all women do. You never heard that?"

"I don't recollect it. I don't recollect that my wife said one way or the other."

"I'm sure it's so," I said, very gravely.

"I don't doubt it. I just don't recollect. We had a boy anyways."

"Where are they now?"

"My folks? The flood got 'em. My mammy too. Ever'body but my daddy."

"Where is he?"

"He died."

It was a long time before I could say anything else. We sat watching each other with such ease and aimlessness that we seemed not to be watching each other at all.

The fire was dying away in the stove and the room was growing colder. As if there had been no interruption I said, "My aunt was the one told me every woman wanted her first child to be a boy. She never got married. She just told me that one stormy night. I used to stay with her a lot when I was little. She was afraid of storms. That night she was telling me about the siege of Vicksburg. It's one of the great sieges of the world, you know."

Mims nodded. "It looks like it."

"She's not my aunt. Did I tell you that? She's my great-aunt. And she's going to leave everything she has to me. Isn't that strange?"

"I can't see nothing wrong with that."

"I mean, you see, she was a teacher and you'd think she would leave something to a school or a church. I don't deserve it. I'm afraid she's very sick."

Mims cleared his throat and tried to find something to say. He could not quite find the words he wanted and finally ended his effort by leaning over and spitting into the cedar ash bucket. Then he added a pinch of snuff to his chew. I thought the maneuver was carried out very neatly.

"Does that taste good?" I said.

"Tastes pretty well," he said.

"I wish I had a pinch."

"You'd be sick."

"I bet I wouldn't. Is it Garrett?"

"No. Garrett's a mite too stout fer me."

I laughed. "Would Garrett make you sick?"

"Wouldn't make me sick. Just spin me around a little. Belikes, it'd have me coming 'round the mountain."

"Could I have a pinch?"

He looked down and rolled the silver box in his hand. "Best not. About time fer bed anyways."

"Sometime? Will you give me a pinch? I sure would like one. With you."

Mims looked from me to the silver box and back again. "What would ya daddy say if I done that?"

"My daddy is dead. Didn't you know that?"

"I didn't ask the Chaplain nothing." Mims got up, stretched. He took the small shovel beside the ash bucket and began to bank the fire.

"Have you seen the battlefield at Vicksburg?" I said.

"Lots of times."

"Really?"

"That's where I'm from. Little ways outside Vicksburg."

"What did you do there?"

"We sort of one-horse farmed. Had a little shop in the wintertime. Done a little work round and about. Me and my daddy."

"Do you know about first cousins twice removed and second cousins once removed and that sort of thing?"

Mims closed the stove lid. "I don't know as I ever had any cousins. If I did they was all back in South Carolina."

"You all by yourself?"

"Belikes, you could say that. I'm 'bout ready to put the cat out. Ain't you?"

"If you are," I said.

At first the bed was terribly cold. I shivered and pressed myself close against Mims, feeling the wonderful warmth all the way down to his sock-covered feet. I could not help smiling at the thought of Mims sleeping in his socks. The guano-sack sheets smelled clean, and Mims smelled clean too, as if he had come out of the springs. Lying there, warm, I tried to imagine the flood, and wondered why people could not move out quickly, well ahead of floodwaters. "How did you get out of the flood?" I said.

"I wasn't there. Me and my daddy was in Bovina, building some cabinets."

"How did your dad die?"

"Heart."

"Was it expected?"

"Belikes, it never is expected. But it wasn't no big surprise."

The wind on the roof became stronger. The sound made me move a bit closer to the warm body.

"Do you ever pray?" I said.

"Yes. When I don't forget it."

"At night?"

"Mostly at night."

"I used to. I didn't stop. But I mean I used to most every night. And now I don't. I can't imagine why you're here. You seem like such a good person."

"Belikes, they's lots of good folks ever'wheres. You don't seem so bad."

"I did an awfully bad thing. But I'm not sorry. I'm not going to say I'm sorry. Because I'm not. Don't you know what I did?"

"No. I jist know you're a capital. But you don't seem like a capital to me."

"Are you a capital?"

"'Sposed to be."

"I don't care. It don't make a difference to me. I don't care." I could hear myself sounding like Mims, but I didn't care about that either. "I'll have to tell you sometime. About me. I hope you'll still like me. I hope they don't change me."

"Hnnnn?"

"I hope they don't change me. I hope they let me stay with you."

"I do too," Mims said.

I turned and put my arm around him. "Can I hug you tight?"

"Tight as you want to," he said.

A long, loud and piteous howl of a single hound rose and was carried away on the wind segment by segment. I drifted into a peaceful sleep, warm and green as spring, thinking how a single howl was far more terrible than the yelping of the entire pack.

17

TIME IS A mystery to me. One week passes so quickly and another lasts forever. When the Chaplain told me I'd be working with Mims, then time began to fly past me as if the whole month was a quick weekend. Then later, the whole year was like the shortest month. Strange as it may seem I was absolutely happy.

Mims usually woke me early in the morning but sometimes I was already awake and would watch Mims's every move. Just about everything he did reminded me of my father. He broke an egg exactly as my father did. He could do something as simple as hanging up a jacket, and with his back to me, I would have sworn it was my father. Sometimes when I helped him build a cabinet, a door, a desk, or anything else, he would mutter something, exactly like my father, and I would never know whether he meant me to hear, to understand, or whether he was talking to himself.

And I would laugh.

Then he would go two or three or maybe five minutes and suddenly say, "What you laughing at?"

"You," I would say.

"What did I do wrong?"

"Nothing."

"Then why are you laughing?"

"Because I'd rather work with you than play with somebody else."

It really was the truth. And the truth will stand when everything else has passed away.

I listened carefully to everything Mims tried to teach me. He taught me a lot. Around Mims, time was not time anymore.

When Aunt Bella died I had been in Olanberg two and one-half years, and it seemed like a short summer. That night the Chaplain came to the Shop to tell me.

He took me back to the Sanctuary to make a telephone call to the Elms. While we waited for the call to be completed—the lines were busy—he seemed more like a friend than a deputy warden and we talked about his family and my family and Mims and some things he would do if he ever became the official warden. He asked me if I had ever read *Erehwon*, which I hadn't, and he got a copy from the shelves to show me.

"See? Backwards it spells 'nowhere.'"

That intrigued me and I said I'd like to read it.

"It's got some clever ideas," he said. "For instance, in this mythical country, if you get sick the government sends you to prison. If you commit a crime it sends you to a hospital. That's not as crazy as it sounds. I don't think we realize how violent we are in this country."

"My mother did," I said. "More and more I can understand why she went back to France. She said her father, my granddaddy, was sick. But I know she couldn't stand the violence and the vulgarity and the lack of artistic things."

"*Ars longa, vita brevis*," he said. "Can you translate that?"

"Art is long but life is short."

"I keep forgetting you had four years in a French school. Their schools are much superior to ours, aren't they?"

"Yes. They are. My mother thought there was a world of difference."

"What's the difference? The teachers? The curriculum? The attitude?"

"I don't know."

"Honors there are more apt to be academic. Here they're athletic. The only-well known student in this country is an athlete, as a rule. The touchdown. The home run. All a part of the great physical myth. If that's not violence it's a first cousin. How long have you been here now? Almost three years?"

"Two years and a half."

"It hasn't been so bad, has it?"

"Nossir."

"You want to go to your aunt's funeral?"

"I didn't think I could."

"Do you want to?"

"Yessir."

"Apple Ass will be here in the morning, I think. I don't know about it. We'll just have to see. I'll leave you here and you can lock up. No, that won't do. The switchboard will close in a few minutes. It's almost eleven. We'll go in the Warden's office. He's got a direct line."

I had seldom been in the Warden's office. When I did go it was usually to take coffee to Apple Ass or coffee to the board of corrections once a month. For the most part, even when the Warden was around, his office was closed and locked. Except for the pictures it reminded me of the boardroom in the Merchants and Farmers Bank building where I had once gone with Aunt Bella. There was a great table with maybe a dozen chairs and rows of filing cabinets along three walls. Above the cabinets were pictures of Olanberg cotton fields during all the seasons: the stark grayness of winter, the rich promise of new plowed earth in the spring, the deep lush green of waist-high cotton in the summer, and the endless sea of white in the fall. Against the fourth wall was the Warden's desk, an enormous piece, that looked like a table with cabinets. The design and the color of the oak was stunning. Much to my surprise the Warden kept it neat and orderly and immaculately clean. I thought the piece was remarkable long before I found out that Mims had made it. From the day I praised the desk highly I had got along very well with Apple Ass.

The Chaplain entered the Warden's office ahead of me, turned on the light, and glanced at the pictures. "You can observe the art collection while you wait."

I could not tell whether he was poking fun at the pictures or not. I thought some of them, from the few glances I had had, were exceptionally good.

"Be certain you lock the door when you leave." He went out.

I looked at three or four pictures and quickly lost interest because my mind was afire with the chance to look into Mims's private file. For months I had sought for some opportunity but had never expected such a windfall. I had some vague knowledge of the system and knew his file would be in one of the cabinets on the east wall. I went around the table, read the labels: ARSON, A & B, LARCENY, MISCELLANEOUS, MANSLAUGHTER...I could not bring myself to open the cabinet. I looked at the picture above, not quite hanging level. It was a wide-angle view, maybe an aerial photograph, of a vast expanse of snow-white cotton with scores of pickers, all bending in unison as if doing homage to the mule-mounted guards in the background.

I moved one hand toward the sliding lock and then turned away and walked on. It would be like stealing something. I could not. No. That was not it. Not my honesty. I was afraid I would get caught, that was the thing. Camp Two or Four or Nine. No Lumber Yard. No Mims. It was crazy. Much as I wanted to know, it was not worth the risk.

I went to the desk and looked at the telephone for a minute or two. I went back to the cabinet. I levelled the picture. I went back to the desk.

I won't do it, I said to myself. To keep myself from walking back to the cabinet again I sat down in the Warden's chair. I leaned my head over the desk. Why didn't the phone ring? That would save me. I should be thinking about Aunt Bella.

"No call yet?"

I jumped straight up. Sweat broke out all over me. I began to cry. Not for Aunt Bella but because I had almost lost Mims.

"That's all right," the Chaplain said. "I understand. I'm sort of restless myself. I never get used to it. When I have to deliver a message like this I know I won't sleep. I walk. Walking is the best medicine there is for depression. Did you know that?"

"Nossir." I was beginning to be all right.

"Yes. When you read the great English novels just notice how much walking takes place. Are you going to read *Erehwon*?"

"Yessir."

"Good."

"Could I read Mims's file?" Cold, unprepared, no explanation. That's the best way sometimes, though I didn't think about it until later.

"Mims's file?"

"Yessir."

"I know everything there is to know about Mims. On good authority. He wasn't here three months until I made him a trusty and put him in the Lumber Yard. His daddy made the best whiskey this side of Kentucky. Nobody paid any attention, nobody cared until a young bailiff got elected who had an old grudge against Mims's daddy—he wouldn't sell him whiskey when he was a minor. The bailiff never forgot. Mims's daddy was set up. By that time his daddy had developed a serious heart condition, and sending him to Olanberg was like a death warrant. Mims had lost his wife. He was alone. Mims took the rap. He's as innocent as you are guilty. You want to know how I know all this. It's not in the record."

"Yes."

"A newspaperman, a writer from the *Vicksburg Daily News*, came up to interview Mims. He told me the whole story, but he couldn't get Mims to say yea or nay. He wouldn't talk about it. A month later his daddy died. If you were faced with the same situation, what would you do?"

"I don't know," I said. After a few seconds I asked, "Why don't you let him out?"

"I'm not on the board of corrections. I'm on the board of maintenance."

"What does that mean?"

"Just a figure of speech."

"Innocent men shouldn't have to stay in prison," I said.

"That's right. And innocent people shouldn't be killed, or raped, or robbed."

"I don't see how he stands it when he's not guilty. I knew he was not guilty. I knew it. And it doesn't seem to bother him at all."

"No. He's free. You could put him in Camp Fourteen and he'd still be free. He's one in a million. One of the unvanquished."

"Looks like you would let him out."

"I would. Didn't I make that clear? I would. But the powers that be, won't. You read their explanation. It is dangerous to substitute judgment from a distance for the firsthand observations of the twelve men good and true. You can't quarrel with that, can you? He doesn't stand a chance for a long time. You might, however."

"That seems awfully unfair to ..."

The telephone rang. The Chaplain indicated for me to answer. I did. The operator said, "Ready on your call to Hammerhead."

I heard the strange voice of a woman. "Hello ... hello ..."

"Could I speak to Brooks?"

"He's not here," the strange voice said. "I'm just a neighbor. There's been a death in the family."

"Yes. I know. Could I speak to Sarah?"

"She's not here. She's with the body. They didn't bring it home. Are you calling about the funeral?"

"Yes, ma'am. I'm Marcus."

"Are you a friend of the family? This is long distance, isn't it?"

"Yes, it's long distance. I'm Marcus."

"The funeral's day after tomorrow at two o'clock, Mr. Marcus. If it's flowers . . . Peterson's Mortuary is in charge. Did you want to leave a message?"

"No, ma'am. Thank you."

I was about to hang up the phone when I heard, "Marcus?" I did not recognize the voice but it was warm and appealing. It sounded like home. "Marcus, don't you recognize me? It's Shelley Raye."

"Shelley Raye!"

"How are you, Marcus?"

"I'm fine."

"Are you gonna come home?"

"I'm not sure. I'll know in the morning."

"I do hope you can." She sounded so warm and sweet I wanted to cry. Not for Aunt Bella alone but for old times, for nights and days, voices and faces, ripe apples falling.

"She loved you so much. We all do, Marcus. We haven't forgotten."

There seemed to be nothing but a faint buzzing for ages.

"The funeral is day after tomorrow at two o'clock."

"I'll call Brooks to meet me in Memphis if I can come."

"All right."

"Bye, Shelley Raye."

"Bye, Marcus."

The Chaplain was gone. I locked the door carefully and went out into the warm night.

Never before had I been so glad to see Mims. He was sitting in his underwear, his snuffbox in hand, his sock feet propped on the cold apron of the stove. He leaned over and spat into the cedar ash bucket which was now full of sand. "You gonna git to go home?"

I sat down. "I'll know in the morning."

He seemed in no hurry to go back to bed.

"You didn't have to stay up," I said.

"Hnnnn," he grunted.

After a bit I said, "You know what you promised me when I'm eighteen. What you'd let me do?"

"Yeah."

"What if I asked right now?"

"Well..." He paused for a long time. "I'd come across, I guess. But you don't mind waitin', do you?"

"No," I said. "I'll wait."

18

FATE LOOKING INTO the future must have marked me down as absent from Aunt Bella's funeral. I missed the early flight from Greenwood to Memphis because Receiving could not find my civilian clothes, which were supposed to be packed in a moth-proof bag and kept on hold. By the time the Chaplain arranged for clothing from a medical attendant the Warden had arrived and so much was astir that I missed the second flight. A few minutes before Hawthorne appeared to take me to Greenwood for the final flight a jeep and a radio squad car came speeding along screaming out a Red Midnight. The Chaplain came in sweating and full of excitement. "I'm sorry to tell you this. There's been an escape from Camp Fourteen. Everything's been sealed."

Which meant that even Hawthorne who had a green nose and a black flag couldn't get past the Main Gate. The Chaplain dismissed me for the day and I went directly to the Lumber Yard.

I found Mims in his garden, which the parching sun had all but destroyed. He was hoeing a row of late corn. His garden had not been too good that summer. First there was too much rain. The showers did not drift in and move on. Rather, the big drops fell like marbles, leaving the tilled earth pockmarked and steaming. Then a dry spell set in and lasted so long the corn and bean and cucumber leaves looked like gigantic and grotesque cigarette papers. Nevertheless, Mims was able to have some of the finest cabbage I'd ever seen. Every day or two I would take several heads to the Sanctuary and the Chaplain shared them with various personnel.

I got a hoe and helped Mims for a while.

"I figured they wouldn't let you go," Mims said.

"No," I said. "It's a Red Midnight."

"Too bad," he said.

"It doesn't matter. Probably better I couldn't."

"I thought of that," he said.

"I was really sort of glad," I said, feeling the sweat beginning to roll down my armpits. Everything was deathly still and unbearably hot although the sun was almost down. We heard the faint barking of the dogs in the distance. The sound became quite clear and then suddenly stopped.

"Leo's got 'em working," Mims said.

I noticed that Mims did not have his chew of snuff. Somehow, in the open he chewed in a different way. But I liked to watch him inside or out. "Where's your snuff?" I said.

"Ah," he said. The sweat rolled off him. He wiped his brow with his forefinger. "This kind of weather, sometimes a good chew gits you to coming round the mountain 'fore you know it." He looked off toward the kennels. "Makes you feel like you're top of that tall hickory with no saddle."

"I'd like that," I said.

"Hnnnn," Mims grunted. "Make you sick."

"I can wait," I said.

We finished the hoeing and went into the shade of the big apple tree where we kept two old chairs. The sound of the dogs rose again, lacking strength, far away, like cowbells in the night. We sat forward for several minutes listening, which was the way Mr. Pollard and my father would sit, foxhunting on Hammerhead.

The sound ceased, but one single vibration seemed to hang forever on the air.

"I'm really glad I couldn't go," I said.

"This might git over with," Mims said.

"In the morning is too late. The funeral's at two o'clock tomorrow. I wanted to go but I'm glad I couldn't. It's not as if I could go and wouldn't. Do you understand?"

He took a big pinch of snuff before he answered. "Yeah. I see that. I understand. Maybe she wouldn't want you to come, knowin' it'd be hard on you."

"I hadn't thought of that," I said. "You can see things better than most people."

"Hnnnn," Mims grunted. He spat the biggest dark stream imaginable.

"You think she wouldn't mind?"

"I think it ain't where you are. It's how you feel."

"I feel awful. I know she'll leave me everything. And it makes me feel guilty."

Mims grunted again. "If that's what she wanted, it wouldn't me. You never ast her for nothing, did you?"

"No. She told me once: sometimes it's harder to receive than to give. She was talking about a lot of things. My mother's trust fund. And love. She was in love once. I guess she had a sad life in a way. I sure did love her."

"Then don't feel bad about what she gives you."

"What if I gave you something? Something big?"

"That's a different story."

"How?"

"Oh," he said, drawing it out for a long time. I could tell he didn't want to answer.

We heard the dogs again, louder and clearer, but somehow different.

"They ain't running no more," Mims said.

"How can you tell?"

"They treed."

"But how can you tell?"

"They on the railroad."

"Reckon they caught him?"

"No. They treed but they ain't nobody there. He musta hopped a freight."

"How can you tell that?"

"If you was talking to me in the dark and you was mad, couldn't I tell it?"

"Yes. I guess you could. You think he got away?"

"Fer now. But they'll catch him. Sure as God made little green apples."

"They might not," I said.

"You don't think God makes little green apples?"

"Yes. But they may not catch him."

"Be a long Red Midnight if they don't."

"You mean everything will be sealed until they catch him?"

"Always has been. No picnic tomarr'."

"Tomorrow is the Fourth," I said. "I forgot about that. Is it true Vicksburg don't celebrate the Fourth of July?"

"True as rain."

"Aunt Bella said they didn't because Vicksburg surrendered on the Fourth."

"It's a fact they don't anyways."

We could hear the dogs coming back toward the kennels.

"I don't care about the picnic noways," Mims said. "Nothing but the Egg. I'd like to hear him. He's sorta funny."

"Yeah," I said. "He's different."

"Belikes, we might go fer a few minutes if you want to. And if Red Midnight gits over with. It will more'n likely. They'll catch him."

"I guess they will," I said. "And he may be innocent, like you."

Mims coughed. I thought he had swallowed some of his snuff.

"You don't know nothing about that," he said.

"Yes, I do. The Chaplain told me. He told me the whole story. It's awful, Mims. I couldn't stand it. It's the most awful..."

"It ain't so bad," he interrupted. "If I wasn't here I wouldn'ta met you. And I wouldn't take nothing for that."

He just grinned and I thought I was going to cry. All I could think of was I wished Aunt Bella had lived and could one day see him. My heart was so full, heavy and light, I had to leave and go upstairs.

That night we were almost asleep when Leo burst into our room and said, "They got him."

"Turn on the light," Mims said.

"Ain't no need to," Leo said. "I just wanted to tell you they got him. I knowed how he got outa here when the dogs treed and went cold. Dead cold. Sheriff got him in a freight car in Itta Bena. Looks like he woulda knowed they'd be lookin' in a freight car."

"Who was it?" I said.

"I don't know," Leo said. "But Red Midnight's over. Air yawl goin' tomarr'?"

"We might," Mims said. "Fer a little while. We might go hear the Egg."

"Holler at me," Leo said.

It was a little past noon the next day when Mims hollered to Leo. And Leo hollered back for us to wait a minute while he got his teeth.

The sun was bearing straight down and the thermometer had to be well over ninety degrees in the shade. It wasn't too bad on Mims and me, however, because I had, with my new free trusty badge, been allowed regular clothes like Mims for more than a month. Poor Leo, small and thin in his stripes, looked cool at a distance but close up we could see the sweat running off him like an icicle in the sunshine.

We got our blue cards at the central guard station and went through the Second Gate to the grove behind the Tag Shop. There was a game under way on the baseball field at the edge of the grove. A pickup with half a dozen armed guards was on the west side of the crowd. A radio squad car was on the east side. Deep in the grove, and well shaded, was a ten-wheeler loaded with a dozen armed guards. Near the ten-wheeler were several long tables stacked with food. There was an ice cream and lemonade stand and a row of water kegs. Prisoners crowded haphazardly about the tables and stands, paper utensils in hand. Some milled about. Some leaned against the trees like farmers at a political rally. Some sat on the back of the bleachers that served the baseball field. In the very center of the grove was a huge platform with chairs and a bandstand and loudspeakers.

As we approached, the Camp Four band, colors flying, was in the middle of "Mama don't 'low no lowdown hangin' around." Leo let out a harsh, piercing cry which he had told us several times was an authentic rebel yell. Nearby a prisoner called out, "Hey...hey...Leo's got his teeth in today. You gonna make us a speech, Leo?" Leo went over to talk to the man.

"We better stick pretty close together," Mims said. "I don't want nothing but some lemonade. You want some lemonade?"

We went to the lemonade stand.

The Egg was the master of ceremonies. He had been for years. He was a small man, not much bigger than Leo, thin, brown, sharp featured, with gleaming white teeth and piercing hawk eyes. Light and shadow played around his dark silvery hair. He was ageless to me. He could have been any number of years on either side of fifty. I had talked to him once when I was listing the books in Camp Two. He had helped me for a while, for no reason, and had told me Victor Hugo was his favorite author, but Fedor Mikhailovich Dostoevski was the greatest novelist in the world by far. He said Dostoevski's name the way I would say John Paul Jones. And he seemed to be acquainted with every book in the place. His name was Ernest Eggenwicker. The Chaplain had told me the Egg had been a college professor and had, perhaps accidentally, killed a neighbor in an argument-fight about a dog. He had declined to be a trusty or a free trusty. Nevertheless, he was now the overseer of the Tag Shop.

While the Camp Four band gave way to the Camp Two band, the Egg took over the microphone to entertain. He had a clear, resonant, dramatic voice. He made a joke out of nothing. A wrong car tag number. How to put a rock in your cotton sack—come picking time—to make the weight quota. The death of the Warden's favorite mule. Tools. Food. Sleep. Sickness. He had a line or two about any subject. Marriage. "I married this schoolteacher. She was a grass widow. At the end of the first month I said: Give me a grade. She said: Wait. At Christmas I said: Give me a grade. She said: Wait. School was out. I said: Give me a grade. She said: You flunked. I said: Flunked? How could I flunk? Excusing when the moon was wrong, I made love to you at least once every night. She said: My first husband made love to me at least twice every night. I said: Huh, I guess you flunked him too. She said: No, he passed... away... before school was out."

The crowd could not stop laughing. But they were really waiting for his annual poem. That didn't come until after the Camp Two band had played five or six numbers.

The Egg took the microphone again. He told three or four jokes while someone sold copies of his poem for a quarter. I bought one and gave it to Mims. Then with some sort of preface so the crowd knew what was coming, the Egg stepped away from the microphone to make his poetic entrance. The crowd clapped and yelled, "The

Egg! The Egg! The Egg!" He made a grand bow to either side and stepped forward dramatically. The crowd was now insane. He had some kind of electric appeal. He could turn them off and on like a lightbulb.

"The title of my composition is 'Apples,'" he said. Then he recited, repeating the title:

Apples

Now let us praise our own triple A's
On this glorious Fourth of July.
Mine sits in the shade of his white colonnade
Surrounded with juleps and rye.

Let us praise him for meat a dog couldn't eat
And sweets meringued with flies,
For tainted old ham and rancid old jam
And biscuits that failed to rise.

Indeed we're aware of the vigilant care,
Thankful for constant guard,
When at meals we sit, or take a slow shit,
Or a sneaky piss in the yard.

We praise him for Annie on each naked fanny,
Though many transgressions are mild
Sparing the rod according to God
Will certainly spoil the child.

The shattering call that comes to us all
Two hours before the cock,
Gives each of the men an hour and ten
To sit on his ass and rock.

But once our sharp hoes are put to the rows
We never look up at the sky.
We fight the good fight against inch-a-night
Determined to do or to die.

I'm certain of this, we would be remiss
If we failed to give him the praise
For letting us stay at the end of the day
For a glimpse of the stars ablaze.

The night count is long, like a tent meeting song,
And often we have an encore.
Though ninety-nine's safe and one be a waif,
Triple A will rescue the hoer.

Triple A I confess as I slightly digress,
Refers to a top piece of brass
That some call a god, and others a clod.
I call him Almighty Apple Ass.

The ovation seemed to be endless. It was still going on when
Mims and I left the grove. Leo was not ready to leave. For my part,
I was depressed. I looked back at the grove and said, "My mother
was right about us."

"Us who?" Mims said.

"Me. This country. Look back there."

"Didn't you like the poem?" Mims said. He still had his copy.

"I'm not talking about the poem, or you either." I looked back
again.

"Don't be too hard on 'em," Mims said. "You been lucky."

I didn't know exactly what Mims meant but I was depressed
more than ever. Any time Mims seemed the least bit out of humor
with me it felt like somebody inside my stomach with a rub board
washing dirty clothes.

Mims put his hand on my shoulder. "Listen. I know what it is. The funeral's going on jist about now. We shouldn'ta come. I shoulda thought. We'll go loaf off under the apple tree. When it gits cool I'll go upstairs and fix us some fried mackerel and ice-cold tea and have you feelin' better in no time."

Sure enough he was right.

19

ABOUT A MONTH after Aunt Bella's death I got a letter from my grandfather saying that Aunt Bella had written him a full account of my troubles. He offered his assistance in any way possible, though he understood clearly from my aunt that nothing more could be done and I was comfortably situated. He also said that in the future I was welcome to his part of the world where personal matters were bright enough but political matters appeared grave and bleak.

I answered with a long and what I hoped was a grateful response. I tried to emphasize that I was comfortable and contented. I did not want to say that I was happy. But I was.

The months went by like weekends. And every month, sometimes every week, I received some document or another from the trust department of the Merchants and Farmers Bank. It came to the point that I detested the sight of the long tan envelopes with their pale green dollar sign emblems. They seemed to interfere with my life.

A week before my eighteenth birthday, I received from Mr. Molock a reproduction of Aunt Bella's will. The photostat copy magnified the peculiarities of her writing, which began in a meticulous schoolteacher hand and drifted midway into a more cursive scrawl. She had printed in block letters: LAST WILL AND TESTAMENT.

My dearest Marcus:

These may not be the last words Grandfather Dixon said to me, but they are the last of his that I remember: "I never tried to take from others. I have tried to keep what was mine." These words had a meaning in my life, perhaps too much meaning. Maybe they will mean for you exactly what they should, neither too little nor too much. Always keep what you have. And remember, what you give away freely is what you keep most securely. I hereby freely give to you on the day of my death all my worldly goods.

Sic: My house and its adjoining sixty acres (more or less), known as the Elms. This conveyance includes all property and any other such items and goods which repose in my house in my possession, personal or otherwise, and such items and goods that repose on or in the land, comprising the cabin, barns, forest, minerals, and any and all other things.

Sic: Any and all securities and assets which repose in the trust fund entitled "Augusta Ann Dixon to Beullah Anne Dixon," such securities and assets now consisting of common stock in Gautney; M & S Railroad; Colfield, Rubel, & Company; Koslo Telephone Company; Northeast & Gulf Power; and Great Southern Life and Assurance Company. There are also various certificates of deposit designating the Merchants and Farmers Bank.

Sic: Honorable Christian Molock shall prepare and render all documents necessary to execute the terms of this will, and any and all such terms shall become effective on the day of my death or on the eighteenth birthday of William Marcus Oday, whichever date is later.

Her mark   Beullah Anne Dixon
Witness: (x) Sarah Ashmore

I think it was Sarah's mark that made me realize for the first time Aunt Bella was dead. I understood too what my father had meant one night when he said he could not fully realize my mother was dead because he had not been there.

Then, the day before my eighteenth birthday, I received from the bank a package of documents as bulky as a Sears, Roebuck catalog. The Chaplain helped me in the proper execution and signing of all the forms. He went with me to Administration to have them notarized. On our way back to the Sanctuary, the Chaplain said, "Apple Ass knows what it's like to be rich. But I don't. Maybe tomorrow you can describe it to me. Let me share the feeling."

I didn't really know what the Chaplain meant, if anything. But the next day my birthday was not mentioned. The day was like any usual day. The Warden quarrelled with the Chaplain. The fields were full of cotton pickers. I had to make four trips to Administration and two trips to Captain Burt's office in Piccadilly. The remarkable and startling exception was my discovering that I had been in Olanberg exactly one thousand days. I discovered it by chance while calculating some possible release dates for prisoners appearing the coming first Monday before the board of corrections. I did not tell the Chaplain because I wanted my account to be fresh for Mims. I was going to tell Mims and at the same time remind him of his long-standing promise to me.

That night, which did not seem like my eighteenth birthday, we sat as usual before the stove listening to the radio. Time passed as easily and pleasantly as creek water across the shadow of a fishing pole. There was no fire in the stove. The day had been warm for October and the night was only pleasantly cool. We had finished with supper, and the fried apple pies which had served as a birthday cake. We sat in that curious harmony, like a very old couple who have long since forgotten that separateness could exist.

Mims turned the radio off. He had not yet got out his snuffbox and I knew it was a game.

"I know what you're doing," I said.

"Do which?" Mims said.

"You're teasing me."

"About what?"

"About what you promised me."

Mims got up and went to the dresser for his snuff. He came back to the rocker, propped his sock feet onto the apron of the stove, opened his silver box and took a large pinch. I watched with my eyes lighted and my face flushed with excitement. I had waited a long time. The blood rose higher in my face, my heart pounded.

"Remember?" I said.

"Remember what?" he said. He leaned back to a comfortable position and surveyed me. With a grunt and a wave of the hand he indicated to me to rise. Obedient as always to him, I stood, now taller by three or four inches than when I had first entered the room. A certain expression of warm-hearted approval flickered in his eyes. He leaned over and spat in the cedar ash bucket and with thumb and forefinger wiped his lips for neatness. His eyes returned to me. "You'll grow some yet," he said.

"You promised," I said.

"How exactly was it?"

"You know exactly how was it," I said.

"I just said when you was eighteen. This is the first day you been eighteen."

"It begins now, doesn't it?"

"I reckon it does if you think so."

"You know how many days I've been here?"

"No."

"Guess."

"Nearly three year."

"One thousand days. Exactly. Today makes one thousand days."

"You're joking."

"I'm not. I figured it up today. Now can I have it?"

"You can have it. But you gonna be sick."

"I might not."

"Ah," Mims said. "Maybe not. One thousand days." He opened his silver box and handed it over.

My hand trembled as I took the box. The sharp smell rose up into my face. At that moment there was a heavy rap on the door.

"That's Leo," Mims said, neither rising nor turning his head. "Grease up your belly and slide under," he called.

The door began to open. "It's the Chaplain," I whispered fiercely, thrusting the silver box toward Mims.

Mims rose quickly as the Chaplain entered. "Sir," he stammered. "Sir, I thought you was Leo."

The Chaplain looked about the room, ignoring the apology. He held a large paper bag. "How's your mustard?" he said.

"Tender as a frog's tongue and thick as molasses," Mims said, hustling about to get on his shoes. "We can pick you all you want."

"I like to pick it myself," the Chaplain said.

In a minute Mims was dressed and the three of us were at the top of the stairs. "You don't need to go," the Chaplain said to me.

"Oh, okay," I said. But it was not okay at all. I could tell the Chaplain was commanding me to stay behind rather than relieving me of a task. I returned to the room and lay down on my bed. I felt my birthday party was being spoiled. Something between me and Mims was being spoiled too. For the briefest moment I thought the old black dog might appear in the doorway. Not the faintest notion of that old bugbear had occurred since my first glimpse of Mims. I kept telling myself that nothing was going to happen. Pretty soon I was almost all right. Then I was perfectly all right when I heard the sound of Mims on the stairway. Within a few seconds he was in the room and had his shoes off and we were seated exactly as we were when the Chaplain knocked.

Mims commenced to laugh in his own hearty way.

"What is it?" I said.

"I was thinking if the Chaplain hada found you pale as a ghost we'd both end up in Camp Four."

His laughter gradually ceased. He opened the box and took a huge pinch of snuff. "Belikes he won't come back tonight." He did not close the box.

I knew the moment had come. In another second Mims would hand over the box and this time we would not be interrupted. All the blood in my body mounted to my face. I was trembling with fear and pleasure. In a strange and mystic way I felt the sharing of the silver box with Mims provided some eternal commitment, a final seal, a perfect union with something. Blushing and laughing, trying to keep up my courage, I took the box from his outstretched hand.

I fingered the damp brown contents. Then, trying to imitate Mims exactly, I took a great pinch, a good bit larger than I had intended, and placed it carefully into my jaw. I tried to return the box casually.

Mims moved the cedar bucket to rest between us.

"If it throws you, you go wash it out before it makes you real sick."

"You mean makes me drunk?"

"I mean if you git to feeling like you was going the wrong way on a Ferris wheel."

"I'm all right," I said. "It's real good." I leaned over and spat into the cedar ash bucket. There was a tiny explosion of ashes. When I raised my head I felt a slight dizziness, like riding high in a swing, and it was wonderful.

We sat for a while in silence. I was terribly proud.

"You think it'll make me real drunk? I don't feel anything."

"You'll be coming around the mountain soon enough," he said.

"You know, I never have understood that song. Who is coming? Is she a bride? She'll be driving six white horses when she comes. We'll kill the old red rooster—and all that. I don't get it."

"You'll get it. I remember the first time I ever had a chew and it made me so sick I thought I might die. And after I got over my sick spell I wanted another chew. Belikes, you've had it enough. I think you ought to go and spit it out. You might be coming around the mountain so fast you'll fall off on your head."

The room began to float. It was a marvelous sensation for a while.

Then I said, "I think I'm fixing to come round the mountain without any white horses. I don't guess that quite makes sense." I know what it is to be seasick. It was like that and then it was not. I felt perfectly all right.

Mims came over to me and put his arm around my shoulders and said, "You better wash it out."

"I'm perfectly all right."

"You better wash it out. I'm telling you."

"I'm all right, but I'm sort of drunk."

"What if the Chaplain came in now?"

"It would be bad."

"You'll be sick as a cat."

"Who?" I said.

"You."

"My head is swimming."

"I'm telling you."

"Whoooo..." I said, not so loud as before. I jumped up and ran into the bathroom. I made a great mess in the lavatory.

"It don't matter, it don't matter," Mims was saying, holding my shoulder. "Wash it out."

He held me while I scooped water into my mouth and over my face. I wouldn't look into the mirror. I felt green.

"Wash your face again," Mims said.

I washed again. Mims let me through the doorway. "Lay down," he said.

I moved unsteadily and stretched out at an angle on his bed. He unlaced my shoes and slipped them off. He wet a towel, folded it neatly and placed it across my forehead.

"That better?" he said.

"Yes."

He kept standing beside the bed with a solemn sympathetic stare. Several minutes passed and he did not move.

I lifted the towel. I could feel something coming back into me, like a cool breeze.

"How you feel?" Mims said.

I sat up. I could see with reasonable clarity. "I did it, didn't I?"

Mims laughed. He looked greatly relieved. He took the towel. "Belikes, I shouldn'ta done that with you."

"How about tomorrow night?" I said.

"Lord," Mims said. "Lord, I done started something."

"You didn't start anything," I said. "I've been asking for three years. I've been waiting to do this for two...no, three years, Mims."

He went into the bathroom.

"Besides, isn't it more fun with somebody?" I called. "Lot more fun than by yourself."

I could see Mims in the bathroom. He scrubbed at his face and looked into the mirror. "Isn't it?"

He didn't answer.

"Isn't it?" I called, louder.

"Belikes, let's git to bed."

When the lights were out and we were in our beds the soft moonlight through the windows made grotesque shapes of the furniture.

"You'll let me have it again, won't you?"

"I guess," Mims said.

I was not sleepy. I remained wide awake and I could tell from his breathing that Mims was wide awake too. I felt my body growing all over. The strange light rose and fell in the room like drifting fog. Mims's coat hanging on the wall looked like a soldier parachuting. The teakettle on the hot plate took the strange shape of a rooster. I fastened my eyes on Mims. The room seemed to be moving and both of us were being snatched backward in time. I tried desperately to scan every feature of the big face which was all but obscure though his hair was golden in the faint rays of moonlight. "Mims, I sure do love you," I said.

"Much obliged," he said.

"I love you more than anybody. When you get out of here, will you promise to live where I do. I'll give you anything. I'll take you anywhere. I'll take care of you. Will you promise?"

"I won't be gittin' out for a long time."

"Will you promise?"

"I reckon. But I won't be gittin' out for a long time. You will, but they turned me down."

"But do you promise?"

"I reckon."

I bolted up. "Did you say I'll be getting out?"

"It slipped. I'm not 'sposed to tell you."

"But I don't want to get out and leave you here."

20

ONE MONTH PAST my eighteenth birthday I rode away from Olanberg in an unmarked prison Oldsmobile driven by Hawthorne. Like a visitor I wore an Oxford-gray alpaca sweater, a blue shirt, tan trousers and black shoes, all purchased for me by Hawthorne a week before in the town of Olanberg. In the backseat was my duffel bag and across the bag lay my topcoat, which I had not yet tried on. Hawthorne had bought the bag and the topcoat in Greenwood the day before and brought them to the Sanctuary that morning.

The car moved at a rapid pace along a straight stretch of Highway 49 toward Greenwood. The vast cotton fields on either side of the road were gray and barren except for occasional unharvested spots which from a distance glistened like the last patches of a heavy snow.

My face felt rubbery as I turned away from Hawthorne and watched the power poles blurring past my window. It was almost noon and I had eaten no breakfast. The thought of food brought a thin wave of nausea to my throat.

The night before had been a brooding, painful interval. I had sat by the unlit stove with Mims, performing the last ritual of the silver box. Insignificant talk and uneasy silence alternated. I had not once mentioned the one thing that weighed on my mind. It was finished. The separation was only hours away. Every act, every word, every image was clothed in a desperate finality. There was no delight in watching Mims take his pinch of snuff so neatly from the silver box. There was no pleasure in the idle chatter about rooster fries which Leo had been explaining that day. Even the silence seemed to attack me with suddenness and violence. What had been so delightful and pleasurable in days gone by became unbearable. I was glad when we went to bed early.

In bed I lay awake and heard the restlessness of Mims. When I finally slept, my dreams were fragmented, marked with alarm and dread. Even when I knew I was dreaming I endured a profound terror. I was relieved, finally, to be awake, to remember that my socks were lying across my shoes at the foot of my bed, to remember that Mims's socks would be on his feet under the covers.

I got up, dressed in the twilight, and sat by the cold stove. It was the first time I ever remembered getting out of bed ahead of Mims. Blue autumnal light pressed against the windows. Early morning noises came from the Second Gate. It was long past Mims's hour of waking but I would not rouse him. A cry came from the kennels or the cabin. It was so quick and brief that I was not certain whether it was the howl of a dog or the yell of Leo.

Mims sat up in bed slowly. Curious shadows crossed his face. For the first time ever I thought the face looked old and pale. The huge gray eyes shone in the twilight, smiled, and the fresh and healthy look returned.

"What time is it?" Mims said, his eyes searching for the clock. "We'll be late for muster." He was out of bed quickly, effortlessly, as if something had lifted him. He stood for a moment, tall, immobile, invulnerable, timeless. Like the Confederate soldier on courthouse square, I thought. Then he started for the bathroom. "I mean I'll be late. Not you. I thought I'd never go to sleep."

I thought: I'm not going to let it be like a funeral; I owe that to him. I went to the bathroom door and watched Mims shave. Then I remembered I would have to get a razor. I couldn't use his anymore.

"You want some coffee?" I said.

He turned his face and winked. "Jist exactly what I want. I ain't much hungry."

The coffee was ready by the time Mims had dressed. We sat at the table drinking coffee, trying to act as if the day was like any other day. Mims abruptly began to laugh. "Leo told me something I've been meanin' to tell you," he said. He placed his right forefinger on the base of his left thumbnail. "What's this called?"

"You mean the cuticle?" I said.

"Yeah. Leo said this feller, a neighbor or something, was in the barbershop and this real nice-looking woman was working on his nails, polishin' and filin', while he's in the barber chair. She tells him to hold still and she'll push his cuticles back. And he says never to mind, they'll be all right when he stands up."

We laughed and laughed.

"Leo made that up," I said.

"Of course," Mims said.

For a moment I felt perfectly at ease. We got up from the table and began laughing again. Mims put on his coat to go to muster.

While Mims was gone I made both beds neatly and placed on my bed all the items I had not already mailed. I left for the Sanctuary before Mims returned.

The Chaplain was not in his office. On his desk was a note to me. "You know about getting all the papers signed. Take one copy and leave the original and duplicates on my desk. Hawthorne will drive you to Greenwood. All the very best, my friend. *Ars longa, vita brevis.* Send me a copy of your first book."

I kept thinking of the note all the way to Piccadilly for Captain Burt's signature. He was still at muster and I had to wait. He was in a hurry, friendly, but cool. I watched the dime on his face while he signed, and while he shook hands and wished me good luck. Next I went to the Administration Building, where nobody knew my name, and then to the Infirmary. The tests at the Infirmary took more than an hour. When I returned to the Sanctuary, Hawthorne was there with the bag and the topcoat.

"I don't want to rush you," Hawthorne said. "But we ain't got no whole lot of time."

A guard waiting for the Chaplain said, "It's you ain't got the time, Hawthorne. He's got all the time in the world."

Hawthorne drove me to the Lumber Yard. I ran up the stairs with my empty bag, saw that Mims was not in the Shop. A desperate, sinking feeling overcame me. I knew that the Chaplain had deliberately avoided our final parting. Perhaps Mims was doing the same thing.

I rushed into our room. Mims sat at the table drinking coffee. I was relieved beyond description. We looked at each other, each with a dry, forced, painful smile. I went to the bed and began to stuff my duffel bag. The packing was quickly finished.

"You want some coffee?" Mims said.

"They're waiting on me," I said.

"Let 'em wait," Mims said. His voice was thin.

I placed the bag beside the stove and went to the table. I put my arm on Mims's shoulder, my fingers caressed the face, the neck. I took a swallow of coffee from his cup. Mims half turned and looked up at me. I drank again from his cup and put it down slowly. I leaned over and kissed him. He stirred as if to rise, but only lifted his hand and I felt the pressure of the big fingers on my shoulder and then the warm hollow of his hand like a gentle collar about my neck. I kissed him again and turned away quickly. I picked up my bag. In the doorway I turned fully around. Mims was standing, smiling. I hurried toward the south stairway. I stopped and looked back. Mims stood outside the room, his hand lifted. I raised my hand and my heart seemed to stop. I hurried down the stairway.

And now, roaring along the highway, I knew that something in me was going to rise up. I could see ahead of us the flashing light that marked the intersection of 49 and 82, on the outskirts of Greenwood.

"Stop a minute," I said.

Hawthorne glanced curiously at me. The intersection was a mile away.

"Stop!" I cried. "I'm about..." The words choked in my throat.

The car came to a quick halt on the shoulder of the road. I opened the door and leaned forward and a stream gushed from my mouth. I sat for a minute, leaning forward and clearing my throat. I took out a large prison handkerchief and blew my nose. I closed the door. I looked at the blinking light ahead.

"You all right?" Hawthorne said.

I wiped my face. "Yes. I'm all right now."

Hawthorne looked back and steered the car cautiously onto the highway. "You're not used to it. You got carsick. Maybe I was driving too fast."

I was almost sick again on the plane, but only momentarily. I had never flown before. When the plane took off into the south wind and banked steeply for its northward flight to Memphis, I felt a weakness in my stomach and a dizziness, and added to that feeling was the awful fear of the other passengers if they should see me repeat before their eyes the incident on the highway. But the plane levelled off smoothly, the dizziness and weakness began to disappear.

I looked out the window for some sign of Olanberg. I saw only the great level grayness and tiny sharecropper shacks anchored beneath curious and drifting alphabets of smoke. I imagined that all the passengers were conscious of me, watching me, knowing I had come directly from Olanberg, precisely aware of the hour I had departed the prison gates. Perhaps they expected me to do something foolish or quite drastic. No one had chosen to sit beside me even though I had felt the plane was crowded. But as I grew more comfortable I looked about and realized there were many empty seats. Nevertheless, doubts and reflections kept flitting through my mind. I hoped the stewardess would not ask me anything. She reminded me a little of Shelley Raye. Not her face. Her face was too scrupulously arranged and too precise. It was her hair. She did have beautiful hair.

She stopped beside me and asked in a very friendly manner, "Would you like something?"

I was puzzled for a moment.

"A Coke or coffee?" she said.

"No," I said.

She smiled and went on as if she had never heard of Olanberg. I turned to look at her hair again. This time, for some reason, I thought of Obie. I knew from old letters of Aunt Bella's that Obie had gone to junior college for a year, failed his grades, returned to Hammerhead and the running of the sawmill. The thought of facing Obie was almost as painful as leaving Mims. I well remembered seeing Obie that day of my father's funeral, standing in the rain, in the center of the old cemetery road, tears running down his face. After that, there was only the note, which I had that morning taken from the dresser and folded neatly into my billfold. I had also taken my father's golden key and stowed it safely in my pocket. Obie knew all about the golden key. If he had possession, I wondered, would he ever in my lifetime give it back to me?

I looked out the window. The great gray levelness had changed to rolling hills. Suddenly I felt chilled and thought of pulling on my topcoat. I had not yet tried it on. But the chill seemed to disappear and I looked out the window again. I would neither avoid Obie nor seek him out. Anyway, Brooks and Sarah would be glad to see me. They were as unchangeable as Mims.

I leaned back in my seat and closed my eyes. I was about to play my game again, to see if I could create the sense of moving in the opposite direction toward Mims. But I checked myself. I might get sick again. And more, I must now, forever, begin to put away childish things. Perhaps my goodbye to Mims had been childish. Maybe I'll always be a child, I thought. I stretched out. I imagined I was stretched out on my bed with Mims only four or five feet away. A phrase suddenly popped into my mind from nowhere, like the click of a lightbulb, and I found myself saying quietly, "Precious are the dead."

A buzzer sounded, and the stewardess was coming down the aisle, pausing to see that each seatbelt was properly fastened. I realized that I had never unfastened my own seatbelt.

I felt the plane descending rapidly and with each curious snapping in my ear I repeated to myself, "Precious are the dead."

I came out of the terminal building and approached the semicircle where the limousines and taxis waited. Soft sunlight fell on the ramp and the shrubs and a patch of white and yellow roses. I turned sharply and found myself bending over the roses, my lips almost touching a boll of petals. I broke off a yellow one quickly, scratching my finger so deeply the blood ran into my palm, yet I did not notice at the time. I hid the rose in the pocket of my topcoat and looked about me. People loaded with baggage were hurrying by. The full and awful realization of freedom struck me. I could feel my body growing hot, my face growing lighter and lighter. I lifted my hand to wipe the sweat away. I hurried toward the last taxi. I looked back twice as if something followed me. I had the curious and strange sensation of being a few feet away, behind, in front, one side and the other, watching myself, seeing the sweat trickle through a wild and panic-stricken face.

I was in the taxi. The hills and the pine trees were passing outside. I remembered that I would not allow the driver to take my coat or my bag. I knew the driver was uneasy about something. Maybe he thought I would not have the fare when the long trip ended. But I could not help it. I was too weak to care, to remember. I could not remember leaving the airport. I could not remember whether I had said the Peabody or Hammerhead. I must have said Hammerhead. It didn't matter. I thought of the ducks in the lobby of the Peabody, my father beside me. I could not remember whether my mother had come along with us or not.

Then there was Hammerhead before us. The taxi had stopped. And Hammerhead did not matter either. It was the cemetery that mattered. The road through the cemetery. Why would anyone think I wanted to go to the sawmill?

We had found it. And I was standing by the cemetery gate and the taxi was gone. It was a young face, too young to drive a taxi. I could not recall the countenance exactly, but it was young. I remembered that.

I could hear the taxi disappearing somewhere on the road behind me.

I looked for the Elms again, knowing I could see it if the leaves had fallen. But there was no trace of house or smoke.

I left my coat and bag inside the gate and started down the old cemetery road.

I stopped suddenly. On the western side, near the old road, a man rose slowly from behind a gravestone and a new grave still littered with flowers. The man took a jumper that hung over his shoulders and began to put it on. The sun was well hidden behind Hammerhead Mountain but its rays seemed to bend in arcs and fall across the man's face. His hand was caught up in the tangled jumper sleeve, and I watched the patient untangling until the big work-worn hand, soft in the fading light, slipped from the cuff like a little animal emerging cautiously from its den. The man knelt among the wilted and ruined flowers and took from the grave a handful of the fresh red clay.

It was the sight of the jumper that sent a wave of uneasiness through me, something akin to a cool, fresh, too-sweet breeze across honeysuckle. A mill worker, I thought, though no one I knew or remembered. The man stood up. He was very tall, with a refined, expressive face not usually seen on a millhand. He was a sawyer, a planer, an off-bearer, I guessed, but not a logger or woodcutter. I judged him to be one of the planers, or probably a kiln tender. There was something friendly about him, some compelling warmth, and I wished I could go speak to him. But there was also a painful need to escape. I wished I had stayed at the Peabody as I first planned. The man might be a stranger, yet he certainly would have heard, would know. And most of all, I wanted no one watching when I went down the old road to the graves of my father and Aunt Bella.

In the stillness I could hear the sound of night birds beginning, and in the distance the faintest sound of a cowbell. For some reason I imagined Shelley Ray driving the cows from the back of the Pollard pasture. I wheeled about with the quickest steps I had used all day and returned up the old cemetery road to the new gate. I took up my coat and bag. When I closed the gate the loud, ringing clang seemed to rise and rise and spread like a covey of quail.

I stopped at the springs for a long time. The minute I put my hands into the bright stream my head began to clear. I washed my face and hands thoroughly and dried with the prison handkerchief. Then I drank with the cup of my hand and the water spilled over my shoes and trouser cuffs.

I climbed onto my old favorite rock and waited, listening to the fall of the water. The world about me and behind me was unreachable, but it was vivid and clear now, like a rainbow. Heavy darkness had set in when I went up the hill and around the house to the front yard of the Elms.

III

The Rifle

21

WHEN I ENTERED the front yard I saw, though the darkness was heavy, that the lawn was neatly mowed and the shrubs and flowers carefully tended. The encroaching grass had been scraped away in the narrow strips on either side of the brick walk. The old honeysuckle bush had been replaced with a bank of azaleas. I moved some distance down the walk, away from the house, in order to get a full view. I dropped my bag at my feet and stood with my coat folded over my hands as if to hide them.

The house in the darkness appeared like a great monument carved from one gigantic mountain of ageless earth, not stone. I imagined I might sink my hands into its sides, take a simple tool and carve an entrance quickly. Yet, it had never seemed so alive, so beautiful and terrible. I stood watching, feeling I could not be any older than I was the day I came from Vingt-neuf Cour du Maréchal Foch. I could hear my father saying, "You finally made it, Oliver." And I was not sorry.

I felt a sense of chill, and wondered how long I had been standing there. The air was crisp and cool, the sky was becoming brighter. The moon was rising. The key would be in a tiny knothole pocket behind the left facing of the door. I could enter without calling Brooks or Sarah. I took my duffel bag to the porch and put it down and walked back to look at the house.

The inside of the house held some inexplicable and consuming terror for me. So I remained standing, afraid and depressed and almost trembling. I put on my topcoat for the first time. It did not seem to fit. It bound my shoulders and made me feel as if I were tied to the spot I stood on. It was easier to remain motionless than to move.

The thought occurred to me that I had never hated anyone. I could not remember a child's face in school, a teacher, a grown-up in Hammerhead, an old face on the streets of Bordeaux that I truly disliked. Certain I had not hated... And I would not allow myself to think the name. But I envisioned the face all the same, saw all of him, as if I had turned my own face northward and my eyes had zoomed in on the fatal hour with my German binoculars. I saw the man coming, not seeming to hurry, but actually looking aside at something and then moving on. He climbed the steep bank at the corner of the cemetery and I was praying: "God, don't let him do it... I'm going to back down..."

"Hey!" A voice shattered the darkness behind me.

I whirled around and saw someone standing a few yards from the nearest elm tree with packages in his hands. The tears were welling in my eyes. I was cold and trembling, but I knew Brooks well enough. I hurried toward him. The package of sodas slipped to the earth and a small paper bag fell on top of the bottles. I grabbed Brooks as if he were my father coming from the sawmill. I felt all the black strength engulf me. And then we were shaking each other and slapping like children.

Walking along toward the cabin I realized in my excitement that I was carrying the package of sodas and Brooks was carrying only whatever was inside the small paper bag. Reading the realization in my face, Brooks reached out and took the package into his own hand. Neither of us said a word about it, though I knew we both felt something significant in the maneuver. We had reached the yard of the cabin and Brooks was calling to Sarah as if the house stood afire.

The front door seemed neither to open nor close, yet Sarah had somehow appeared almost instantly on the porch, holding up her hands and crying, "Stop! Now you stop just where you at. I wanta see you coming close."

We stopped while Sarah continued to gaze at me.

"I got to git ready for you. Lawd, Lawd, I ain't ready. You got to come slow. Come on easy." She motioned to me. "I got to git my mind ready."

I walked slowly onto the porch. I lifted her into my arms, and as though a signal had been arranged, Brooks opened the door and I carried her into the house, her arms locked about my neck and my face pressed against her face.

I stood her down in the firelight before the hearth. She backed away and looked at me. "You big as Brooks nearly," she said. "But you still my baby. You all we got left." Turning to Brooks, she said, "He all we got left, honey. Pull him up a chair."

Brooks placed a cane-bottomed chair near the hearth.

"I don't want to sit down," I said.

"Well, you going to whether you wants to or not," Sarah said. "You take off that overcoat and warm yo'self and we 'bout to have supper dreckly. Brooks gonna help me and it'll be fast."

I took off my coat, sat down and stretched out my feet on the hearth. I looked into the soft firelight, remembering times I had often been there as a child, straddling a chair before the hearth wondering why Brooks and Sarah always had better fires than the ones at our house or the Elms. I got up, turned the back of the chair to the fire, as I had done in those other years, and sat down again straddling the cane bottom that sagged and squeaked. My mother had never allowed me to sit in a chair that way. But my father didn't mind. Sometimes my father would do it himself and my mother would explode in a mixture of English and French.

I could hear Brooks and Sarah in the kitchen and could smell the rich aroma of country ham frying.

"You want some coffee?" Sarah called. "Brooks don't want nothing but Co-Cola if they's to be snow on the ground."

"I'd rather have Co-Cola," I said, knowing that Sarah called every kind of soda a Co-Cola.

"What kind of Co-Cola you want?"

I smiled at old times. "Pepsi."

Then I remembered the yellow rose. "I'll be back in a jiffy," I called. I ran out of the house and hurried to the Elms, took the rose from the duffel bag on the porch and hurried back.

I entered the kitchen holding the rose up like a precious stone. "I brought this for you."

Sarah took the rose with a cry of surprise and real delight. In a few seconds she had it in a vase and was moving dishes of squash, beans, fried sweet potatoes, ham, pickles to make room for her present, mumbling, "You always done the sweetest things. I tole Brooks they ain't gonna change you. Well, we ready. Less you wanta wash yo' hands."

"I washed at the springs," I said.

Sarah made me sit down first. Everything in the kitchen was so quiet I could hear the fire popping in the living room. "Been so long since you eat from this table, be nice if you was to thank the Lawd," Sarah said.

A flash of crimson filled my face. I said what I had always said at Sarah's table. "God is great, God is good, and we thank Him for this food."

"Amen," Sarah said. "Say amen, Brooks."

"Mama, I'm hungry."

"Brooks."

"Amen," Brooks said.

Something about Brooks reminded me of Mims. I felt at once an immediate happiness and a faraway sadness. I helped myself to the fried sweet potatoes first because I knew that Sarah had prepared them solely for me. I tried to erase from my mind everything outside the room. I reached out to my left and to my right, touching Brooks and Sarah. I withdrew my hands quickly, trying to hide the strange embarrassment I felt. It had something to do with the feeling that I would be welcome no matter what I had done.

"What happened to Cleo and Aunt Bella's Buick?" I said.

"Buick settin' up in the barn on blocks and Mama won't let me touch it," Brooks said.

"And Miss Bella give Cleo to Mr. Pollard," Sarah said.

"Not to keep," Brooks said.

"Yes. To keep. To take care of," Sarah said.

"Keep means forever," Brooks said.

"Don't always," Sarah said. "This case, to feed and look after and ride till the time comes. You was willing."

"I wasn't neither," Brooks said.

"Mr. Pollard was. Glad to he said. But he just keepin' Cleo. Brooks ain't good with hosses. He good with mules."

"Hosses too," Brooks said.

"No you not. You 'fraid of hosses. Ain't with mules though. I know."

"Hosses ain't like mules," Brooks said.

"No. Cause mules more stubborn. Like you," Sarah said.

"Hoss liable to do anything," Brooks said. "No warning. Mule, he tell you what he gonna do."

"Hoss tell you too but you won't listen," Sarah said.

"They speaks a different language," Brooks said. "They speaks French. A hoss, one ear go back, you don't know. Maybe he lookin', maybe he listenin', maybe he gonna run. A mule, one ear go back so fer, and he gonna kick the shit outa you."

"Brooks!"

"What I say?"

"You heard yo'self. Oughta git me some soap and wash yo' mouth out. Befo' company, like that."

"I didn't go to do it."

"Git up. Walk around the table."

"Mama."

"Like I say. Git up."

"Mama, I near forty years old."

"Don't care if you Methuselah. Git up."

He got up and walked around the table. He remained standing.

"If you done," Sarah said, "you go open that house and turn him on some heat."

"I'll go with him," I said.

"You ain't finished," Sarah said.

"Yes, I have. It was so good, Sarah. It was just wonderful. Fried sweet potatoes and everything." I took a last bite of pickled peach.

"Them peaches come from ya daddy's orchard," she said. "Brooks try to keep things up. But he workin' at the mill some now."

Brooks and I started out. "Brooks, you stay long as he wants," Sarah said. "That house git awful big when you can't hear nobody else breathing. You make a pallet and stay long as he wants. Tomarr's Saturday. You don't have to work."

The moon had risen and the sky was full of stars. The air was almost cold now but I carried my coat over my arm, feeling no chill because of the food and the walking. The sound of the springs was like a distant church choir. I stopped to urinate.

At the back porch Brooks pulled a ring of keys from his pocket. He chose the right key almost without looking. He unlocked the door, pushed it back for me to enter, then saw that I was some distance behind.

"Go ahead," I said. "Might be somebody in there."

Brooks laughed. "That's not what you scared of." He entered and turned on the hall lights. He continued down the hallway and through the house, turning on lights.

I went upstairs. I opened the door and turned the light on in the big south room. In spite of the beautiful patchwork quilts that served as counterpanes, the five beds, spaced exactly, reminded me of graves. And, excluding Aunt Bella's quilting area in the corner, the room still looked as if the Dixon boys had left that morning for Shiloh and Vicksburg and Gettysburg. I don't know why I had entered the room. What I was looking for was not apt to be there.

I crossed the hall to what I thought of now as my room, where Aunt Bella had kept so many items connected with my father. Although, on the day between my father's death and his funeral, she had made Brooks bring all my father's clothes and store them in the closets in her own room downstairs.

The room smelled fresh and clean. I did not find what I was looking for but I did stand for some time looking at an old slingshot that had belonged to my father. Aunt Bella knew every time I took it off the wall. I turned out the light and went back downstairs.

Brooks was waiting for me with the duffel bag. He led the way to Aunt Bella's room. "Mama fixed this room for you," he said. He placed the bag on Aunt Bella's old Singer sewing machine. I opened the closet door to hang up my coat and saw all my father's clothes. Then I knew Aunt Bella's room would be all right with me.

I undressed, leaving my sweater and shirt and pants on the cedar chest. I pulled back the bedcovers: an embroidered sheet, two patchwork quilts, and a quilted Rose Garden spread. I propped the lace-trimmed pillows against the headboard and got into bed.

"I can git me some quilts and make a pallet," Brooks said.

"No," I said. "Just turn off the lights and sit down a minute."

Brooks turned off the lights in the hall and in the room and pulled a chair beside the bed. I lay propped against the headboard watching Brooks's eyes.

"I don't mind making a pallet," Brooks said.

"There's no need. I'll be asleep in a little while."

I moved down in the bed and pushed one of the pillows away. The soft eiderdown of the pillow made me think of the rockers beside the stove. I heard the clock strike in the living room. Mims would be going to bed now.

"It's all over now," Brooks said.

"Not all of it," I said.

"You not out for good?"

"Yes. It's all over in that way. I just meant something else."

"I got the package you mailed," Brooks said.

"Good."

"Put it in the kitchen."

"Good."

"On the shelf behind the stove."

"Good."

"You didn't wanta come home."

"No."

"I don't blame you. I tole Mama you won't come home. Go to Paris, France, or something. She said you bound to come. Bound to. She knows things."

"Yes. She knows things."

"She said he ain't studyin' France. Ain't studyin' nowhere in the world but here. I hushed."

I pulled the cover to my chin and lay very still. Soft moonlight seeped through the windows, choking the room with an awful silence. I was so glad Brooks was there, almost like Mims, yet I felt a sharp sense of guilt in keeping him there. Black people were kinder than most people, I thought. They know how to suffer. A great light burst inside me, flashed like a star, a heartfelt knowledge not clear enough to be spoken. The luminous blot burned for one bright moment and died away, not entirely but faded to a flame so tiny and flickering that other thoughts overwhelmed it.

"I couldn't find my rifle," I said. "What reckon happened to it?"

"I ain't seen it," Brooks said.

"It was mine."

"I ain't seen it," Brooks repeated quietly.

"It was the last thing Dad ever gave me. They had no business to keep it."

"I don't know," Brook said.

"It's somewhere. And I'll find it."

"Bound to be somewhere," Brooks said.

"I'll find it."

I lay very still again. The only sound was my deep slow breathing. Brooks sat watching, motionless and silent, not a breath of his could be heard. Clouds passed over the moon and the room grew darker. Brooks waited for a long time. He thought I was asleep. He got up like a shadow and left.

Through the window I saw him go off the porch, but I had not heard the back door open or close. I watched his dark form move away.

I lay down again. Indescribable terrors moved in on me, like the first awful night in Piccadilly. Worse. More horrible. More real. More unendurable. I wished I could smell the cedar in the Shop, taste the snuff with Mims. Everything would be all right. My life would be ordered. There would be things I had to do. In a few hours muster would come around. I wouldn't have to think about my rifle. Or Obie. Facing Obie. I wouldn't have to face the people at Tanner's Store. Or Dr. Ziddie, who would probably live till the last soul passed away in Hammerhead. Doctors rarely passed away. That was such a strange expression: passed away. Nothing ever passed away. Blacks knew better. Sarah never said anyone passed away. She said, "Passed."

"Whatever happened to Miss Fairfield, Sarah?"

"She passed," Sarah would say if I asked her.

But I wouldn't ask her, wouldn't have to. Aunt Bella had written that Miss Fairfield had passed away sitting at her desk in front of twenty-eight children. Forty years in Hammerhead Consolidated. Passed away. That was a nice way to put it. But it was all wrong. She had simply passed and I would never have to tell her anything at all about Olanberg, the way I had had to tell her everything about Bordeaux. I wondered what her face had looked like when she first heard about what I had done. "Mercy!" That was her favorite, and that was probably what she said. "Mercy, children!" I could hear it very clearly. And long before that: "Oh, mercy, Oscar Baron, it's I before E, except after C, or sounded like A, as in neighbor and weigh. Can't you remember that?"

Miss Fairchild had passed. But she had not passed away. I saw her floating in the clouds. Now why? You tell me why the day my father died the taxi driver went to Miss Fairfield's room. How did he know she had been my favorite teacher? I hadn't been in her room for four years. You tell me why he went to Miss Fairfield's room. No answer. There's no answer to a lot of things.

If I could only be in the Lumber Yard, hear Mims snoring, I would not be asking questions and seeing people floating in the clouds. Mims never really snored like other people. No more than deep peaceful vibrations. They had never bothered me. They made me sleepy.

I turned on my back and gazed at the ceiling. I saw old faces. The Chaplain, holding onto his cigar, was talking to Mrs. Galloway, comforting her, while Obie hid his face in her apron laughing.

I must be dreaming. I turned on my side. Their words walked through the moonlight. Somebody's words. "Oh, mercy, Shelley Raye. It's I before E . . ." Had Miss Fairfield ever taught Shelley Raye? I could ask Aunt Bella if I could only wake up. I dreamed I was sleeping. I sat in the moonlight above the quilted Rose Garden spread and watched. "Red Midnight! Red Midnight! William Marcus Oday has escaped. Red Midnight!"

Then I was awake. I was cold. I sat up in bed and knew that only the sheet covered me. The room was very light. I could see the bright Rose Garden design on the spread lying on the floor. I heard Sarah in the kitchen. I knew it was Sarah. Brooks never made that much noise.

"Oh, mercy," I said.

I wondered whether my old underwear would fit, my old shirts. Then I thought about my father's clothes.

22

I WROTE A short letter to Mims, and Brooks mailed it for me. I didn't go to Deer Forks. I didn't want to go to Deer Forks. Days passed by and I had been no farther from the Elms than the cemetery. Sarah came each morning and sometimes fixed me fried mackerel patties for breakfast. I set no alarm clock. No one called me. I was usually awake when Brooks left for work and would hear him walk along the back porch and step off onto the ground and go off whistling with his lunch pail under his arm. I would stay in bed until I heard the seven o'clock mill whistle blow. Often I wished I could have gone to the mill with Brooks.

With the sound of the mill whistle I would get up quickly and put on one of the half dozen pairs of khaki pants which belonged to my father. Sarah had taken up two full inches in the waist and seat of each pair and they fit me very well. I also wore my father's shirts, which were a size too large, and a dark gray suede jacket that Aunt Bella had given him for a birthday present. The sleeves of the shirts and jacket were of the right length for me and I rather enjoyed the loose and unhampered feel of the clothes.

I spent most of the days in the upstairs northwest room making it into what I thought of as a studio-den. Brooks helped me on Saturdays and Sundays, though sometimes he and Sarah went to church. I took the bed out. Brought a rug from the front downstairs.

It was a deep rich tan with a beige croker-sack design, the newest rug Aunt Bella had owned. Sarah made me drapes and curtains. The room had enormous single-pane double windows on the north and west sides. I robbed other parts of the house for chairs, lamps, pictures, a couch, books, and other odd pieces. I used the desk in Aunt Bella's office. And the typewriter. I left everything that belonged to my father. Brooks caught the bus to Koslo for things Sarah suggested and to cash a check for me.

Usually I ate breakfast alone. When the mill whistle blew at noon I promptly left whatever I was doing and went to the kitchen to have lunch with Sarah. I always had to ask her to join me at the table. At night the three of us ate together without my having to suggest it.

I had been home almost a week before I went back to the cemetery. I had expected some deep emotion to overwhelm me. But I stood at the foot of the two graves, in the old road, in a state of surprising calm. It just seemed to me there was nothing anybody could do about it. I liked Aunt Bella's gravestone. She must have left instructions. It was almost like my father's except the name DIXON was in big letters. I didn't stay long. I returned slowly up the old cemetery road and as I fastened the gate the mill whistle blew for noon. The mill whistle always made me nervous. I hurried to the Elms and found Sarah waiting for me. We ate in strict silence. She knew I had been to the cemetery.

When the meal was finished she began to wash the dishes and talk for the first time about Aunt Bella. "Dr. Ziddie tole her she ought to go, but he so old and cranky nobody won't hardly listen. Finely I just bundle her up and Brooks toted her to the car. She didn't weigh nothing. Couldn't hardly git nothing down her but what Dr. Ziddie left. I stayed in her hospital room. They didn't make me leave till the last three days. And then I didn't leave. I had on my white uniform and they let me stay in that little corner where folks waits. It was a nurse at night let me go in when I wanted to, and one in the day sometimes. One wouldn't, little mean-eyed heifer. Except I slipped. She always knowed when I was in the room without looking, eyes closed. 'Sarah, you take care of Marcus,' was most of the talk. The last day the mean little ole woman was there. She come and said to me in that little corner where folks waits, 'You don't need to wait no more, Auntie.' I said, 'You mean Miss Bella done passed?' She nodded so sharp I thought her cap would fall off. I wouldn'ta picked it up neither. But I didn't leave. She went back down the hall and I went to Miss Bella's room. Sheet done pulled up over her face, and I pulled it back. I said, 'Miss Bella, you was good to me and Brooks. You was always good to ever'body. I don't know why the Lawd takes good folks and leaves the bad. But you can ask Him y'self cause you gonna see Him, Precious.' They come and moved me over by the winder and took her out. I come home to dress. We went back to the funeral home and I stayed all through. Me and Brooks too. It was real nice and lots of peoples. Mostly women. And me and Brooks rode right behind the hearse. Mr. Obie come."

She stopped washing dishes, but she kept her back to me. Tears ran over her hands. The room was entirely still. After a moment I got up and took my plate to the sink. As I turned away, Sarah said, "You gonna see him sometimes. Ain't no need to worry about it."

"I'm not going to tell him I'm sorry," I said. I stopped at the table and looked back at Sarah. "Do you know what happened to my rifle?"

"What rifle? What you talking 'bout?" she said, as though I had never done anything and Olanberg did not exist.

"The one Dad gave me. The one I used."

"Oh," Sarah said. "I don't know nothing 'bout it. Fore or since."

"It's mine. It belongs to me."

"You better be thinking 'bout a lot of other things 'sides that."

"I do think about a lot of other things. But I want my rifle."

When the work was finally completed in the studio-den I sat down one morning to write something. I did not know what I wanted to write. I felt no great urge about anything, no special enlightenment, and no particular anger. I simply felt that writing something was the one thing I could do entirely by myself, and I was going to have to do without Mims. I got up and stood looking out the north window. Had it not been raining I would have gone to the springs and perhaps beyond, deep into the woods toward Dixon Creek. But the rain was already falling lightly and the skies were dark and threatening a downpour. Heavy clouds floated so low they seemed at times to be hung in the tops of the tallest pines. The great splash of color was all but gone from the hills. I could see in the distance the bare branches of a tall oak jabbing a cloud. I thought of my father carrying a pitchfork of hay over his head. A single leaf fell and floated earthward slow as a handkerchief. The soft weird light intrigued me, but the grayness, the barrenness and rain depressed me more and more. In another week, perhaps two, when the leaves were totally gone, I would be able to see the whole cemetery through the north window.

I drew the curtains, sat down at the desk again and began another letter to Mims. The first one was not what I had wanted and neither was the second. I wanted to write: I love you...I love you...

I crossed out words and sentences and rewrote as if composing a poem. I finally threw everything away and started a new letter. I wrote rapidly in a small neat hand, sometimes cursive and sometimes printed. I wouldn't think of typing it.

> Dear Mims,
>
> Every day I thought I would write you again. But I waited thinking each day would find me in a better mood and I could say what I feel. Right away I started making some changes at the Elms. You ought to be here to help me. The room upstairs

which I've told you about I've made into a studio-den. It's all finished and this morning I was standing by the window and could almost see the cemetery. When the leaves are all gone I can see it plainly.

I thought of you several times this morning and felt bad that I had not written again. It's cold and raining and if it's the same there you're probably working without lunch. You can have a lot of fried mackerel patties for supper.

We've had a prediction of snow. Remember what a snow we had that first day or night I saw you? It looks different there because it's so level and unhindered, not much chance of great white monsters. Wish it would snow here today. Maybe it would cheer me up. I might go hunting. I haven't done anything except work on my room project. Or been any place. I don't know what people think. Or what I expect them to think. I really wish I was there. I sure have missed you.

If it did snow I wouldn't have my rifle. The one Dad gave me, etc. I thought they would send it back to Aunt Bella but it's not here. Surely they have no right to keep what is mine. In a few days, maybe this week, I'm going to see if I can trace it. I guess start at the sheriff's office.

I'm enclosing you a little Christmas present. Don't think I had forgotten you. I just wish I could handle everything the way you do. If you ever need anything you can write me or somehow manage to call me. The Chaplain would let you use his phone. But if you need anything I'll send it or bring it or something. Remember your promise. When you get out I'll take you to New Orleans. Or anywhere. But I'm going to do something. Just remember your promise. I will write again soon but please do let me hear from you. No matter how short it is.

Sincerely,
Marcus

Wrapped in a separate sheet I enclosed five twenty-dollar bills. Later, I thought I should have mentioned the amount in my letter, for safety reasons. But I had already sealed the letter when the thought occurred to me.

The mill whistle finally sounded for noon and I went to the kitchen. Sarah had fried sweet potatoes and stew for lunch. I ate not because I was hungry but to avoid Sarah's questions.

While we were eating I asked Sarah a great many details of how she made stew. She was at last tired of explaining and said, "I don't know how I makes it. Sometimes one way, and sometimes another."

"Can you make Brunswick stew?" Mims had told me lots of times that he liked Brunswick stew almost as much as he liked fried mackerel patties.

"Kill me a squirrel and you find out."

"I don't have my rifle."

"Brooks got one."

"But that's not mine."

"You ain't gonna git yourn."

"How do you know?"

"They takes things like that. It's gone."

"Gone where?"

We could hear the downpour of rain outside.

"How come you can't forgit it?"

"Because I don't want to forget it."

"You better."

"Well, I'm not going to."

"You more stubborn than Brooks. Besides you can't go huntin' no way. It's raining."

"The rain's going to stop."

"You don't know about the rain. Might rain forty days and nights."

"It's going to stop and turn cold. Colder."

"You better git out if it does."

"Out where?"

"Anywheres. Set inside like you been, you gone turn yeller."

"All right. Where do you want me to go?"

"Anywheres. I done tole you."

"The post office?"

"Post office good as none."

"When it stops raining I'll go to the post office. I've got a letter to mail."

"Who you write a letter to?"

"A friend."

"Yo' girl friend?"

"No."

"What happen to her?"

"Who?"

"One brought ya books home that time."

"I don't know. Maybe she turned yellow. Turned into a pumpkin."

"Find out."

"I don't want to find out. The only thing I want to find is my rifle."

"Sometimes you near worries me to death."

"I just want to find out. How does that worry you?"

"All over. That's how. Won't git outside long enough to pick a mess of winter mustard greens."

"I'll pick you some mustard greens. When it stops raining."

"I already picked 'em for supper. I knowed it was gonna rain."

"You heard it on the radio."

"Radio ain't nothing. They don't know. I know when it gonna start raining cause my bones aches and itches. Ain't nobody know when it gonna stop. Might rain forty days and nights."

"Then we'll all be goners."

"No. Lawd ain't gonna do it with water no more. Fire."

"Is that so?"

"True as a rainbow. That's the sign. Cove-nut."

"Sign of what?"

"That He ain't gonna do it with water no more."

"Oh, I thought a rainbow was just the refraction and reflection of the sun's rays in water."

"You ain't nothing but a child," Sarah said. "It's the good Lawd's arms around you. That's what a rainbow is."

Later in the afternoon the rain stopped. I went to the post office. I did not want to go. I had intended giving the letter to Brooks for mailing the next morning. But once the letter was finished and the gift enclosed I had a great urge to send it along. A day of delay seemed unthinkable.

The rain had ceased completely and the air had turned much colder. I felt the cold, yet I was not uncomfortable. The errand itself, having something I must do, was a sort of pleasant gift to me. And the increased coldness meant I was less likely to encounter someone. There would be no idlers on the sidewalks and around Tanner's Store.

As I approached the store and the post office I saw no one and was greatly relieved. I would, of course, have to speak to Mr. Pettigrew but he was such a small and terribly shy person, never inquisitive, that I felt quite prepared to face him. He was often away from the post office because of sickness. He had been gassed in the war. On the days he was sick, his wife, much younger and very pleasant, ran the post office. She often ran it for a whole month at a time. She had a wonderful complexion and hair like Shelley Raye. She read a great deal. Once I had heard her say, not to me, but to some-one in the lobby writing a postal card, that she had read everything in the high school library once and several things twice.

Now, as I crossed the road to the post office, I suddenly thought of the remark as an exaggeration. She must have meant all the novels, I reasoned, and surely not the histories and biographies and such. It was the sort of exaggeration Mims would never make.

Mims never exaggerated anything. I must have been thinking about Mrs. Pettigrew because I had a presentiment that she would be working.

As I reached the sidewalk the post office door opened and a woman came out. I remembered suddenly, as if pulling a scene out of an old dream, I had seen this same woman do this identical thing. She wore the same black sweater, holding it tight with one hand and holding a newspaper with the other.

I pulled the letter from my pocket and pretended to read the address and allow her to pass on. Instead, she turned and stared at me and waited. I tried to remember her name, to remember where she lived. Some flash of recollection from long ago placed her in Tanner's Store, with a bushel of beans to sell. She was somehow kin to Nellie Gray.

"You picked a bad day to come out of your shell," she said. "I asked Cousin Nellie if anybody'd seen you. We thought you'd gone back."

I tried to smile.

"You don't know who I am, do you?" she asked.

"No, ma'am."

"You been gone so long. I mean with your mama and all. That's why you forgot me."

I could do nothing but stare.

"Well, I know who you are. I spoke to you the first day you come home in that taxi. Don't you remember? I thought the world and all of your daddy. Harmon did too, but he can't work no more. Rheumatism mostly. And just plain wore out. I told Cousin Nellie— talking about Harmon one day—that pulling that crosscut saw and fightin' them logs for above thirty year wasn't like handing out pinto beans and chill tonic. It's took its toll. Harmon's stove up so he can't hardly walk up here. Which leaves me to come for the mail. I say mail when all we ever git is the paper. He reads ever word. You remember him, don't you? Harmon Littlejohn. That's my husband."

I continued to stare blankly at her.

"You ought to remember him. He was the one nearly done it. No, he wasn't. He had more sense. He knowed it was wrong. Said so. Do you know he was always on your side? Did you know that?"

"No, ma'am," I said. I was on some kind of merry-go-round revolving so fast I didn't dare jump off. I wanted to cry out, run away, free myself from the awful burden of going over it and over it again and again. Olanberg had been entirely safe that way.

"Lots of other folks too," she said. "Me for one. You know what I mean about Harmon, don't you?"

She saw my bewilderment, understanding and not understanding, the agony of memory on my face, no doubt.

Forcing her words as if to drive the point home, she said, "Why, Harmon was driving the mules that morning. He was the one wouldn't do it."

"Oh," I said.

"He wants you to come see him."

That'll be the day, I thought, standing rigid and motionless, staring straight past her.

"He'd come see you but it's worse than I'm telling it. His rheumatism. He has to crawl up and down them steps which ain't knee high. The porch steps. He thought the world and all of your daddy." She looked up at the skies. "Reckon it's gonna actually break down and come a Jim Dandy snow?"

"I hope so," I said.

I darted inside the post office and closed the door behind me. Then I realized my abruptness and was ashamed. I opened the door to say some parting word and saw Mrs. Littlejohn disappearing down the sidewalk. For a second the flat gray levelness of Olanberg appeared before me and I saw her as a prisoner trying to escape.

I could almost hear the cry of the bloodhounds, the sirens announcing Red Midnight.

I felt the warm air of the room escaping past me. I closed the door and went quickly to the postal window.

"Just a minute," a woman's voice called from the semidarkness behind the cage.

Mrs. Pettigrew appeared at the window. I was astonished at the face, the woman herself. She had been so fine looking and now she looked as old as Harmon Littlejohn's wife. I would not have recognized her in some other place. I put the letter and a quarter down in the window. "I'd like a stamp, please."

She smiled. She tore off a stamp from a wide sheet, wet it on the sponge beside her and placed it on the envelope herself. She carefully counted out change. I waited for her to say something. She stood smiling.

"Thank you," I said.

"You're welcome," she said, and that was all.

I turned away. I was glad I didn't have to go over it again, but I felt empty, cheated of something. I paused and looked back at the window. I had to say something to her. "Mr. Pettigrew has you working for him today."

The smile faded slowly from her face. "Is that you, Marcus? I didn't recognize you. No, I'm working for myself. Hubert passed away five or six years ago. Six this spring."

I drew a deep breath and kept looking at her. She began to smile again. "That's all right. You just didn't know about it."

"No," I said. "I didn't know about it."

"It was right after your mother left. Doesn't seem that long. But time gets away. You wasn't here at the time."

"Do you still read all those books?" I said.

"No. My eyes bother me. I can't read much anymore."

She shouldn't be old so quick, I thought. "It's nice to see you."

"Nice to see you too, Marcus."

I went out. I could not believe that Mrs. Pettigrew could look so old. Maybe it was the way the light and the shadows fell. She still had beautiful hair.

I walked along slowly, feeling a faint sense of triumph. The letter was safely posted and I was safely through two conversations. It felt good to be outside. If I had my rifle I might go hunting and bring Sarah a squirrel. I looked off into the deep stretch of woods. The leaves were probably too far gone for still hunting.

There was nothing like the winter woods right after a heavy rain. The smell. The sudden and distinct crash of one small drop of water on a dead and fallen leaf. I was about to feel an easiness inside. Then the mill whistle sounded, like all of time shot from a Roman cannon, exploding and splintering, falling around me. Fine bits and pieces struck my face. It was beginning to snow.

The old black dog came out of the woods, threatened me with its long red tongue and ghost eyes. I hurried. Sweat broke out all over my body and I could hear the loping draw nearer and nearer.

I suddenly turned into the woods and walked and walked. With every step I intended to turn back. The loping behind me continued. But if I kept on, never looking back, it would always be behind me, never quite reach me, though I could all but feel the hot breath, as if I stood with my back to a fire.

I was streaming with sweat, and the woods had grown dark. I saw a light ahead. I climbed the hill, clinging to the branches and small bushes to keep my feet from slipping. I could hear the roaring of the springs behind me. I looked back and saw the deep prints of my shoes in the snow.

I stepped onto the back porch and opened the door. Sarah was in the hallway facing me.

"Lawd, have mercy!" she said. "Where you been? You wringing wet."

She brushed at the snow on my shoulders. She found a broom and swept the snow from my shoes.

For some reason I was holding the golden key in my open hand. "You're not going to take this away from me, are you?"

"I ain't gonna take nothing away from you, baby," Sarah said. "Come on in the house and git warm."

23

THE SNOW WAS so heavy that the mill was closed. I was glad for an excuse to stay inside. Sarah found an old pair of my father's gum rubber boots which she wore between the cabin and the Elms, and Brooks wore them each day when he went for groceries and the mail.

I spent most of my time refinishing a beautiful old bookcase I found in the barn loft. It reminded me of a bookcase Mims had once made for the Warden. It had a secret compartment on top, almost the length and width of the case itself and to a depth of five or six inches. When unlocked, the top folded back easily. A cleverly designed facing hid the lock and made the top appear, even on close inspection, to be a solid piece of walnut. Most of my books were still at Deer Forks but Aunt Bella had had books all over the house in corners and on shelves and in various small cases. I wanted to make a special collection for my studio-den.

The snow was still on the ground when I put the finishing touches to the bookcase. I was testing the lock and unfolding the top as Brooks entered.

"What you gonna hide?" Brooks asked.

"My secret journals," I said.

"Where they now?"

"I don't have any now but I might have a few some day. Or love letters. Or money. Everybody ought to have a secret hiding place. Don't you have a secret hiding place?"

"All I got is a hole in the mattress and nothing to hide. I got you some mail."

He held out two letters. One from Mims and one from the Merchants and Farmers Bank. I quickly opened the letter from Mims. It was in pencil on ruled tablet paper, written in a large scrawling hand. I had trouble reading it.

> Dear Marcus,
>
> How are you fine I hope. I got you first letter and you Christmas gift allso and feel like I am rich. I wood give you a hug if you was hear. I was puny a few days and wen to infermery. I eat to much frid mackrell paties I guess. Ha! Guess who is new docter. He is from Vickburg. One who use docter us. I allready treeted Leo at the store. It is a plasure to be rich and abel to treet folkes. Ha! You said you mised me. I allso. It will never be the same hear. Write me more and I will anser better next time and more. Yours truely.
>
> Mims
>
> P. S. Forgive this is so short. It tuck most last nite.

I read the letter three or four times. I was instantly transported into a different world. I laid the bank letter aside because I did not want anything to interfere with my sudden dose of happiness. I went to the north window and read Mims's letter again. When I could have repeated every syllable I put the letter in the secret compartment of my bookcase. I didn't mind what Brooks saw.

"You act like somebody done give you a new car," Brooks said.

Plans were whirling in my mind. "I told you I was gonna get a new car. I am. I might let you have it some Saturday night." I paced about the room, full of energy, bubbling over with good will and plans.

"When you gonna git it?"

"Right away."

"Right away is a road. And roads is long."

"Before Christmas."

"You won't let me drive no new car."

"Yes I will. Of course, I will. You won't even have to ask. I'll pitch over the keys and you can head for Beale Street for all I care."

"You joking at me."

"Why would I be joking?"

"Cause you ain't got no new car."

"I'll have one by Christmas. Maybe real soon."

"What kind?"

"What kind do you like?"

"You bound to be joking now."

"You know more about cars than I do. What kind do you like?"

"Was me, a Dodge."

"All right. A Dodge."

"I'm gonna see."

"That's right, you gonna see." My mind seemed to be going in all directions. I needed to do something to quiet myself. "Help me move this bookcase."

We found the right spot for the bookcase and then set about to collect books from various parts of the house. I carefully selected armloads for Brooks to carry upstairs. I made selections, changed my mind, sometimes stood reading for a quarter of an hour while Brooks patiently waited. By supper time I was more or less satisfied with my collection.

At the table Brooks said, "Tell Mama about the new car you gonna git."

"What new car?" Sarah said.

"He gonna git one. Tell Mama."

"That's right," I said.

"Huh," Sarah said. "All you needs is a tricycle. You ain't going no place."

"A Dodge," Brooks said. "Ain't it gonna be a Dodge?"

"That's right. A Dodge," I said.

"He gonna loan it to me. And I'm gonna head for Beale Street," Brooks said.

"I Beale Street you," Sarah said.

"He said." Brooks pointed to me.

Sarah pointed to herself. "And I ain't said."

"I slip off," Brooks said.

"Dodge," Sarah said. "What both yawl needs is a little ole toy truck on the floor and some toy soldiers." She got up and handed a deep-dish pie pan to Brooks. "See can you find some snow ain't melted and I make yawl some snow cream."

That night I slept extremely well. When I awoke I heard Brooks going to work. I though of Mims's letter and ran upstairs to read it again. There lay the bank letter which I had completely forgotten. I ripped it open with some feeling of anger because it was keeping me from Mims's letter. It was a request from the trust officer to come to the bank at my earliest convenience.

After breakfast, dressed in the clothes I had worn away from Olanberg, I walked to Hammerhead and waited outside Tanner's Store for the morning bus to Koslo. Patches of snow remained in shady places but the day was not cold. Gusts of wind, almost warm, whipped up old wrappers and trash and turned the patches of snow into little clouds of smoke. While I waited a few people passed me, sometimes nodding, sometimes giving a mere glance and passing on quickly. I recognized three of four of the faces but could not remember a single name.

I saw the bus approaching and felt a great relief that I would now be able to escape the conversations I had expected while waiting. I boarded the bus and dropped a quarter into the proper slot.

The bus was not crowded. Five or six whites sat in the forward section and about an equal number of blacks sat in the back. I moved down the aisle to the last row of seats in the white section. As I sat down I noticed the sign over my seat dividing the white passengers from the black.

Two people came out of Tanner's Store and hurried toward the bus. They appeared to be mother and son, a boy of fifteen or sixteen, I judged. The woman had the tired, drawn face of a sharecropper's wife. She paid both fares. The two passed by several empty seats and came to the last row in the white section, directly across the aisle from me.

The bus moved on. I gazed out the window at once-familiar spots that now seemed foreign and strange. When I glanced back across the aisle I saw that the woman and boy had been observing me. The boy continued to stare but the woman turned her gaze away quickly, flushing with country shyness. The boy was much older than I had thought, perhaps twenty or more. There was a tight, almost angry look in his face. His mouth was open in a careless half-grin, revealing long, irregular front teeth and one short protruding eyetooth on which the corner of his lip seemed to hang. He continued to stare at me until the woman drew his attention to something outside in a field of dead cotton stalks.

The bus stopped often at crossroads and country stores until all the seats in the white section were filled except the one beside me and the one aisle seat in front of the boy. In the black section the passengers were crowded together and four or five were standing.

I furtively searched the faces of the new passengers for ones I might recognize. Suddenly I realized the boy and woman were in a quiet but heated argument.

"Yawl let Troy," the boy said.

"I didn't let Troy do nothing," the woman said. "He done it on his own accord. He was free, white and going on twenty-one."

"He wasn't twenty-one yet," the boy said.

"I said going on. Same as," the woman said. "No, sir. You're not traipsing off no thousand miles. Job or no job. Brother or no brother up there."

"Gary, Indiana, ain't no thousand miles," the boy said.

"Well, seven hundred then."

"Six hundred. Ain't even six hundred," the boy said. "And Troy makes more a hour than he used to git in a day at Koslo."

The bus stopped at a country store. A very old Negro woman and a very old Negro man boarded the bus with great difficulty. The woman carried a worn and tattered satchel from which she finally extracted a knotted handkerchief and from the handkerchief the fares. The two reeled down the aisles as the bus began to move again. I was certain that one or both of them would fall. But here and there along the aisle a hand reached out to steady one or the other. I got up and offered my seat to the old couple. I took the satchel and held the old woman's arm until she was able to turn and fit herself into the aisle seat. She looked up gratefully to me.

"I didn't lose my hank'chief, did I?" she asked.

"No," I said. "It's there in your hand."

She located the handkerchief and looked up again, her old face full of warmth and laughter. "Lose my hank'chief done lost all my Christmas."

"You don't want to do that," I said. I moved to the seat directly in front of the boy.

"I ain't no nigger lover," the boy said, not very loud but above a whisper. I heard it distinctly.

"Shut your mouth," the woman said.

"I just said I ain't one," the boy said, louder. "I know who he is."

"I said hush," the woman said.

"I know who he is. He ain't gonna do nothing to me," the boy said. "He ain't gonna do nothing."

The woman raised her hand slowly. "If you don't shut up, Deward, I'm gonna slap you square in the mouth." She leaned forward to speak to me. "He's just that-a-way at times. He don't mean no harm."

I turned. A broad grin spread across the boyish face, something mysterious, secretive, something not quite right in the dull eyes. "That's all right," I said, and turned forward again.

"I didn't mean no harm," the boy said.

"You didn't mean no good neither," the woman said. "Them people is old and can't stand up with this old bus rockin' around them curves."

"I know who he is anyway," the boy said. "I know what he done."

"Hush, you don't know nothing about it," the woman said.

"Troy told me," the boy said. "In the graveyard with a rifle."

"Troy don't know nothing about it neither. You hush," the woman said.

"Troy went to school with him."

I tried to think of someone I knew named Troy.

"Shut up," the woman said.

"He's gonna buy me a bicycle when he gits home. Fer a Christmas present."

"You keep on, and I'll tell Troy not to buy you nothing."

"It ain't gonna be mine total. But he's gonna let me keep it. What you gonna git me?"

"Nothing if you don't hush."

"I don't want nothing if you let me go back with Troy."

"Troy can't take care of you. He's got to work."

"I can take care of myself. I'm older'n him."

"What if you have a spell, a thousand miles away and all by yaself?"

"It ain't no thousand miles. Ain't even six hundred."

"Hush. Who's gonna help ya daddy milk?" She looked out the window and rubbed it with a little doily-like handkerchief. She sighed. "We nearly there."

The boy stood up. The woman pulled at his arm. "Set back down. We going on acrost the railroad. We ain't payin' no uptown prices."

The boy sat down.

"Court square," the driver called.

The bus stopped at the corner near the whittlers. A dozen passengers, all white, moved toward the door. I was behind all of them. When I reached the front row of seats the driver said, "What was you tryin' to pull back there?"

I actually did not know for a second what he meant.

"You know where they're 'sposed to set. I'll be lookin' fer you on the way back," he said.

"You kiss my ass," I said in French. And in English I added, "I won't be going back with you."

"Fine with me, Buster," the driver said.

For three or four minutes I stood on the corner watching the whittlers. Near the end of one bench an old man carved away on a block of cedar, shaping a crude horse. He leaned forward, his spectacles hanging at an angle across his sunken face. From time to time he brushed away the end of a ragged scarf wound about his long thin neck. The motion was slow and soft as if he brushed away a fly. He had to be eighty, I thought. But his hands were full and strong, amazingly young, almost free of wrinkles. They looked like Mims's hands at work. I moved a few steps nearer and continued to watch him. Finally the old man knew that he was being watched. He looked up and smiled.

I returned the smile and hurried on past the Confederate monument toward the bank. I felt that something important was about to happen. Not something ominous so much as inevitable. A presentiment. I had several things to do: see the trust officer, buy some clothes at Meade Brothers, buy a car, get a car tag and apply for a driver's license at the sheriff's office, look at some gifts at Bates Jewelers. I wanted to get everything done because I was certain that something was going to happen.

Sure enough, before midnight I was in jail.

24

IT MUST HAVE been about eleven o'clock when the deputies woke the jailer, who was not Mr. Fancher. He took me to the end of the hall, near the Back Room, and gave me an extra blanket. He wore nothing but long-handled underwear and unlaced shoes. I don't believe he said a single word to me but he was not unpleasant. He reminded me of Harley Oldham, Juanita's father, dark and stocky and silent.

The jail was as quiet as the Elms. I slept with my clothes on. It must have been too cold for flies but the same old smell of urine was there.

Stella came to my cell early the next morning. She started out cool, like the first time. "I guess you're surprised to see me back," I said.

"Lots of people have a habit of coming back," she said.

"Maybe they like your cooking," I said. I meant to be funny. I didn't mean to offend her. But I could see that I had. "Where are Mr. and Mrs. Fancher?"

"Mrs. Fancher lives on their farm at Antioch. Mr. Fancher is deceased."

"I'm sorry," I said.

"Do you want some breakfast?" she said. "It's in the Back Room."

"No, ma'am, I don't want any breakfast. But I wish you would call Mr. Molock for me."

"You can call him yourself at the regular time. At ten o'clock." She turned away and then turned back. "Oh, I'll do that for you."

"I sure thank you, Stella," I said.

I thought she was going to say something else, ask me something, but she answered, "You're very welcome."

It was past ten o'clock and I was getting very hungry when I heard Mr. Molock. He was coming down the hall with Stella.

"He's downstairs," Stella said.

"What's his problem?"

"Burglary and larceny."

The sound of footsteps ceased. "Are you sure?"

"That's what's on the books. I wasn't here last night when they brought him in."

"Seems awfully strange."

"That's how he's booked."

"Have you talked to him?"

"We spoke. That's all. He didn't want any breakfast. He asked me to call you."

"Well, we'll just have to see. People with grandchildren shouldn't be surprised at anything. Except I'm always surprised you never look any older."

"I certainly feel older, Mr. Molock. I'm awfully tired of this place."

"You ought to be able to find something else."

"I've tried the plants and everywhere. Two or three places told me they couldn't hire me because I had a college degree. I don't know why that's a hindrance, but it seems to be."

"That's a shame."

"Whatever it is, I didn't get a job. And I'm not going north. I'm not going through that. He's in here."

Stella unlocked the door. I was sitting on my bunk fully dressed except for my shoes when Mr. Molock entered. Stella went away without relocking the door.

"Yet, we meet again," Mr. Molock said. "*Ça va?*"

"*Ça va.* I didn't know anyone else to call," I said. I was about to sneeze. I took out my handkerchief and pressed it against my upper lip under my nose. That usually works for me, but I sneezed anyway.

"I hope you didn't catch cold," he said. "Sit down."

I sat on the bunk. Mr. Molock took off his topcoat and sat down, smiling. He looked away, and about the room, as though he might discover something significant. "You're the last person I expected to meet here this morning. What in the name of heaven have you done?"

"I took my rifle."

"Your rifle?"

"It belongs to me. They kept it after the trial."

"Took it from where? The sheriff's office?"

"From Kewlit's Gun and Bicycle Shop."

"You broke in and stole it?"

"No. I took it."

"Do you know what you're booked for?"

"Yes. The sheriff told me. A deputy did."

"Where is the rifle now?"

"Hidden."

"Where?"

"Where nobody's likely to find it. The deputies couldn't. They tried hard enough. They searched my house without a warrant, which is illegal."

"Have you been studying law while...while you were down there?"

"I read a lot of books. Some were law books."

"A little knowledge is a dangerous thing. You've heard that expression, haven't you?"

"Probably."

"Did you admit taking the rifle? Admit to the deputies you took it?"

"Yes. I told them the truth."

"Let me help you with your legal education first. Then we'll try to begin at the beginning. That was probably a search incident to an arrest for the purpose of discovering the fruits of a crime. If that was the case a search is permissible without a warrant. I don't happen to agree with it. But that's the law. Now tell me how this whole thing started."

"It started when I came back home and couldn't find my rifle."

"You expected it to be at home?"

"Yes. It's mine."

"What made you go to Kewlit's?"

"I bought a new car yesterday and I had to get a tag and a driver's license. While I was in the sheriff's office I saw Miss Whitfield. I remembered her from going there with my dad to pay taxes. And I thought she might know about my rifle, and I asked her. She said she was sure it had been buried and she saw right away I didn't know what buried meant. She explained that meant it had been sold. And she might have a record of the sale date but she wouldn't have a buyer's name. She thought about Mr. Wooley who was a deputy at the time and he's a gun expert. She called him and he thought a Mr. Lokey had bought it. She called Mr. Lokey for me who said he had sold it to a Mr. Leatherwood who had sold it to Mr. Kewlit. I went to see, to ask."

"And you found it and took it?"

"Not then. I asked Mr. Kewlit about it. He can't hear too well, and he can't speak English very well. But he finally understood what I wanted and sure enough he had it. He just cleaned it a few days ago. It looked brand new. But he wouldn't sell it to me. He had promised somebody to keep it until Christmas, a Mr. Barnett. If Mr. Barnett didn't buy it Mr. Kewlit would sell it to me."

"Didn't that seem fair enough?"

"It's mine. I kept telling him it was mine, that I would pay for it, that I would pay him double or whatever he wanted but it was mine. He wouldn't listen to me. He said he didn't understand. I couldn't understand why he couldn't understand. I kept yelling it was mine, yelling so he could hear. I wasn't mad then. But he wouldn't let me have it. He only wanted thirty-nine dollars and a half for it. Finally I left."

"Without the rifle?"

"Yes. I could have just walked out with it then. He isn't big as . . . well, he's a very small man. He certainly couldn't have stopped me. I had it in my hands holding it. But I felt sorry for him in a way. I put the rifle down on his work bench and pointed at it and yelled again that it was mine and walked out. I went to get my new car and still had to wait. About an hour, I guess. All the time I was waiting I got worse and worse. I kept thinking it wasn't right. Not if I was willing to pay. I got my car and went back to the shop. I went in. The door was not locked. It definitely was not locked. The front door wasn't. The back door was. I don't know where Mr. Kewlit was. I called three or four times. I went into the back room. I tried to look in the back, outside. But the door was locked. The rifle was still on the work bench. I took it and went home."

"Where did you put it?"

"I hid it."

"And nobody knows where except you? And you're not telling?"

"No. I'm not telling."

"We've been through something like this before, you no doubt remember?"

"Yes, I remember." I pulled out my billfold and brought out the note Obie had written to me. I held it up. "I still have it."

"Well, I'll be damned," Mr. Molock said.

I replaced the note in my billfold. Mr. Molock seemed distracted by the whole procedure. "What did you think about Olanberg?" he said.

"How do you mean?"

"You wouldn't want to go back, would you?"

"I'm not telling where my rifle is, if that's the price."

"What if I told you that rifle doesn't legally belong to you, not at all."

"I would think that's your opinion."

"It's not an opinion. It's the law."

"Law is opinion."

"I mean there's a statute. A specific statute."

"Well, my dad gave it to me. It was the last thing he ever gave me. The law can go to hell."

"Do you realize what any judge or jury is almost certain to do?"

"They can't do any more than they've already done. And I'll still have the rifle."

"You'd give up everything for that?"

"What do I have to give up, except what my father gave me?"

"How about your aunt Bella? She certainly left you plenty and you know I know."

"If she were living, you think she'd want me to give it up?"

"You tell me. Would she?"

"I don't know. But my father certainly would not."

"You still have a remarkable attachment to your father."

"That might be because of him. He was a remarkable man. In my opinion, anyway. If I didn't defend what he gave me it would be like not defending him."

"But the laws must be obeyed."

"What laws?"

"All laws. Whether you agree with them or not."

"What do you do when you disagree with the law?"

"I obey it."

"Do you drink whiskey?"

"Yes. Occasionally."

"Here in this county?"

"Well...yes."

"That's against the law."

Mr. Molock looked away. He picked up his coat and held it in his lap.

"Isn't it against the law?" I asked.

"It is."

"But you think you have a moral right to do it?"

"Something like that."

"I think I have a moral right to my rifle. I'll pay for it. If you ran over someone with your car they wouldn't take your car would they?"

"No. Do you know what's going to happen to you?"

"Not exactly."

"I'll go to the justice of the peace. He'll set your bond and bind you over to the action of the grand jury, which meets the first Monday in January. In all likelihood they will return a true bill against you. Which means you are indicted. There will be a trial and I can almost assure you they'll send you back to Olanberg. Is the rifle worth that?"

"I don't know what it's worth. I don't know what anything is worth. If it means enough you should be willing to pay and not consider the price. Bread is worth more to a man who's starving. That's how the world is run. That's how the rich stay in power. The rich don't pay too much for a loaf of bread. They can go home and eat cake."

"You're pretty well off. But you don't like the rich?"

"I don't like the power they have."

"The rich don't run this country," Mr. Molock said.

"Who does then, the lawyers?"

"The people," he said. "This is a democracy."

"Democracy doesn't really work. It just works well enough for people to think it works."

"The people rule."

"That's absurd. Who tells the black people to sit in the back of the bus? The blacks? Do the blacks tell the blacks where to sit?"

"That's just an unfortunate custom."

"It's not a custom. It's the exercise of power by the powerful. The indecent exercise of power."

"You're a very disturbed young man, aren't you?"

"What if I am disturbed? People ought to be disturbed. I'm not going to be a slave. If I was black I wouldn't sit in the back of the bus. Some day somebody is going to say, 'I'm not going to do it.' The sooner the better. Let all hell break loose. That's how I feel. They will not get my rifle."

"Did you send for me to give me a lecture?"

"I sent for you to get your advice but I don't have to take it."

"I don't have to take your case either."

"I know that."

He stood up. He took a long time in putting on his coat. "I can't make up my mind whether you're childish or a step ahead of me."

"The best bet between the two is I'm childish. But children are not always wrong."

"I'll post your bond. Give me an hour or so. You'll be free until January. Then . . . surely I've made it clear what the consequences are almost certain to be." He started out and stopped. "I'm on pretty good terms with the prosecutor. A new one. We can stop this right now if you take the rifle back. What do you say?"

"No."

"All right. If one bleak January day you stand before the bar and hear the judge give you two, four, five years at Olanberg...wouldn't you dread it more this time?"

I looked up at Mr. Molock a long time before answering. I had to smile. "I wouldn't dread it at all," I said.

25

THE GREAT LEVELNESS stretched out before me like an eternity, and the car seemed anchored, forever barred from the distant horizon. I drove on through the soft light and the grayness almost in a trance. Beyond the haze and the thin wisps of clouds the pale sun hung like a paper moon behind sheer curtains. There was very little wind and the day was unusually warm for Christmas. I thought of taking off my coat, the car had become too warm, but I did not want to delay for one second. I was happier than I had been for weeks.

Past Tallapalo River the sharecropper shacks began, all exactly alike, hovering near the road with no sign of life except the smoke hanging on the rock chimneys and the tin tops as though a crop duster had made its run along the edge of the right-of-way.

For a month I had known I would go to Olanberg on Christmas Day. In spite of careful planning I was running somewhat behind schedule. Ahead a vast stretch of swamp appeared. From oak and cypress the Spanish moss fell in great waves, almost golden in the weird light. It made me think of Shelley Raye.

When I had passed the swamp I saw the water tower of Olanberg mushrooming from the great gray levelness, and wondered whether the guards would spoil the appearance of the Christmas present by opening it at the Main Gate.

I turned off the highway slowly and onto the road leading to the entrance. A terrible misgiving seized me. My driver's license had not yet been issued and I had only the stub of the application, which might not be sufficient identification.

A guard stepped out to block my passage and said, "Driver's license."

I handed him the stub. The guard turned and handed the stub to a free trusty, who looked cautiously, then copied down the name and number. He returned the stub to the guard and said, "I don't know."

"I think it's all right," the guard said. "What's the package?"

"A Christmas present," I said.

"All right. Straight ahead at the Second Gate. You'll have to go through S. and I. Pull over to the right there at the guard station. They'll have to open your package and inspect the trunk of your car. Here's the white card. They'll give you a blue card for the Second Gate."

"I'm not going through the Second Gate," I said.

"Who do you want to see?"

"The Chaplain."

"What nature?"

"What nature?"

"I mean what's the nature of your business?"

"I have a Christmas present for him."

The guard looked at the free trusty and back to me. "All right. Long as you're this side of the Second Gate all you need is the white card. You know where his office is?"

"Yes. I've been there lots of times."

"Kinfolks?"

"No."

"You're not newspaper, are you?"

"No. A friend."

The guard looked at the car. "Brand new, isn't it?"

"Yes."

"Smells brand new. Nice."

I drove on, past the Administration Building, past the Infirmary. I stopped before the Sanctuary. I had intended seeing the Chaplain first, but my mind was changing. It was ridiculous to go to the Sanctuary first. I might be delayed by the Chaplain. I looked back toward the entrance, then moved the car along slowly toward the central guard station where three or four cars waited. I neared the fork which led to the Circle of the Guards. I stopped the car and held the white card out the window as a guard came toward me.

"You'll have to wait a while," the guard said. "We ain't lettin' but twenty in at a time."

"I just want to go to the Lumber Yard," I said.

"Okay," the guard said. "Round the circle and to the left."

I started to drive off.

"Hey," the guard said. "I think Leo is out with the dogs. But you can see. Might have to wait fer him. It ain't no Red Midnight but I think he's runnin' 'em."

"Thanks," I said. I drove away quickly. I got out at the corner of the building, thought of locking the car, and smiled. I looked toward the kennels. There was no sign of Leo or the dogs. I could smell the cedar beneath the shed. I looked up. The building seemed taller now, much taller and grayer too, as if it had passed a lifetime of long winters since I had last seen it.

My heart was pounding with dual pumps of joy and sorrow, for my mind was more focused on the moment of leaving Mims than the moment of meeting. A curious, fleeting notion came to me that I might ask the Chaplain if I could spend the night. It would be cold before dark. I saw myself and Mims sitting by the stove and listening to the radio, and Mims taking his pinch of snuff and offering his silver box and placing the cedar ash bucket between us. Maybe it would turn real cold by bedtime and I could crawl under the covers beside Mims and put my arm around him.

I ran into the building and up the steps. The Shop looked as it did the first time I had seen it, clean and orderly as a well-kept kitchen. I thought I smelled mackerel patties, but perhaps it was only the rich odor of the wood. I rushed toward the north stairway.

With my hand on the doorknob I paused, listening for any sound inside. My heart now pounded only with happiness. I turned the bolt and burst into the room. The shock was sudden and powerful, as if Mims had been stretched out dead on the cold linoleum. The beds were stripped. The sheets and blankets were folded neatly on one bed. There was no quilt. The dresser was bare. Kitchen utensils were stacked beside the sink. No sugar bowl, no salt and pepper shakers, no pickle jars, nothing sat on the dining table. I knew Mims was gone.

I ran out of the room, leaving the door ajar. Flying through the Shop and down the stairway I knew that I must control myself. At the corner of the building I managed to stop running. I looked toward the kennels hoping to catch a glimpse of Leo, but the cabin seemed deserted, not the faintest trace of smoke.

My hand shook as I inserted the key into the ignition. Maybe he's in the Infirmary, I thought. He was sick once, his letter said. Or he could be with Leo. There could be all kinds of reasons the room looked deserted. He can't be gone. Maybe for some reason, like repairs, he had temporarily moved in with Leo.

I approached the central guard station slowly and saw the cars waiting. Surely to God Mims had not done something and been put behind the Second Gate again.

I turned toward the Sanctuary. I parked and went up the steps slowly, trying to breathe deeply and drive the fire out of my body. At the door I looked back toward the Second Gate where the people waited as if some great disaster hovered over the vast levelness. All of it seemed so horrible and unbearable without Mims.

I entered the hall and knocked on the Sanctuary door.

"Come," the voice inside said.

Then I remembered the present.

I opened the door. The Chaplain stood behind his desk smoking his cigar. "I've got something for you," I said quickly. "I didn't know...if...if...you'd be in here today. I'll get it."

I ran out of the building. "What a lie...what a lie," I whispered. "On Christmas Day. No wonder Mims is gone. But I didn't want to seem crazy."

The Chaplain was standing in the doorway. He stepped back toward his desk for me to enter. "Oday...Oday," he said, as if to make certain the name did not escape him.

I put the present into the Chaplain's hands. "What's all this about?" he said.

"A present," I said.

The Chaplain led the way around the cabinets into the kitchen area. He placed the package on the table and sat down. His eyes squinted through the cigar smoke. I sat at the corner of the table.

"This is very thoughtful of you," he said. "I shouldn't be surprised. But I am. Presents always surprise me. You mind if I open it now?"

"I want you to," I said. I wanted to get it over with and come to the vital subject of Mims.

The Chaplain opened the package carefully and drew out a magnificent silver set: a large tray, a pitcher, eight goblets, a sugar bowl and creamer. He was clearly stunned. He made several unintelligible grunts in search of words. "Oday, why did you do this?"

I was ready to make my speech. I had it all prepared: They may send me back down here and I just wanted you to know that I'm not a burglar nor a thief. It's the principle of the thing. I will not be run over.

And not a word would come out. My mind was full of the vital question: What's happened to Mims?

"My wife won't believe this," the Chaplain said. "She...she... I don't know what she'll do. Nothing under the sun could please her better. She's never had anything like this. She's here for Christmas. Do you know what she's been doing this morning? Grading term themes. The teachers in this country...they deserve..."

I was not listening. Was Mims sick or gone or behind the Second Gate or with Leo?

"You want some coffee?" the Chaplain said.

"No. No, thank you," I said. "I was just wondering about Mims. I didn't find him..."

The Chaplain got up. "Well, I'll tell you about Mims. Pretty good story." He went to the sink and ran water over the burning tip of his cigar, then placed it in a soap dish. I could not see his face but I thought it was frowning. I waited breathlessly. Something awful had happened to Mims. He was probably behind the Second Gate now.

The Chaplain turned to face me. "Do you remember that writer on the Vicksburg paper? Mims was his special project. He never let up and he finally got the governor's ear. Mims has graduated."

"He's gone?"

"This morning."

I breathed deeply. It was almost like hearing that Mims was behind the Second Gate. "Where did he go?"

"To Greenwood."

"Why did he go to Greenwood?"

"To catch a bus home I suppose. Or somewhere."

"He didn't say where he was going?"

"No. He can go wherever he likes. Inside the state. He has thirty days to find a job and report to any parole officer. I suppose he went home. Just a guess. Did he know you were coming today?"

"No. I wanted to surprise him. Maybe the doctor knows where he is."

"I doubt it. But he might."

"Could I ask him?"

"If he was here you could. He's on his way to Little Egypt. Christmas dinner with the Warden. It wouldn't do to call him there."

"No," I said. I held the corner of the table, wrinkling the oilcloth. I wanted to jump up and run out.

The Chaplain began to rub his hands over the silver, leaving his fingerprints. He held a goblet up as if it were a mirror. "Why, I think most of Mims's folks are in South Carolina," he said.

"I don't think I could stand it here now," I whispered.

"What?" the Chaplain said. He took his handkerchief and rubbed his fingerprints from the goblet. He saw that I was looking away from him toward the door. "What's worrying you? The war? I've got a boy a little older than you. He wants to go. Is that what's worrying you? It can't be money."

"No. My childishness."

The Chaplain laughed. "That shouldn't worry you. Most of us remain children all our lives, searching for a more satisfying toy. Yes. Never really knowing how to love and how to sing. You know, when you were here I envied you. Now that you're out I envy you more. I always wanted to write a book. I used to write a sentence now and then that I thought was brushed with the shadow of greatness. But a book? No. Better stick to the urges of the average man. You know what his greatest urge is? To defy gravity. Fortunes, automobiles, athletic stars, skyscrapers, guns. They all come from the basic urge to defy gravity, to break the bonds. I couldn't write a book. I couldn't write a really good sermon. I'd have a decent sentence here and there. Once a year a good paragraph. 'What is more beautiful than two lovers sharing an apple without a knife?' That's from one of my sermons. The only thing I remember in it. You could write a book."

"I don't think I could do anything except something foolish," I said. "I barely know how to exist."

"*Cogito, ergo sum.* Can you translate that?"

"I think, therefore I exist," I said. "Could you help me find Mims?"

"When?"

"As soon as possible."

"Well, we'll know where he is in a few days. As soon as he finds a job. Or doesn't find one."

I got up. "Would you let me know? Call? Or write me? Could I call you?"

"Of course."

I held out my hand. "Merry Christmas."

"Merry Christmas to you," he said.

I started out. "Thanks again for such a present," he said. "I've never had one from a graduate before."

"I'm glad I did it," I said.

In the car I drove slowly toward the gate trying to find the white card. My eyes searched the seat, the floorboard. My hands fumbled in my pockets. I could feel the sweat in the edge of my hair. The world of freedom seemed to hang on the card. Don't panic, I thought. It's here somewhere. At the gate the guard was holding out his hand for the card, while I was fumbling furiously with my coat pockets. Sweat poured down my face. "I can't find the card," I said.

"Ain't it there on the dashboard?" the guard said.

My hand trembled as I delivered my ticket to freedom. The guard saw and smiled. "Ain't no great big matter," he said. "We wouldn't keep you if you'd lost it. Be surprised how many do."

At the highway I wanted to turn south, go in search of Mims, but even in my distress and dejection I realized the sane thing to do was to go home, get myself clear of the charge against me if I could. The thought of being in Olanberg now, without Mims, was terrifying. I wheeled the car sharply and sped north toward a dark bank of clouds that seemed to block the road. The old black dog was sitting behind me, whining. I drove faster and the whine grew louder.

Far ahead vultures circled, as if their wings scratched the dark wall of clouds. A few drifted down lazily and bounced softly on the narrow strip of pavement. The black lumps of winged coal held their places stubbornly while the car raced nearer and nearer like a stallion bearing down on a flock of chickens. I was determined not to slow the car. The black bodies appeared like a sign, an omen, a presentiment, and they seemed unwilling to give way until the last mutilated cell had been devoured. In the final seconds of safety their huge wings began to spread and the dark bodies rose awkwardly, like unattended umbrellas in a violent wind, and the car roared on through the gray haze and the Spanish moss.

The rain commenced, a heavy driving downpour that wiped out the distant outline of hills and beat on the hood and the windshield like falling gravel. It was another bad sign, I thought. I remembered my mother's accident. I slowed the car considerably.

The rain stopped. The sky grew brighter. The green patches of pine appeared near and far like friendly faces. At the intersection of highways 6 and 51, beside the bus station which was also a filling station and a grocery store, I located a telephone booth and made my call. While I waited in the booth the old smell of urine and flies came back to me. Though there was noise from vehicles I opened the door and stood as far outside the booth as I could to talk.

"Mr. Molock?"

"Yes."

"I'm sorry to bother you on Christmas Day."

"That's all right."

"This is Marcus Oday."

"Marcus? What are you doing in Batesville?"

"I've been to Olanberg. To see my friend."

"Yes?"

"I was calling to tell you...to say...well, I'm sorry about the rifle. I want you to get me out of it if you can. I'll give back the rifle. I'll do whatever you say. Anything..."

Mr. Molock laughed. "Well. You're coming to your senses. You saw the place again and it doesn't look too attractive, huh?"

"Something like that. But if you can only get me clear I'll do what you say."

"You're in Batesville now?"

"Yessir. On my way back. Do you think there's a way..."

"A way?"

"A way to get me clear?"

"I can't promise that."

"I understand you can't promise. But I wanted you to know I'll do anything you say. I couldn't stand to go back down there, Mr. Molock. Your office will be open tomorrow, won't it?"

"Yes. I'll be there."

"Is there anything you want me to do?"

"Yes. Tell me in particular why you changed your mind so suddenly."

A long silence occurred.

"Seeing the place again? Just that?" he said.

"Yes. Seeing it again. There was something else but I can't explain."

"No need to. I just wondered. I'll call you as early as I can tomorrow. You keep handy. Where I can get you."

"Yessir. I will."

I closed the door to the telephone booth, started toward the car, turned and pushed the door open so the fresh cool air could invade the booth. The sun had come out strong enough to cast my shadow faintly.

I bought gas and asked the distance to Koslo, which I already knew, and the ticket agent, irked with the business of pumping gas in his Christmas clothes, did not. Inside, I paid for the gas and bought a Coca-Cola and a package of Nabs.

At the counter end of the room an elderly white couple, apparently man and wife, travel weary, waited on the oaken bench with a suitcase between them. At the far end of the room a young black woman, plump and smiling, struggled to control three children crowded about her on the bench. The smallest child, a five- or six-year-old boy, pulled at the woman's fingers, pleading for a Coke.

"You hush," the woman whispered. "You can't spend ever'thing before we git there."

The child sat down, nestled closely against the woman and kept his big dreamy eyes fastened on me while I finished my drink and Nabs and looked about for the empty bottle rack.

"Set it anywhere," the ticket agent said.

I paid no attention to the ticket agent and kept looking for the bottle rack. I found it at the end of the waist-high partition that separated the white waiting section from the colored. I placed my empty bottle in the rack, went to the drink box, got four Coca-Colas, and took them to the woman and the children. The woman smiled with surprise and a touch of embarrassment. She said, "Say thank you to the man."

The children smiled shyly and nodded. They did not say anything.

The ticket agent kept watching me all the way to my car. He watched me as I drove away.

For several miles I thought of the timid black faces and the way all three of them clutched the pale green bottles with both hands.

The sunlight came through the windows and warmed the car. The old black dog disappeared, lost somewhere in the hills that moved past me.

It was almost sundown when I crossed the bridge over Dixon Creek and entered the long curve that led to the first hillside houses of Hammerhead. Without thinking, without plan, I suddenly turned onto the gravel road toward Deer Forks. I would have to go sooner or later, as I would have to meet Obie, and now, with the sun sinking red in the west, the time was as good as any I could forecast. The road was surprisingly smooth. It had been graded recently, which I knew was because Mr. Pollard always stood in with the county road supervisor.

Wisps of smoke came from the Pollard chimney. Reddish levels of light struck the fields and pastures and buildings like hurled water. Weeds grew in the land leading to our house. I pulled into the yard and past the house and stopped at the lot gate where the old pear tree, bare and robbed and dispirited, stood as changeless as the Confederate marker on courthouse square.

I got out of the car and, turning my head slowly, made a quick appraisal of house and barn and fields. After my father started work at the sawmill, Mr. Pollard would usually mow our cotton and corn fields once or twice a year for hay. Later, my father rented the land to the government and the agent wouldn't let Mr. Pollard mow. That was why the fields were so overgrown. Yet, everything except the fences looked well enough. It might have been the magic spell of sundown, which I had always loved, the curious moment when most of the light of the world seemed to fall near me, solid and heavy and colorful and almost touchable.

I went to the lot gate and felt it, shook it. The same planks, the same nails, the same hinges, the same cedar posts my father had touched. My mother would never let me sit on the lot gate, not even on the cedar posts. It seemed strange now that she had objected when my father never minded at all. A few times he might have said, "Watch it, Oliver."

I laughed and the sound made me think of a ripe golden pear falling from my favorite tree. My mother often put quilts under the tree to keep the pears from bruising.

I unchained the gate and swung it back and forth to see whether the hinges creaked. They did. Like rats in a hole. I kept swinging the gate, deeply amused. It was my gate, I thought. I could swing it as long as I liked. And I kept swinging it, sensing the rapid change of light.

"What on earth are you doing?" a voice called.

Shelley Raye was coming across the pasture on Cleo at a moderate pace. Rider and animal looked unreal, gliding through the twilight like something hurled from a merry-go-round. She wore a pale blue jacket. About her neck was a bright green scarf that covered the white collar of her blouse. Her trousers were a shade darker than Cleo's silky roan sides and her cordovan boots a shade darker than Cleo's feet. She stopped the mare between the gate and the pear tree. The last rays of the sun shone on Cleo's face and on Shelley Raye's golden hair. She had never before seemed half so beautiful to me.

"Hey you old sourpuss," she said.

"Hey yourself," I said.

"If I was on the ground I might give you a little hug."

"Pull up closer and I'll climb onto the gate post," I said.

"No. I won't give you anything," she said. "You're on my list. I'm mad at you."

"Real mad?"

"Lukewarm. But we know how long you've been at home. And not a peep out of you."

"It was pretty inconsiderate," I said. "How are you?"

"How do I look?"

"You look like Christmas. You look wonderful, Shelley Raye." She really did look like a young girl to me, though she was almost old enough to be my mother. I opened the gate, stepped through and began to rub Cleo's nose and forehead.

"New car?"

"Yes."

"What kind is it?"

"A Dodge, Shelley Raye. Can't you tell?"

"I can tell it's green."

"To match your scarf."

"With that to ride in maybe you'll let us keep Cleo."

"You can keep Cleo."

She tapped Cleo's neck gently. "She's getting old and I know how to treat her. I love old things."

"You do?"

"I always have. You know that."

"How's your mother and father?"

"The same. Daddy with a bad back and Mama with a little bit of everything. But we manage. Had the biggest crop this year we've ever had. I was the boss. Really. Daddy lets me. Nobody objects much."

"I remember how you used to boss me around."

"You needed it."

"Need it or not I got it. I was afraid of you."

"Aw, hush."

"I was. And you know it. I minded you better than Mother."

"Nonsense."

"Not nonsense at all. I thought you were blood kin and had a right to boss me until...you know..."

"You're crazy, Marcus."

"I know that."

"But I still love you. I'm glad you're home. And you better come see us. We're family from way back and you just might need us."

"I'll come see you."

"I didn't mean that last part the way it sounded. What I meant was, we are kin if it's not blood and we want to see you when you feel like it."

"I'll come. I want to."

"I've got to go. They'll wonder what's happened to me."

All the while I had hardly ceased to pat and caress Cleo, feel the bridle, adjust the bits, run my fingers through the flowing mane. I stepped back and Shelley Raye, with the slightest movement of hand, wheeled the mare around. Looking back she said, "I'll be disappointed if you don't come take care of this place."

"I'll take care of it," I called.

The twilight soon swallowed the last glimmer of flowing scarf and mane. I was glad I had no key and could not get into the house.

26

WHEN I REACHED the Elms the house was dark. I entered and
went directly to the back porch searching for the light in Sarah's
cabin. There was nothing but darkness. They were at church, at
some Christmas gathering, I guessed, but it did not lessen my
misgivings.

Though I knew there would be plenty of food in the kitchen I
went upstairs without eating anything. I stood at the north window
looking toward the cemetery. The rain was falling lightly in the
heavy darkness and I imagined that time had unreeled backward
and I could see the winding road through the cemetery and the one
fresh grave and the deep wagon ruts running over it. I heard myself
say in a whisper: Murderers shall not inherit the kingdom of God.

In the bookcase I found the large family Bible which had
belonged to Aunt Bella. I looked for the words I had whispered but
I could not find them. Perhaps they were not really there. Turning
the pages in a random sequence my eyes fell on the family record
of births and deaths. My mother's was there. My father's was
there. Aunt Bella's birth was there but not her death. There were
all sorts of strange names recorded in the beautiful handwriting of
Aunt Bella and question marks beside a number of dates. I tried to
memorize all the names and dates. When I thought I had succeeded, I closed the pages on my thumb and began to recite the

list. I did not miss one name or date. I began to feel more anchored in time and space.

A faint realization of hunger came to me. Downstairs I made a simple sandwich of ham and cheese. I cut the sandwich into two triangles and thought of my meeting with Shelley Raye. I had been terribly wrong. I should have gone to the Pollards. I should have seen Obie. I finished my sandwich and went into the living room.

Some mysterious power directed me and I could not resist. I dialed Obie's number. I could hear the phone ringing and with each ring I hoped there would be no answer. Yet I let the phone continue ringing as if I had no more control over the ringing in my ear than the raining outside. What would I say? Wild and bizarre ideas went off in my mind like Christmas fireworks. "Precious are the dead, Obie. Do you read the Bible? Where does it say a murderer shall not inherit the kingdom of God? I looked and couldn't find it but I know it's there. I've looked for so many things I couldn't find but I know very well they are there. Everything is there, Obie, if we could only find it. I have your note..."

Someone was saying, "Hello. Hello."

"Hello," I said. "Could I speak to Mr. Galloway?"

"Mr. Galloway ain't here."

Of course Mr. Galloway was not there. I knew where he was. It was not Lizzie's voice either. Why had I not said Obie.

"Obie. I want to speak to Obie."

"He gone to Arizona."

There was a long silence.

"Gone to see his mama. She stays in Arizona now for her arthritis. He goes ever Christmas."

"When will he be back?"

"He most generally and usually stays a long time at Christmas. Mr. Hilburn handle all the business while Mr. Obie gone. Was you speaking of business? Mr. Hilburn the man for that."

"No. It's something else. Where is Lizzie?"

"Oh, she hepping her husband now. They using two teachers."

There was a long silence.

"Thanks."

"You welcome."

I cradled the receiver and stood wondering more sensibly about what I might have said to Obie. A telephone call was not the way to do it anyway. Was I speaking of business? Yes, very serious business.

I wandered about the house for a long time before going to bed. Time had never seemed to pass so slowly. Twice I went to the back porch to look for Sarah's light and found nothing but darkness. When I finally did get into bed I remained wide awake and kept imagining that if I opened my eyes and looked through the window I would see bright daylight instead of the heavy rain-swept darkness.

I was so tired of thinking about Mims and where he was, about not seeing him, that I decided I would play a little game of beginning with my first memory and seeing how many events I could place in exact order. The first thing I could remember in my life, absolutely the first thing, was holding to the bib of my father's overalls. And then pushing my hand into the watch pocket, my hand was small enough then. It had gone all the way in, had hung, and I could not get away, could not with all my might pull away.

A heavy burst of rain woke me in the night. I had slept on my hand and it was numb. I clenched and unclenched my fingers rapidly to restore the circulation, and wondered whether Sarah and Brooks had come home. The second time I awoke I felt very tired. It was morning, too early for Sarah. I dressed and went upstairs and tried to read.

It aggravated me that I had got up so early. My early rising would not bring Sarah any sooner, would not open Mr. Molock's office a minute earlier, and certainly would not undo any of yesterday's sad failures. I thought: I'm like somebody swimming across the whole river, desperate to reach land, any piece of dry earth, when the river bank behind me is only ten feet away.

I heard Sarah arrive. I was so glad to hear her I would not go down right away. I waited as long as I could. When I reached the foot of the stairway I could smell the coffee strong as I ever had at Vingt-neuf Cour du Maréchal Foch. I sat down at the table.

"Where's Brooks?"

"We late and he already gone," Sarah said.

"You must have stayed up dancing last night."

"On Christmas Day? Won't catch me shaking my feet. I was at church."

"It lasted mighty long."

"Had cause. Was a play and a sermon and a social."

"What kind of social?"

"Food social. What kind you reckon in church on Christmas night?"

"I thought you might have had a baptising."

"You need baptising. That's what you need."

"I've been baptised."

"With what?"

"Fire and brimstone."

"You make light of the Lawd and you git some fire and brimstone. For real."

"I'm not making light."

"You and Brooks too."

"What's Brooks done?"

"Went outside 'fore the sermon end last night."

"Maybe he didn't like it."

"Don't make no difference where he like it or not. You 'sposed to listen to the Word."

"What is the Word?"

"Love is the Word. You don't have the Word you don't have nothing. It's a time fer all things. A time to be born and a time to die. A time to weep and a time to laugh. A time to moan and a time to dance. A time to kill and a time to heal."

"Where does love come in?"

"Come in all through it."

"Well, maybe."

"Ain't no maybe to it. I know. You ain't got ya times right."

"What's wrong with my times?"

"Read on and you see."

"Read where?"

"Ecclesiastes is where. Whatsoever is done is done forever. Ain't nothing gonna be taken away, ain't nothing gonna be added. Jist start ever'day new with the Word. That's all you can do."

"How have I got my times all wrong?"

"You trying to undo. Ain't nobody can undo. Not me or you or the preacher or the Lawd. The Lawd Hisself don't try to undo and we best not. Jist start with the Word. Now look, I done got ya eggs too dry."

"Oh, that doesn't matter."

She placed my breakfast before me. I felt some strange sort of relief and was suddenly hungry. Sarah could often do that to me, make me hungry simply by the way she moved about in the kitchen.

"How's ya friend?"

"He's fine."

"That's good. I think 'bout all them pore peoples locked up on Christmas Day. Maybe some ain't 'sposed to be there. Nobody caring. Law ain't always right."

Sarah grew silent. I ate slowly.

"But you better be right with the law," she began suddenly. "You done showed 'em you ain't afraid. No need to show 'em again."

"I've been thinking about that."

"You keep on thinking 'bout it. Law can act like chillren, and you can't 'spect chillren to have more sense than grown-ups."

I finished my breakfast and went upstairs. I took the rifle from the secret compartment of the bookcase and looked at it for a long time. I stood it against the bookcase and went downstairs. I had intended to tease Sarah about hiding her money, for I had given money to her and to Brooks for Christmas presents. But the telephone rang as I reached the kitchen doorway. There was no waiting for Sarah to answer. I ran into the living room and grabbed the telephone.

"Hello."

"Oday?" It was the voice of Mr. Molock.

"Yessir."

"Could you come to my office right away?"

"Yessir." There was a brief silence. "Do you want me to bring the rifle?"

"Bring the rifle?"

"Yessir. I will if you say so."

"No. That wouldn't do any good now. Listen. Bring a check made payable to Randle Barnett. No, wait. You can do that in my office. Bring a check blank and meet me in my office about nine or a quarter after."

"Yessir."

I left immediately. The whole world looked sad. The low-hanging clouds, the wet fields, the dead cotton and corn stalks, everything was depressing. Yet, I kept thinking Mr. Molock wouldn't be wanting a check if things looked so dark. I said to myself: Please let him work it out, Lord. Something said back to me: The Lord has a billion things to worry about besides a stolen rifle. I didn't steal it, I said, but all right. Just take care of Mims. He may be wet and hungry and no money in his pockets. Then I remembered my Christmas present to Mims. Take care of him anyway, I said.

I drove all over Koslo. The pigeons were there. The whittlers were there. The faded Christmas decorations were there. What a great change in them from the day before to the day after. I kept driving around court square. The pigeons seemed to be as anchored in their places as the whittlers. I wondered where the Honor Roll of the Confederate Dead was kept.

When the courthouse clock struck nine I parked and rushed up to Mr. Molock's office. He was not there. His secretary showed me a seat and gave me a copy of the *Commercial Appeal*. She was a large woman with iron-gray hair who looked about as old as Mr. Molock. She moved quickly, reminding me of Obie's mother as she went from her desk to the files and back several times. Finally she seated herself at the desk, lifted the glasses that hung about her neck, and began typing so fast I forgot what I was supposed to be worrying about.

She typed eight or ten legal-size pages while I tried to figure out the fewest number of days I could reasonably wait before calling the Chaplain about Mims. Then came the nauseous reminder that I might be seeing the Chaplain face to face very soon. I was on the verge of asking about Mr. Molock when the secretary said without looking at me, "He shouldn't be much longer. He's in the prosecuting attorney's office."

In a little while the courthouse clock struck ten. I was about ready to run down the stairs. I could feel the sweat on the inside of my thighs.

"Don't worry," the secretary said. "He might have stopped for coffee. I imagine he'll find a way. He's mighty interested in you."

"Thank you," I said.

"You pique his curiosity some way or other."

"I imagine I just pique him," I said.

"No. He's very fond of you. I don't know anybody else in the world who could have him working on Christmas night."

"I'm sorry to cause him so much trouble," I said.

"Oh, he's used to it, I guess. We'd be in trouble without trouble, wouldn't we?"

She said it in such a way that it sounded all right. I began to feel better.

We heard him on the steps at last. I couldn't help jumping up. His hair was standing out behind like a lot of white flags in the wind but I couldn't read a thing on his face. All I could think was I should have got him a Christmas present.

He closed the door and said, "You're a poet, aren't you? I want to recite you a little poem I wrote."

"Oh, Christian," the secretary said. "Don't do him that way. Tell him. He's been on pins and needles."

"No. Not before I recite my poem. I wrote it. I want to get an expert opinion."

I was nearly dying.

"He couldn't write 'Mary Had a Little Lamb,'" she said. "I do all the writing around here. Tell this man something, Christian. I already know. I can see it. Tell him."

"She's not going to let me recite," Mr. Molock said.

She said, "You're all right, son. Relax. He won your case."

"Thank God," I whispered.

"You're thanking the wrong person," Mr. Molock said. "The Lord wouldn't do what I've done. But it is over. Finished. And I'm a good mind to give you a long lecture. But I don't have time. You can keep the rifle. The bill of sale is in Sarah Ashmore's name. Don't ask me how I did it."

"I don't want to know. I'm just thankful. I won't ask you anything about it." Only later did I realize fully the rifle was to be truly mine.

"You won't have to ask him," the secretary said. "He'll tell us all about it anyway."

"Well, it was pretty clever," Mr. Molock said. "Pretty clever and pretty simple. Legal too. Now I always figure three major factors in most cases. One: fairness. Two: greed or prejudice. Three: vanity. Mr. Hewlit was fair from the beginning. Mr. Barnett, well, he liked the hundred dollars profit. And Mr. Castleberry, the prosecutor, I egged him on to run for D.A. and told him I'd support him. Which I was going to do anyway. Now you write me a check payable to Randle Barnett for one hundred thirty-nine dollars and fifty cents. I don't have the nerve to tell you to your face what I'm going to charge. I'll mail you my bill."

On the way home I saw that the clouds had lifted considerably. I don't care what he charges, I thought. I'm free. I can go to Vicksburg. I'll find him. Somebody will know where he is. Only he might have gone to South Carolina. Then what? Still, they'll know sooner or later. Somebody will know and I'll find him. The Chaplain will help. Then a tiny ray of hope charged my memory: The Chaplain had said Mims could not go out of the state.

I rode along in the valley between contentment and worry. I thought of stopping at a country store, where life seemed always so well arranged, but I drove on. I thought of turning onto the Smith Bridge road, a shortcut to the Pollard farm, but I drove on. I entered Hammerhead and thought of stopping at the post office, but I drove on.

When I turned into the yard at the Elms I saw the figure sitting on the front steps, a bag and a pasteboard box beside him, his arms resting on his knees, his hands folded, his big gray eyes looking up, smiling. The first thing in my mind was: I bet he's got his patchwork quilt in that box. I leaped out of the car and ran. The great commotion brought Sarah to the door. As she opened it I was pulling Mims into the house.

IV

The Journal

27

EVERY DAY I showed Mims something at Deer Forks that had a special place in my heart and soul. Every tree in my father's orchard, every old hoe or plow stock, almost every piece of furniture in the house, a tub, a washpan, the very same well rope my father bought the day I told Mr. Galloway to kiss my ass. The swimming hole on Dixon Creek, the fishing grounds where Obie and my father and I had last fished. It took a long time but I got to everything day by day and one by one.

Mims had arrived the day after Christmas. It may have been a mistake but I took him to Deer Forks that very afternoon, even before he had a glimpse of my studio-den. We saw that the old orchard, in spite of some attention from Brooks, needed pruning badly. We climbed into the barn loft and saw pieces of the sky where the roof had blown loose or blown away altogether. We roamed through fields waist high and shoulder high with grass and weeds and sprouts. We crossed fences that sagged to the ground. We inspected every room in the house, which wasn't too bad, because Sarah and Brooks had come occasionally to open the doors and windows for airing or build a fire for drying.

I enjoyed every hour, even every minute, with Mims, but a lot of the sights depressed me. Not Mims. He talked about pruning the orchard, and reroofing the barn, and mending the fences, and clearing the fields. He was like a child at an ice cream picnic. There was no keeping him at the Elms, not even for one night. By sundown his quilt covered the bed I was born in.

We had supper that night at Deer Forks. It was as much like old times as anything could have been. We had fried mackerel for one thing. We built a roaring fire in the living room and stretched our feet on the hearth as if it had been the old stove apron.

I don't know what time I left for the Elms, and I don't know exactly why I left at all. I think I wanted Mims to feel that he was in full possession of Deer Forks and could do with it whatever he liked. Or maybe I wanted the pleasure of coming back the next day. Anyway, I left sometime after midnight and sometime before the roosters started crowing at the Pollards'.

From January first to Easter I don't think I missed a day going to Deer Forks. Sometimes I spent the night. Sometimes I spent a day or two.

I never told Mims to do anything. He pruned and mended and repaired and cleared to his own satisfaction. I helped at times and other times I was probably a hindrance. I know he liked my being around. My biggest help, though, was giving him every tool, and a new pickup, and the finest pair of mare mules Mr. Pollard could find at Koslo, and a new pump, and a telephone.

One day I was late getting to Deer Forks because I had been writing in my journal from early morning to mid afternoon. Right after Mims came I had started keeping a journal. I thought it would be helpful for a project I had in mind. Jonathan said it would be a good idea. Some of it was of no consequence, and maybe of no interest at all to anyone else. I tried to put down everything. For example, I wrote down how Mims would not say Shelley Raye. He just said Shelley. Very soon everybody was saying Shelley instead of Shelley Raye.

But I was late that day because I was trying to capture in my journals some kind of notion I had about him. I didn't capture it, but I did get this down: Measuring time by the sun is complete foolishness. You might as well measure happiness by the brightness of the sun or sadness by the heaviness of rain or worry by the thickness of fog. Time is a thing of the heart, a temperature of the blood. A clock cannot give you a sense of time any more than a thermometer can give you the age of a patient.

So I was late getting to Deer Forks. It was a warm day, for March was coming in like a lamb. I found Mims breaking a piece of corn ground. I noticed he did not have his chew of snuff and I asked him about it. He said, "I was waiting for you." I helped myself to as much as he did and couldn't believe how drunk it made me. Not sick but drunk.

I suppose in one sense I was drunk from Christmas to Easter. Lots of time at night, when we sat before the fire, it was so much like the old good times at the Lumber Yard that I could almost hear Leo's bloodhounds howling. I didn't have a worry in the world. If Shelley came over, which she did pretty often, I would usually go and wash my mouth out. Mims never would.

At first I was jealous of Shelley. And then I got used to it. The three of us started going every few nights to different restaurants for catfish. Shelley knew all the places: Shiloh, Pickwick, Iuka and a dozen more. I was surprised how much Mims enjoyed it. I had always thought he was less inclined to go out in public like that than I was. Occasionally Mims and Shelley would call me unexpectedly to meet them someplace. I always went even if I had already eaten at the Elms. If I was writing I'd put it aside. They usually came in the pickup instead of Shelley's car. I knew they went sometimes without calling me but it didn't bother me much.

Nothing really disturbed me until Easter. Actually it was the Saturday before Easter Sunday. It was not Mims's fault. He is the most agreeable person in the world. I say most, not one of the most. But Shelley has always been bossy. She told me to meet them at Pauley's, which is an old hotel converted into a catfish restaurant on the banks of the river at the corner of Shiloh National Park.

I didn't mind meeting them. That was not the point. The point was I had asked Mims, not Shelley. I had my own curious reasons for wanting to take Mims all by himself. At first I thought if she was going to barge in at least we could all go together. I could pick them up or Shelley could come by in her car. Yet, I know I shouldn't blame Shelley too much either.

Pauley's sells antiques as well as catfish and she wanted to go in the pickup to bring back two chairs and a mirror. She had a good reason. She always has good reasons.

But I had something special to tell Mims, and I didn't want anybody else around. I thought it would be nice to tell him in a restaurant, over catfish and hush puppies. Not Pauley's necessarily, any good place where I could hear Mims laugh. Mr. Molock had been working on the plan for more than a month. He couldn't get a pardon but he did get a commutation of sentence, which was almost as good. At least Mims would never have to report to a parole officer, or anybody, again. That's all I had. Something else that pleased me as much as anything, Mr. Molock believed my account of Mims's misfortune.

Anyway, I met them at Pauley's, and I had a good time for Mims's sake. When Shelley went to deal with old lady Pauley for the chairs and mirror I told Mims what Mr. Molock had done. For a minute it was like leaving him at Olanberg, his eyes were so sad.

"What's the matter?" I said. "You're supposed to be happy."

"I didn't know you had something to tell me. I woulda come with just me and you," he said.

"It's done. Mr. Molock got it done I mean. That's all that matters," I said.

He pressed his fist against the back of my hand, very hard and warm. I thought I could feel his heart beating. "I wouldn't hurt you for nothing in the world," he said.

"Hurt me? In what way?" I said.

"No way," he said. "I wouldn't for nothing in the world."

I helped them load the chairs and then I helped put the mirror into Shelley's lap after she was seated in the pickup cab. And she was right. The mirror was a long rectangular thing with back braces and there wouldn't have been room for me comfortably.

I stood by my car for a long time after the pickup was gone. Then I sat in the car for a long time watching the river flowing north and thought of Aunt Bella explaining how the Rebels really whipped the Yankees that first day at Shiloh and with one more little effort—and if Albert Sidney Johnston hadn't got killed— could have pushed them into the river and nobody would ever have heard of Grant. But, alas, time and tide and one fatal night of waiting had changed the history of old lady Pauley and all her customers.

I don't know why I went back into Pauley's. I didn't want the coffee I ordered at the counter. I might have wanted to see what it was like to go in alone. Nobody else was going in or coming out alone.

I sipped the coffee slowly and looked above the counter at the battlefield pictures of the Peach Orchard and Bloody Pond and the Old Church and Pittsburg Landing. When I turned a bit to get a better view of the Hornet's Nest at the end of the counter I heard someone say, "You're not going to speak?"

Facing me, in a booth not ten feet away, was Obie. A burning numbness spread from head to foot. I tried to move and to speak and was paralyzed. I was finally aware that Obie was drinking a beer and that a man sat in the same booth, across from Obie, lifting a coffee cup and looking up at me.

"I didn't see you," I said to Obie and went toward the booth. But I thought: "I'm not going to say I'm sorry."

Obie said, "Scoot over, George."

I went back to the counter, found the cup, and got it to the booth without spilling any coffee. I sat down beside George and looked at Obie, whose eyes were red and far away.

Obie said, "George, you know who this is?"

"No," George said.

"He's richer than all the Galloways and Hilburns put together," Obie said. His speech was thick and almost drunken. "This is George Hilburn, Marcus. My bodyguard and manager and brains."

I was in a daze.

"George is a Yankee," Obie said. "He knows German machinery. We've got a German slicer. You know what a German slicer is?"

"No," I said.

"Tell him," Obie said to George.

George laughed.

"You don't have to laugh. I'm very serious," Obie said. Then to me he said, "I wrote you. Don't you remember I wrote you?"

"No," I said. "I didn't get a letter from you."

"Shit a mile," Obie said. "I don't mean a letter. A note. I didn't come see you, but I wrote you."

"Yes," I said. "Yes, you did."

"George," Obie said. "This is a pretty good guy but there's one thing bad wrong with him."

Obie waited for George to ask what was wrong but there was only silence. Obie said, "I'm sorry I said that about the bodyguard."

I didn't remember anything about a bodyguard.

"He said I was his bodyguard," George said. "His mother's in Arizona and he's just got back. Actually I'm his wet nurse."

"You don't understand," Obie said to George.

"What don't I understand?" George said.

"You don't understand nothing about it," Obie said.

"Okay," George said.

"You know what's wrong?" Obie asked George.

"With what?" George said.

"With him," Obie said.

"No," George said.

"He loves too much," Obie said. "Love. You know what that is, George?"

"Not exactly," George said.

"Ask him. He knows. But he can't tell you. Nobody can tell you," Obie said. He drank half of his mug of beer. "Why didn't you come see me?"

"I don't know, Obie," I said.

"It's all right," Obie said. "I've got something to tell you if you ever do come."

"I will," I said.

"Are you coming to see me?" Obie said. "I'm thinking about joining the army air force. Thinking."

"Yes, I'll come see you," I said. I got up.

"Remember, I wrote you," Obie said.

"I remember. I've still got it," I said.

"You've still got everything," Obie said.

As I turned away George said, "What was that all about?"

"None of your goddam Yankee business," Obie said.

I don't know what made me do it but I wheeled around and went back to Obie's table. I pulled the golden key out of my pocket and held it up. "Do you remember this?" I said.

"Yeah," Obie said. I thought he was going to cry.

I dropped the key on the table. It bounced with a sharp clear tingling sound. Obie picked it up and turned it round and round in his fingers. "Samson...Samson..." he said. Then he put the key into his pocket.

I was moving away. George said, "Could I venture to ask again what that's all about?"

"Yes," Obie said. "And I'll venture to tell you again it's none of your Yankee business."

Most of the way home I thought about Obie and wondered whether he got drunk very often and if he was really serious about joining the air force. But when I got into bed I began to think about Mims.

There must have been a full moon, for the blue light came through the window like early morning. Even with my eyes closed I knew the room was not very dark. I was trying to piece together, like a patchwork quilt, everything from my first glimpse of Mims on the porch at the Elms to the moment he and Shelley drove away from Pauley's with the chairs and crazy-shaped mirror.

I saw Mims at work with his hat high on his head, his jumper hanging on a post, his overalls unbuttoned at each side, two or three staples in his mouth, a crowbar in one hand stretching a bright new strand of barbed wire, a claw hammer in the other hand. I saw him on the ditch banks with nothing but a kaiser blade and a poleax, fighting briars taller than his shoulders and saplings larger than his thighs. I saw him behind the mules dragging the cotton and corn fields so the turning plow could cut through the over-grown weeds and grass. I remembered a hundred little things, how Mims still put on clean socks when he went to bed. Everything seemed perfectly in order. But something was wrong. Something spoiled everything for me, like my mother's speech that night at the Bolentines'. I liked the Bolentines better than anybody in Bordeaux. Jean Claude and Marie Christine, twins exactly my age, and monsieur and madame and the maid. I liked everything about the Bolentines. They lived one block down from us on Cour du Maréchal Foch and one night they gave a dinner party for my mother. My grandfather was there. And the LaGardes. In the middle of the dinner, Madame LaGarde asked my mother something about America. My mother in rapid French unloosed a speech that astonished me. I cannot translate exactly, can hardly remember half of it, but I did get up and leave the table. Had my grandfather had authority over my golden key I'm sure he would have taken it away from me for the rest of my life. I think my mother never knew I had left the table, she was so transported. "Ho," she said. "It is the most violent country in the civilized world. Murder, rape, drunkenness. Profanations and infringements and outrage. No ceremonial signs of consideration, no social courtesies, barbaric church services. Music! A cornstalk fiddle and shoestring bow! No sense of opera, art, wine, painting. The schoolchildren can hardly read or write or calculate. No consideration for the blacks or the poor. No sense of history. They think all the great battles of the world occurred in the American Civil War. Ho!" And she burst into tears. I came back and sat down at the table again. I could not bear to see my mother cry.

Yes, something was wrong, and I knew it had nothing to do with seeing Obie. I could not go to sleep. Two or three times the old black dog appeared in the moonlight. I saw the face in the window. I was so depressed I thought several times of going upstairs to read or scribble something. The room grew darker. After a while I heard distant thunder.

Then the rain came, gentle and steady, and I went to sleep thinking how wonderful it would be for Mims's early corn, if the field did not wash.

When I got up next morning the whole world was dew-bright and fresh. But I was so tired I felt I had been walking all night long.

At breakfast Sarah began to grumble at me. "Something done pulled you out on the wrong side of the bed," she said. "You got to where you be like Brooks on Sunday. Git up late and when you git up you cross as a pair of galluses."

"I haven't said a word," I said.

"At's how I know you cross. You better eat cause I'm gonna be in church for noon, enduring and after. Be no big dinner today."

"What's the big doings at church?"

"Don't you know it Easter Sunday?"

"I forgot."

"You forgot something awful important. Easter more necessary than Christmas."

"Why is that?"

"He rose! Didn't have Easter wouldn't be nothing to tell the world."

"What do you want to tell the world?"

"Love. Jesus loves you. Jesus loves ever'body. And that take some doing. Love ever'body."

"You ever seen anybody who loved too much?"

"I seen more didn't love none. At's what I worry about, the none. The much don't worry me. Ain't seen no muchers noway. Git that full of love you go up like a balloon. Be resurrected. I don't know nobody been resurrected. Nobody but Jesus."

"I saw Obie last night."

"That why you so cross?"

"I'm not cross."

"All sunk in. What's he telling you?"

"He didn't tell me anything."

"He got more troubles than you got."

"How do you know?"

"Brooks know. You don't have to tell me."

"I can't tell you. I don't know anything."

"Brooks know."

"Knows what?"

"He got more troubles than you got."

I started out of the kitchen. "I hope you find a lot of Easter eggs."

"Ain'ta looking for no Easter eggs," she said. "I looking for the Word."

I put on a sweater and walked down to the springs. The day was cool and bright. Above me, in the deep shadows of the woods, the early dogwood exploded in pink and white patches. The sweet smell of honeysuckle drifted by and I could hear far down the hollow the swarming cry of the blackbirds, like rusty hinges on a thousand swinging gates.

I climbed onto my favorite rock and listened to the water from the springs and wondered whether the stream was truly weaker now or whether it was only my imagination. For a while I was a bit chilled and thought I would get up and go to Deer Forks. But the sun grew warmer and I stayed on and on. When I did get up I turned away from the house and walked in the valley along Dixon Creek. I found the old tree where Obie and I had once gone to sleep after a bellyful of muscadines and the hickory tree where, with my father along, I had bagged my first squirrel with his magnificent rifle. I went around the edge of cypress swamps and entered the cemetery at the spot where the old western gate had been. For a very long time I stood in the old road seeing how far away I could read the names on the tombstones. Here and there homemade bouquets of flowers decorated a grave. I wished I had gathered something from the woods, if only a single flower for each of the two graves I had come to see. I might have found something in a matter of minutes but I made no effort. I stood looking at the shape of the mounds, thinking about what Sarah believed. The dead shall rise, truly and surely. The horn will blow and in the twinkling of an eye the earth will open and the living shapes come forth. I wished I could believe it.

As I started up the old cemetery road I looked toward the patch of Galloway graves, the irregular height of the stones. Some day there will probably be a rule to make all grave markers uniform, like Shiloh, I thought, and then all the beauty will be gone. For a moment I thought I might go look at *his* grave, *his* marker. I had never seen it. But the urge to look passed quickly and I knew people would soon be coming to church. I went home and read in one of Aunt Bella's old McGuffey readers until I went to sleep and the falling book woke me.

It was almost mid-afternoon when I left for Deer Forks. Mims was not at home. The pickup was there and the house was unlocked but Mims was not to be found inside or at the barn or in the fields. I walked about the place for almost an hour expecting any minute to find something terribly changed. The old pear tree near the lot gate was in full bloom, as if determined to be ahead of all the other trees within sight. I knew that come October the limbs would be breaking with huge golden horse pears so large they would hardly fit into a Karo syrup bucket. But October seemed a lifetime away. Time was fooling me again.

I was tired of walking and aggravated that Mims had not returned. I went to the house and sat on the west end of the porch, leaning against a post where the sun would strike me and keep me warm.

I must have fallen asleep. The sound of a car door closing suddenly brought me to consciousness. Half a minute later Mims came around the corner of the house, from shadow into sunlight. He stopped for a few seconds and looked toward the fields, not yet seeing me. The sunlight struck his face at a peculiar angle giving it an expression of softness and of marble. An easy fire was glowing in his eyes. I thought I had never seem Mims look so young and powerful and handsome. He wore a dark pin-striped suit, a wine-colored tie and a blue shirt. His shoes sparkled in the sunlight.

When he saw me he said, "Where've you been? We called you three or four times this morning."

"I didn't feel too good," I said. "I just walked around one place and another."

He unbuttoned his shirt and loosened his tie. His face took on a serious and somber look. "Let me git this Sunday rig off."

As he went into the house I thought he looked like my father coming home from the Peabody Hotel. I sensed something strange in his eyes, his face, his whole attitude. I felt something extraordinary was approaching.

In a few minutes he came out and motioned me to follow him. He had changed all his clothes to everyday wear. In the shadow of the porch his dark blue overalls, unbuckled at the sides, looked black. He wore a new straw hat, one I had never seen before. We went toward the patch of corn, a five-acre strip of well-drained ground which Mims had planted on Good Friday. He wanted to make sure the rain had not washed the rows down, I thought.

"You didn't git miffed at us, did you?" he asked.

"About what?" I said.

"Last night. And today."

"No," I said.

Mims stopped and laughed. "She thought you mighta had your feelings hurt."

"It was something else," I said. For a moment I felt we were outside the Lumber Yard, going toward the kennels, and I had nothing to worry about.

He pulled the silver box from the bib of his overalls and took a pinch of snuff. He held the box open for me. I kept looking at it.

"Make you feel better," he said. "They's something I want to ask you about."

I took a big pinch while he held the box. The old feeling was back again and I was almost drunk with relief. The chairs, the mirror, Obie, everything at Pauley's seemed far away and unimportant. I could almost see Leo and hear the mournful cry of the hounds.

We stopped at the fence and looked at the corn rows as if the tiny blades were already pushing through to sunlight. The rain had not washed the rows at all.

"I tried to tell her," Mims said. He spat neatly over the fence. "I said you just had something you wanted to do. Belikes, you did. So we went to church."

"You haven't asked me anything," I said.

He turned away and again spat over the fence in a way I never could. "You know how old I am?"

"Yes," I said. "The years and the months and the days."

"I'm old enough to be your daddy and then some."

I laughed. I did not feel Mims was that much older than me at all. Sometimes I didn't think he was any older.

"I could stop," he said.

"Stop what?"

"I could leave," he said. "If you want me to."

The thought jolted me. He saw it.

"I mean I would, if they's some reason," he said.

"What reason?"

He did not answer then. We stood leaning against the fence so long I could tell the sun had moved. He put his hands under the bib of his overalls as if he intended to stand there until the corn sprouted unless the heavy thing in his mind was settled forever. Not far away from the fence a killdeer startled us with a plaintive and penetrating cry and fluttered off in a broken-winged caper.

"You two go back a long ways," he said quietly. "If you think it ain't right for me and Shelley...my record...where I been and all...I wouldn't do you no harm for nobody."

"You're not doing me any harm," I said.

He moved so that the sunlight came over my shoulder and flooded his face.

"You don't mind?" he said.

I felt a dizziness, almost like that night before the stove when Mims had first let me share his silver box. I said, "I don't mind at all. I'm glad. But I do love you more than anybody in the world."

I expected him to smile. But he didn't. There was a strange expression on his face, as if his whole being burned with anger against something far away and overflowed with infinite kindness for everything near at hand.

"I mean it," he said. "I wouldn't do you no harm for nobody. And I'll never love nobody more'n I do you."

His words spread, as limitless and boundless as the sunlight, while I wondered in a vague and unwordable way what strange star-paths had led the two of us to that moment.

28

THEY WERE MARRIED in August, late one afternoon, at the courthouse in the office of the justice of the peace of the first district. The justice was a very old man, almost six feet six, having once been six feet seven, he said. He told Mr. and Mrs. Pollard the ceremony would be number nine hundred and eighty-seven for him and showed them the number in a large black book, his own private marriage journal which covered four years and seven months.

The whole business was done in four or five minutes. Mims had bought the license in the circuit clerk's office the day before, and the ring from Bates Jewelers, and the orchid from Latch's. There were three other couples waiting to be married, two from Illinois and one from Kentucky.

Shelley wore a soft yellow dress that billowed about her arms. Her hair hung in golden waves hiding half the dark blue collar that circled her neck. On her face was a bright, yet almost sad, expression, like the orchid she wore. Mims wore a white silk sport shirt and tan trousers. He stood with his shoulders straight and rigid, his head back, reminding me of the choir leader years ago at Cumberland Baptist. I watched Mims's face while the justice read the vows in a very solemn manner. It was over and Mims took her hand and grinned. Then he kissed Shelley on her cheek, and she kissed him and her mother and her father. I held out my car keys to Mims. He took them without a word. I was so glad he didn't say anything, not a word. His look was all I wanted, the faintest wrinkle about the eyes. We had already talked about the car the night before.

"You two git out of here before I start crying," Mrs. Pollard said.

"Bye, everybody. Goodbye, Marcus," Shelley said. And they were gone.

I gave the justice twenty dollars. He asked me if I wanted change and I told him I did not.

"Mighty fine," he said, and motioned for the next couple to step forward.

"Let's go somewhere and talk it over," Mrs. Pollard said.

"We can go to Boyd's," Mr. Pollard said.

"I'm not going to no beer joint," Mrs. Pollard said. "My feet can make it to the Coffee Cup."

I didn't want to go anywhere to talk anything over but I was afraid of Mrs. Pollard as usual.

"The Coffee Cup is closed," Mr. Pollard said.

We went across the street to Boyd's and ordered three Coca-colas. Mrs. Pollard asked the waiter for a straw and then asked me, "What do you think about it?"

"Pretty late to be asking that," Mr. Pollard said.

"Well, I trust Marcus," she said. "You know where they're going, don't you?"

"Yes, ma'am," I said.

"The Smoky Mountains, which sounds pretty expensive to me. And the ring he give her, and the orchid. I was just wondering about his finances. It got me to worrying and I wanted to ask you about it."

"I'm not the one to ask about that."

"You the one that knows. Now tell me about him."

"About him? I have the highest regard for Mims, the very..."

She interrupted me. "We call him Howard. You call him Mims?"

"I always have."

"You met down there?"

"We did."

"I don't believe nobody is sent to prison that's innocent. Do you?"

"Yes, I do."

"Shelley said how you liked him. I guess she's right on that part."

"I don't know what Shelley said. Nobody's perfect. But he's close enough for my standards."

"Do tell. What's his finances?"

"The business arrangements I've had with him, or will have, I wouldn't want to discuss with anybody."

"You the one who brought him here," she said. "You shouldn't mind a few questions. From the family."

"Yes, ma'am, I do mind." I moved to get a paper napkin and she thought I was about to leave.

"You set yourself right down," she said. "I've pinned diapers on your little behind and Shelley Raye's been a sister to you. You can't high-hat me. You didn't want her to marry him. Look me square and tell me you did."

"What I want has nothing to do with it."

"She was bound and determined, but still and all, you could answer some questions."

"That's enough," Mr. Pollard said. "It's done and over with. You might as well like it as lump it. We give our permission."

"He had your permission, not mine," she said.

"He had my permission because that's what she wanted and she's twenty-one past and plenty. I can't live her life. Let's go home before my back starts killing me."

"Your back?" she said. "What about me? I ain't no spring chicken. Lord, I don't know what we'll do."

"She ain't going to the moon," Mr. Pollard said.

"How do you know?" she said. "No telling where they'll settle. In time. Do you know, Marcus?"

"No," I said, but I thought I knew.

"He's got the finest crop I ever laid eyes on," Mr. Pollard said. "Bar none."

"Because Marcus poured the fertilizer to him," she said.

"Fertilizer ain't all of it," Mr. Pollard said.

"Go ahead and take up fer him," she said.

"My god, what do you expect me to do? You had a chance to speak up before now."

"It never come to me before now. Some but not all," she said.

"Well, you didn't speak so just forever hold your peace. My god, he ain't had a chance."

"Oh, you'd put sugar in honey. Besides, you don't have to take the Lord's name in vain. In a beer joint at that."

"You keep on and I'll order a beer," he said.

"Over my dead body," she said. "That's one thing. He said he didn't drink. But I don't know."

"Can't you take his word for nothing?" Mr. Pollard said.

"I'd rather hear it from Marcus," she said. "I trust Marcus."

"Marcus has told you he don't want to talk about it. It's over and done with and I'm ready to go before my back starts killing me."

"Your back? If I pulled these shoes off, four cobblers couldn't git 'em back on. I ain't going nowhere till Marcus tells me what he thinks. He ain't told yet."

I hadn't meant to say it. But my head was swimming the way it did when I took a big pinch from Mims's silver box in the broiling sun. "I think it'll be wonderful. Had you ever thought he might have been innocent?"

"There," Mr. Pollard said. He pushed himself up from the table.

"Innocent?" she said.

"Some day I'll tell you all about it."

"There," Mr. Pollard said. He pulled her across the seat and waited for her to get up.

"You've eased my mind a little," she said. She tested her weight on the floor. "But these feet, they ain't much hope fer them. Lord, I don't know what we'll do."

Mr. Pollard helped her stand, and after she was standing she pulled her arm away from him and said, "Don't go straining your back agin. I don't know. All that cotton'll be busting open like a skillet of popcorn before they git back. I don't know what we'll do."

"We'll find some pickers. They won't be gone that long. Two weeks at most," Mr. Pollard said.

Two weeks sounded like forever to me.

"I didn't have two days," she said. "I reckon you remember that."

"Peabody," he said.

"Peabody my foot, if I should say such a thing. Which reminds me you can politely stop at Pipkin's and git me some corn pads. It was not the Peabody, Marcus. It was the Gayoso. One night. And trot back. You do actually think it? What you said?"

"I do," I said. We were waiting at the counter. I moved ahead of Mr. Pollard to pay the check.

On the way home in the pickup I wondered why Mrs. Pollard had waited so long to talk to me about Mims.

After supper I went to Deer Forks and fed the mules, remembering to put a handful of salt in the corner of each trough, and slopped the hog. Not real slop. I stirred some shorts into a foot tub of water and poured them into the trough a little at a time, the Hampshire sow was so greedy. I figured she already weighed over three hundred pounds, a good fifty more than her littermates which Mr. Pollard had kept.

The house was not locked. I went into the kitchen and sat at the table and opened a quart jar of cucumber pickles which Shelley or Mrs. Pollard had canned. The room was terribly hot and still but the cucumber was as cold as spring water, and very crisp. I think alum made it crisp. I saw Mims's silver snuffbox on a shelf behind the stove. I took a good pinch and went outside where it was much cooler and I could hear the night sounds better. But it wasn't much fun. None at all, actually. I pumped a handful of water and washed my mouth out and went home.

I found a copy of *Bleak House* and couldn't remember where I had got it. I started in the middle of the book, lying in bed, reading slowly, word for word. It made me sick at heart the way he puts things together, every little word in place, like plums hanging so thick you think every branch will snap. And I was angry with myself for not being able to put one paragraph together that would bear rereading, and for not being able to put Mims and Shelley out of my mind.

Finally I turned out the lights and lay with my ear pressed on one pillow and the other pillow wrapped in my arms. I could hear the steady pounding as if my heart pumped all my blood onto the pillow. I felt so awful that everything began to seem funny to me. Completely silly. Silly words went through my mind. I got up and wrote a silly poem. It was funny for a little while, so funny I thought I would go upstairs and type it. Then I began to be ashamed and to drift off into the darkest corner I had ever known.

I got into bed, and from that corner of deep despair something told me to pray. I did. I said the prayer over three or four times: God, let them be happy. I felt I was praying for the wrong thing. But I went to sleep.

Sarah had to wake me. After breakfast I went to Koslo to the library. Jonathan had given me his list of the world's ten best novels: *War and Peace, The Brothers Karamazov, Madam Bovary, Vanity Fair, Père Goriot, Fathers and Sons, Crime and Punishment, The Red and the Black, Les Misérables,* and *Great Expectations.* I found the seven I had not read. At the desk the woman said, "You can't check out seven books."

"Why not?" I said. "Most of them haven't been checked out for years."

"You simply can't," she said. Her tone was not disagreeable. She pondered the situation, trying to come up with a solution. "If they were for more than one person..."

I thought about saying, "They are for seven people. For me, my father, my mother, Aunt Bella, Mims, Shelley and Obie." But I actually said, "They're really for me."

"Then three is the limit," she said.

"Which three do you suggest?" I said.

"I'm not that well acquainted with them," she said. "There's one other thing you could do if you're a mind to. You could check out three and rent the others. A nickel a day. Seventy cents for fourteen days."

"That's fine," I said.

"Seventy cents for each book."

"That's fine."

"I'm sorry to charge you but I don't know any other way."

"That's fine."

She began to stamp the cards. "What do you think about the third term?"

For a second I thought she was asking about a book.

"Roosevelt," she said.

"Oh," I said. "It's all right with me."

"I'm against it," she said. "Like as not he'll get us into a war that's none of our business. But I can't stand the Republicans. You don't like Republicans, do you?"

"I don't know. I don't know any."

"Old man Cartwright is one, they say. Runs the hosiery mill. But I never met him. There. Two dollars and eighty cents. I bet I've not got change."

I was back home and upstairs reading *Père Goriot* when I suddenly realized that the librarian resembled the Chaplain's wife a great deal. I thought about it for a long time. Odd things like that would come into my mind and keep nagging at me, the way Sarah kept nagging about my staying upstairs so much. For a week I hardly left the studio-den except to eat and sleep and go to Deer Forks to feed the mules and hog.

Mims and Shelley had been gone a week and two days when the postcard came from Blue Ridge. Brooks brought it in and gave it to me at the supper table. It was a picture of an old mountain house. In Shelley's handwriting was the message, "Having a wonderful time. Don't forget to salt the mules! Ha. Ha." The reminder about the mules was funny and sad too. That day in the courthouse, when the justice had called us to step forward for the ceremony, Mims had turned to me and whispered, "Don't forgit to give the mules a little salt along this hot weather."

Sitting at the table, looking at the card, I almost cried. I don't know what it was. Some awful meeting of joy and sorrow.

Until the postcard came I had commenced to feel a certain tinge of satisfaction in not having heard from the two, in being left completely alone to enjoy my sadness. For the marriage had brought a definite cloud. I could not deny it and did not wish to deny it. No matter how happy I wanted to be for both of them I did feel a final and ultimate exclusion. It was something like leaving Olanberg that morning, the wonderful matter of being free and the awful business of leaving Mims, both emotions rolling together deep inside me.

I watched Sarah meticulously scrubbing at the dishes in the sink. Surely she had her moments of joy and sorrow but I doubted that both came to her at the same time.

"I'll be glad when they git home," she said.

"Why?" I said.

"Cheer you up. Settin' up in that room like a sulled possum. I don't know what you do upstairs all time noway. Would wear me out. I'd take me a trip."

"You? You won't even go to Memphis."

"I got things to tend to. Didn't have things to tend to, dig up my jar under that tree, take a trip so long couldn't make a round trip ticket to fit."

I jumped up. "Ah, hah! You finally told me. You buried your money under a tree."

"Lota trees in this world."

"What kind of tree is it?"

"None yo' business. I got two jars now and ain't..."

Brooks came in from burning the garbage. Sarah pointed the handle of a skillet at me. "He been night walking for a week," she said. "Like Papa. Brooks, you 'member how Papa went night walking through the yard in broad open daylight like he looking fer something. Like he asleep. Don't hear nothing. Don't see nothing. Just go on looking. You been doing the same thing fer a week."

"Me?" I said.

"I ain't talking about the man in the moon."

"I'm busy. I'm writing," I said.

Brooks said, "He a artist, Mama. Artist have they ways."

"Ways," she said. "I tell you 'bout them ways. You step off the end of the world some morning. Brooks, you go git me..."

I never knew what she wanted Brooks to get. The telephone rang and I ran into the living room. All along I had thought Mims would call. My hand trembled with great expectations as I lifted the receiver.

"Hello," I said.

"Hey, old man." It was Mims's voice. I was not at all ashamed to be so glad. "Jist wanted to call," he said. "You holding everything down?"

"I'm just fine," I cried. "I'm just great. Where are you?"

"Up here somewheres. In the mountains. I don't know."

That was Mims. I loved his not knowing. He hadn't changed. But it also seemed desperately important to know exactly where they were at that very moment. "Well, ask Shelley," I said.

"She's downstairs buying a wood churn. Wait a minute."

He must have gone to the window and looked out at some sign or other, for after a few seconds I heard him lift the phone again and say, "It says Gat-lin-burg."

"I sure miss you all," I said. "Tell Shelley I salted the mules."

"Yeah," he said. "Is ever'thing all right? We had some rain?"

"A Sears Roebuck."

"Do which?"

I laughed. He could always make me laugh at the way he would say: Do which? "Just what you ordered," I said. "A slow all-nighter. Thursday night."

"Did?"

"You ought to see the crops. You won't be able to gather them."

"You gonna hep me? Like you promised?"

Nothing he could have said in the world would have made me happier. "You bet," I said. "When are you two coming home?"

"Jist a minute. Shelley's back. I'll let her tell you."

I heard the transfer of the phone and then a voice from the playhouse of my childhood. "This is Queen Cleopatra, is that you, Mark?"

"Goose," I said.

"Gander," she said.

"Did you get your churn?" I said.

"Yes. But I don't have a cow."

"I salted the mules," I said.

"Good," she said. "You always were dependable. Have you missed us?"

"A bushel every day and a wagon load at night. When are you coming home?"

"Probably Saturday."

"Be careful."

"We will. Bye-bye. Did you want to speak to Mims again?"

"No. Just tell him bye."

I was so happy I could not walk away from the telephone. I remained rooted as if the conversation continued, drunk with the joy that Mims himself had called me and delighted with the feeling that Shelley was not going to hide Mims from me after all. I don't know what I had expected. The mind and the heart and whatever else it is that shapes our tomorrows can play some funny tricks. Now I was certain there would be no hiding, no walls, no closed doors.

I left the house and walked with happy strides down the hill to the springs. I sat on my favorite rock and longed for the old rainbow to come back again. I was remembering something Mims had said.

I had stayed at Deer Forks the night before they got married, because Mims asked me to. I always stayed when he asked me like that. Shelley didn't come over at all and we had a much better time than I had expected. We stayed forever on the front porch because the night was so hot. Sometimes we talked and sometimes we just sat there with nothing to break the stillness except the little spurt when Mims spat all the way across the porch. Patches of dew glistened in the heavy sea of cotton. I thought we could almost hear the ripe bolls cracking. I was both sad and happy. I felt there was some final, important thing I needed to ask Mims before we went to sleep, for after tomorrow it would be different.

"Mims," I said, "does the Bible say a murderer shall not enter the kingdom of God?"

"I don't know nothing about things like that," Mims said. "The Bible can git me all mixed up. What about King David? I jist have my own notions and they may be wrong."

"What is your notion?" I said.

"If you stay a murderer in your heart I guess it means what it says, but if you ast God to forgive you then you wouldn't be one any more," Mims said.

"Is that the way it is?"

"It's my notion," he said.

"You think I ought to say I'm sorry?"

"No," he said.

We were quiet for a long time. The night sounds were as regular as the ticking of a clock. Then Mims added, "When the time comes, you can't keep from saying it."

Sitting there on my favorite rock, longing for the old rainbow, and actually seeing in the darkness the outline of the water path that led down to Dixon Creek, I knew the time had come.

I just said quietly, though anybody near could have heard me: "God, will you forgive me?"

I don't know why the springs seemed to cease flowing for several heartbeats. Perhaps the sudden gust of wind, drying the sweat on my face, blew the sound away from me. I just know I never felt so peaceful in my life. The only regret I had was that I could not begin anew with my father and my mother in that bright old time when the world was as pure as the springs.

When I got up I went toward the cemetery, not thinking of the cemetery at all. I went past the edge of the swamps and crossed the road, and on the knoll at the edge of the sawmill yard I saw beyond the sycamore tree a light. I went toward it like a moth.

From the edge of the sawdust pile I saw Obie in the office, like a schoolboy long ago, in the big house, at the kitchen table, struggling over a jigsaw puzzle. I entered and he finished writing down a set of figures before he looked up.

Finally he raised his head and seemed not at all surprised. He laughed.

"Sit down," he said.

I sat in the nearest chair at one corner of the desk. He got up, came around the desk, and sat in the other chair a few feet away. He sat almost sideways, slouched back, his leg hanging over the arm of the chair. He appeared to be completely relaxed. Strange, so strange it seemed like a vivid dream. I felt I had to come to help him with an algebra lesson.

We must have sat looking at each other for a full minute.

"Well," he said, almost smiling, almost laughing, but doing neither, simply moving his face enough to bring back all lost time.

"I came to tell you I'm terribly, terribly sorry," I said. "And... and I've never said that before. But I am terribly sorry. If I could die this minute and undo it, I would."

I could not go on. But that was all I had to say. His face was so old and beautiful. I sat there and cried. And he did too.

After a while, with the slightest movement of his body, he took the golden key from his pocket and handed it to me. At last he got up and hugged me in a way he never had before. I knew I had been forgiven and I wanted to leave while the world was perfect.

As my hand pushed on the screen door he said, "Marcus?" The way he said it, the sound was wonderful.

"The thing I wanted to tell you: he asked me to do it. He was afraid. Maybe he did a lot of things because he was afraid of something. I was so mad with him for asking me to drive the wagon, teasing me, and almost ordering me, I finally yelled at him and said, 'Go drive the goddam thing yourself and I hope he shoots your ass off.' It's not much fun remembering that's the last thing you ever said to your father."

We just stood and looked at each other.

"I've been to Arizona and I've thought about the air force. But I can't run away from it. You can help me. You can help me forget it. And I want you to try."

"I'll do anything for you," I said.

I walked through the cemetery, along the old road, and I was not afraid of anything. There were no ghosts. No black dog. There would be no Red Midnight for me ever again.

I started my book that night. When I get tired of writing I go to Deer Forks. If it's not exactly like the Lumber Yard used to be it's near enough. As for Shelley I like her more and more. I think her hair gets more beautiful every day, and she told me not long ago she washes it with Octagon soap. They sure are a happy two. I guess Shelley deserves it almost as much as Mims.

Sometimes I meet Obie at the mill office at night and read him pages of my book. He astonishes me with his understanding, but then we go back a long way. He knows more about me than Mims does. I'm calling the book *The Prisoner of Olanberg*, mostly about Mims under a different name. After that I may do one about Obie.

Or one about my grandfather. It's strange how sometimes somebody you think is going to die outlives everybody. Last week I got the longest letter I have ever received from him. Maybe because I had written to him at some length about my book. I think he's got a lot more confidence in me now. He ended his letter with: "In these narrow and crowded paths we tread in the wilderness, how can one foresee the consequences of the slightest turn toward some more inviting shade? There is no compass. When I acquiesced in your mother's return to Bordeaux I foresaw no great harm. I made the decision with my heart. I must continue to do thus. Mathematics cannot apply to such matters. Neither sale nor purchase price can be stamped on human emotions. We must trust our hearts. When I assisted you in your return to America against your dear mother's wishes, I did that because I thought you not only belonged then with your father, you also deserved to share the bright hope of a rising young land, young like you, albeit restless and untamed rather than violent. I do and should love both you and America. And I am persuaded that age will bring to both of you a golden crown."

He would make a good book, but I'll think about all that after I've finished *The Prisoner*. I'm not the least bit afraid of failure. I'll surprise the Chaplain one of these days. In fact, I might shock him in more ways than one and send him something brushed with the shadow of greatness.

I told that to Mims the other night while Shelley was fixing us some fried mackerel patties. He said, "Watch it, Oliver." He sounded exactly like my father.